A Famous Good Marrying Scheme

Jan Ashton

Quills & Quartos
PUBLISHING

Edited by Julie Cooper and Regina McCaughey-Silvia

Cover by Hoja Design

ISBN 978-1-956613-45-2 (ebook) and 978-1-956613-46-9 (paperback)

For Emma, who has inspired me with her marrying schemes and wedding plans.

Table of Contents

> **"** A famous good thing this marrying scheme, upon my soul! A clever fancy of Morland's and Belle's. What do you think of it, Miss Morland? I say it is no bad thing. **"**

Northanger Abbey,
Chapter 15

CHAPTER
ONE

September 1812

Fitzwilliam Darcy smoothed the fine linen of his trousers and stared up at the painting hanging directly across from his seat. The artist and his subject, likely the first master of Netherfield, lacked imagination; like the estate itself, the portrait had no inspired thought, no spirit or colour. His own imagination was overly active but his hopes were growing dull.

It had been a discouraging three days back in Meryton for two bachelors eager to shed that title. Any expectation of a rapid exchange of love and devotion after a ten-month absence from Longbourn's parlour had fallen to the wayside. Elizabeth Bennet could not even look at him, let alone grace him with a smile.

Frowning, he turned away from the portrait to see Netherfield's current tenant sprawled on the large sofa. *Perhaps this cursed place saps everyone of energy and initiative.*

"Bingley, you have my blessing and encouragement. Why have you not spoken to Miss Bennet?"

His friend, his eyes fixed on a tapestry as if he were counting its threads, turned and looked at him as if startled by the question or by the very sound of Darcy's voice breaking their shared silence. He let out a long sigh before answering. "There was not a spare moment. She was blushing and Mrs Bennet did not ease her talking."

"Mrs Bennet is conscious of the silences that fall between her guests and her family. Especially between her eldest daughter and her supposed suitor."

After shifting uncomfortably on the cushions, Bingley replied quietly, "*You* have never been in love. You do not understand the awkwardness and shyness that come over a man when he wishes to speak his heart to a lady."

Every fibre in his being wished to shout aloud about the encyclopaedia he could write on the subject of unrequited love, tied tongues, and the irrational foolishness of a man desperate to give his heart to a lady, but Darcy managed instead to direct his frustration and anger into the grip he held on the chair's arm.

"No, I suppose I do not." He took a breath and went on. "Yet we have returned here and reopened the house so that you could lay yourself at Miss Bennet's feet and ease my guilt, and thus far the only progress I see is in Miss Catherine's needlework and in the quantity of biscuits turned out by Longbourn's kitchens."

Bingley sprang up from the sofa and sauntered to the fireplace; seizing a poker, he began stabbing vigorously at the flaming logs. Darcy, ever mindful of the embers that singed Pemberley's rugs when his friend was in residence, rose from his seat in readiness.

Bingley turned, hot poker in hand. "She is so beautiful, and every time I look at her and wish to speak—to ask to speak to her alone—I seize up and worry it is too soon, that she is not prepared for or would not welcome my proposal."

Not prepared? Dear God Almighty.

Darcy took the poker from Bingley and hung it back in its place. "Miss Bennet has spent a year thinking only of you, just as you have thought only of her. Relieve her suffering and your own, and ask her to marry you. If you fear her refusal, tell her you would like to marry her but will wait for her answer if she needs time to have a think on it."

"Do you think she would need time?"

Bingley, good man that he was, looked for all the world like a boy hopeful of another serving of pudding. It pulled at something in Darcy, reviving the nagging guilt he had felt for months.

"I think not, and her mother and sister would agree with me that she cares deeply for you."

After a deep breath as if to fortify his own decisiveness, Bingley nodded. "All right then. We will ride over tomorrow and I shall ask her."

With that, Darcy made his own decision. "I shall ride out with you but then I am for London. My cousin has asked for my assistance with some matters while Lord Matlock recovers from his illness."

"But—"

"Do not be uneasy. You have made your vow." He waited for Bingley's nod. "I have held you back too long from the business of your proposal. When I return in a few days' time, I expect to see heart-shaped clouds floating above Netherfield and Longbourn."

Bingley guffawed. "That you will, my friend! That you will."

—— o o o ——

He was grateful when Bingley carried his exuberance off to his bed, exhausted from all the thinking and worrying and anticipating and riding he had done that day. Darcy craved solitude for himself, not to think about his past or present circumstances—he had done enough of *that* over the previous year—but to consider how he might move on.

He had arrived at Longbourn three days prior, desperate to lay eyes on Elizabeth Bennet, to see her restored to the happiness that was her right. Their last meeting had found her in agony, weeping over the fate of her youngest sister. He had attended to that sordid business and now he had paid full reparations by returning Bingley to her eldest and most beloved sister.

And yet she could not even look at him, let alone grace him with a smile. Elizabeth had not walked the paths near Netherfield where he had chanced upon her a year ago nor hinted that she might be found elsewhere should he wish to speak to her. No; she had discouraged him from any further overture—even claiming imminent rain should keep their party from walking out from Longbourn. Whatever friendship had been forged in two days at Pemberley was forgotten. She could not forgive him for the circumstances that led to her youngest sister's patched-up marriage; he could scarcely forgive himself. She hated him, again, and for all new reasons. Or worse, perhaps his presence—or the lack of it—mattered to her not at all.

Bingley, at least, was welcomed by Miss Bennet's smile and Mrs Bennet's enthusiasm. Yet the man had yet to do a thing about it! It was infuriating! Some part of Darcy wondered whether Elizabeth only awaited her eldest sister's betrothal to truly engage with *him*, but thinking about that only deepened his annoyance with Bingley.

He would like resolution, if not to the muddle that was his own romantic *débâcle*, then at least to that of his friend. He had to make right the affairs of at least one Bennet sister.

Tomorrow he would leave for town and leave Bingley to his happy fate. Once he had word of an engagement, Darcy could make plans to travel to Pemberley and find sanctuary there with Georgiana.

It will have to do. It is not the best of outcomes but it is all I have.

—— o o o ——

The sun was bright and high in the sky, though it was not nearly as high as the hopes carried by both men as they rode towards Longbourn. Darcy had packed lightly for his journey to London. His heartache weighed more heavily than the case he carried; it held only a spare pair of gloves, a flask of whisky, and his correspondence.

Bingley's cheerful optimism, bolstered by Darcy's encouragement the previous evening and reinforced again at breakfast, ought to have been contagious. But Darcy, chastened by Elizabeth's silence and solemnity of the past few days, felt himself immune from any happy assurances. He would bid his farewells to the Bennets and offer to carry any letters to the Gardiners; unless he saw some sign that Elizabeth wished him to remain or that she wished to converse in any manner less formal than he had yet seen, it would be his last act of goodwill. Much as Bingley wished him to remain until he had his answer from Miss Bennet, Darcy lacked the patience necessary to stay in company until that time finally arrived. He would return in a week, which he deemed sufficient time for a proposal and the ensuing raptures, dinners, and calls devoted to it.

I am a coward, unable to share my friend's joy yet desperate to see the smile on his new sister's face.

A sudden gust of wind hit him just as Bingley cried "Stop!"

He turned to see Bingley's beaver flying off his head and into the air. It bounced along the tips of the tall grass before it sank and disappeared into the wind-whipped field about twenty yards away.

"Can you believe this wind?" Bingley exclaimed as he climbed down from his horse and started making his way through the waist-high grass towards his hat.

Darcy tugged his own hat a little tighter, biting back his reply as the breeze carried the sound of voices with it. *Was that a scream?* He turned away from Bingley and looked towards Longbourn, still another mile away.

"Lizzy, h-help!"

"Jane!"

Bingley and his hat were forgotten. Darcy kicked his heels and sped off, racing across the meadow towards the sound of their voices. Hearing splashing, he spurred his horse in the direction of the stream. Upon reaching it, he saw the Bennet sisters: Miss Catherine was half in the water, shrieking as she held onto the footbridge; Miss Bennet stood dazedly in the middle of the stream, holding one hand to her head as the other pulled at her skirt. Elizabeth was stepping carefully down the bank, reaching her hand towards her younger sister and looking fearfully at the elder one.

"Miss Elizabeth, be careful!" Darcy jumped off his horse and ran towards them. She stepped back onto solid ground as he threw off his greatcoat and plunged into the water, wading through its thigh-high depths to reach Miss Catherine.

"All is well," he said, looking to Elizabeth as he reached his arm around her younger sister. "Let go of the footing, I have you." Miss Catherine fell into his arms and he lifted her the few feet to the grassy pasture, where she collapsed, sobbing. Darcy turned to Miss Bennet, realising for the first time that she, unlike her sister, was soaking wet. He averted his eyes and strode through the water towards her.

"My loot," she said woozily, still cradling her head with one hand. "No. I mean, my shoot. Boot-shoe. It is trapped. In the mud."

He gained her side and bending over, immediately plunged his hands beneath the water, under where her skirts floated. The boot was caught under a stone, but with three quick tugs he pulled it free. Miss Bennet gasped, losing her balance and, Darcy quickly realised, her consciousness. Catching her in his arms, he carried her to water's edge, laying her next to a shivering Miss Catherine. He manoeuvred himself out of his jacket and draped it over the girl's shoulders. Elizabeth leant over her elder sister, murmuring her name as she brushed damp hair off her cheeks. When he heard her gasp and saw her fingers had come away covered with blood, Darcy thrust his handkerchief at her. She unfolded it and held it to Miss Bennet's head while Darcy stood up, breathing heavily as he ran back to retrieve his greatcoat. He returned and lay it over Miss Bennet; still crouched, he looked at Elizabeth. Her clothing was dry, but she was pale, her movements swift and sure as she tended to her sisters.

"Elizabeth, are you harmed?"

She looked up at him, her dark eyes clouded with unease, and shook her head. "No, I had already crossed when the—"

The sound of pounding hooves broke through their shock.

"Darcy, what on earth are you about, leaving in—" Bingley, his eyes wide as he took in the scene, jumped down from his mount and moved towards them. "What has happened?"

Darcy stood and turned. "Ride to Longbourn! Bring a carriage for the ladies. Miss Bennet has been injured!"

CHAPTER
TWO

The chaos which ensued at Longbourn was no match for the ongoing tumult in Elizabeth's mind. There was shouting from Hill and wailing from Mrs Bennet, doors flung open and slammed shut, and then murmured voices in the corridor as she began gently but desperately undressing her still unconscious sister. Elizabeth could hear Kitty sobbing to Mary in the next room about her own near drowning. Over and over, her reflections centred on how quickly an ordinary morning walk had turned near tragic.

Distracted by thoughts of the silent, nearly unreadable Mr Darcy, Elizabeth had been walking ahead of her sisters as they returned home from the Lucases. Jane—her own happiness certain to be sealed in the coming hours—was listening to Kitty natter on about the bonnet Lydia took from her when she and Mr Wickham had left Longbourn some ten days earlier.

And then suddenly, there was barking and screaming and splashing.

The events were a blur—the Gouldings' dog chasing a small red fox and Kitty shrieking as she stumbled into Jane. Suddenly Jane was in the water, stumbling as she regained her feet. Elizabeth stood frozen, astonishment warring with amusement as she attempted to determine the severity of what had occurred. Then came Kitty's panicked cries and Jane's obvious distress. Just as Elizabeth had turned towards Kitty, *he* had appeared, fearless as he took in the scene and then took command of it.

If Jane had not swooned in his arms, I might have.

Had Mr Darcy not come across them, Elizabeth was certain she could have convinced Kitty to climb back up onto the bridge or helped her swing herself to the embankment. Then she could have gone to Jane, pulled her boot out of the muck and tugged her to walk out of the water...assuming she did not swoon. Unfortunately, it was apparent that Jane was injured.

Mr Jones arrived quickly and gave Jane a thorough, wordless examination; he asked Elizabeth to explain the sequence of events and said nothing more. When he finished, she led him to the parlour to announce his findings to the worried group assembled there. The apothecary's unsmiling appearance served to further upset Mrs Bennet, who began weeping anew. Mr Jones, like Mr Bennet, ignored the display; his stern expression turned more severe. A damp, grave-faced Mr Darcy reached a hand to still Mr Bingley, whose foot was tapping a frantic rhythm on the carpet. Elizabeth was dismayed to see that neither refreshments nor a warm blanket had been offered to Mr Darcy, who stood in his wet boots and jacket near the fire.

"Miss Bennet has a bruise on her head, and a small cut," Mr Jones began. "Those, as well as her swollen ankle, require bed rest for at least the next few days. Time will tell," he continued, turning to address Elizabeth and Mrs Hill rather than the mother of the injured lady. "Keep Miss Bennet still and warm and keep a cool cloth to her head in case of fever. The injury to her head may make her restless. Oh, and it is vital that she be kept calm. To that end I shall leave a—"

"Now, now. Jane is not one for dramatics," interrupted Mr Bennet, plainly uninterested in hearing more warnings from the apothecary. "We shall not see thrashing about the pillow from her."

"Papa," Elizabeth began, before worry and mortification rendered her speechless.

A pale Mr Bingley, clearly restless with the need to be of use, began pacing.

The ensuing silence, beyond Mrs Bennet's wails, was filled by Mr Darcy, who apologised if he had, by any manner of his rescue, worsened Jane's condition. Mr Jones shook his head and assured him that a bump on the head, a sprained ankle, and torn stockings were likely the worst of it. "The Bennets are sturdy girls. A cough, a fever, and a broken bone here for Miss Elizabeth has been the worst of it."

Mr Darcy and Mr Bingley excused themselves; the latter was eager to remain but the former, obviously as uncomfortable in his muddy clothes as he was with the intemperate company, begged his leave.

"Darcy is to London today, although his plans may be altered," said Mr Bingley. "If there is anything I can do, anything I can procure for Miss Bennet to alleviate her discomfort, please—"

"If you would like, I will send a note to my London physician," offered Mr Darcy. "He has some expertise with injuries to the head. I benefited from powders he prescribed when I was thrown from a horse a few years ago."

"Another heroic gesture."

Elizabeth cringed; her father's graciousness lacked the sincerity such an offer deserved, but Mr Darcy ignored it, replying, "Agreed then."

Elizabeth could not see him in full as her father stood between them, but she thought perhaps Mr Darcy was speaking to her. *For why would he wish to engage with a father who mocks such a generous offer?*

As soon as the door closed behind the two gentlemen, Mrs Bennet began her complaints.

"I am wrung out with worry for my dear girls, rescued from certain death! Mr Bennet, you must speak to Mr Goulding about that mongrel!"

It was not certain death, but it was certainly mortification that once again it had been Mr Darcy who arrived at the key moment and played hero to her family.

Mr Bennet, though appreciative, declaimed Mr Darcy's actions as heroics worthy of one of Mrs Radcliffe's novels. "And for one of Meryton's silliest girls and her sister!"

Shamed by their performance, Elizabeth moved quickly back to Jane's chamber.

———o o o———

"I shall leave a tincture I have prepared in case Miss Bennet's head pains her in coming days," Mr Jones said for at least the third time, hoping to gain the attention of her parents. Unfortunately, Mr Bennet took the opportunity of Miss Elizabeth's departure to find his own study, and he was left with only Bennet's wailing wife.

However, upon the exit of her husband, Mrs Bennet thankfully ceased her theatrics—an apothecary alone, apparently, was no worthy audience. "A tincture?" she repeated, but only vaguely, her attention divided between him and Mr Bennet's closed book-room door.

"Yes," he said. "For her head. She is bound to suffer a megrim after such a bump, and my remedy is a good one."

Mrs Bennet looked at the bottle he held with sudden attentiveness. Too late, Jones recalled just how interested she could be in 'remedies'...he always watered down whatever he prescribed her. He must ensure Miss Bennet alone received the medication; fortunately, he knew how to accomplish it.

"The medication is of a special nature," he prevaricated. "In such cases as these, the beauty of the victim could be negatively affected."

Mrs Bennet gasped in horror.

"But as long as Miss Bennet is given a spoonful daily until all pain is gone, you can prevent her from losing such attraction as she possesses. I know you will take care that she receives it."

The apothecary donned his hat and hastened off to see to an ailing tenant child, confident that he had done everything he could.

———— o o o ————

How Elizabeth wished her father had not been so facetious, so irreverent in his thanks to Mr Darcy. How Jane would have blushed had she been awake to hear his words! They were fortunate in Mr Darcy's timing and his quick actions. Did her father not realise what might have been? Death and injury needed no grand build-up; it often was swift and sure and came with little warning.

Elizabeth leant closer to her sister and pressed a fresh cloth to her brow; Jane's steady breathing came as a relief after the worries stoked by Mr Jones's visit.

Her mother, undoubtedly as concerned over her daughter's health as on bemoaning what might have been had she died before she was betrothed, could be heard crying. "Thank heavens for Mr Bingley!"

It was Mr Darcy who rescued my sisters. Mr Darcy who arrived in time to help Jane at the worst moment of her life. Elizabeth tucked the counterpane around Jane. *It is Mr Darcy who takes charge but has no need for conversation with me.*

After days of silence between them, today's encounter had led to Mr Darcy's soaking, followed swiftly by embarrassment as he once again saw her family at its worst while saving two more of her sisters. It was difficult to sort out her feelings on the situation, but Mr Bingley's words had all but destroyed her hopes.

'Darcy is to London today.'

He had come to say goodbye. He is leaving Meryton. Had my sisters not been in danger, he already would be gone. And now he remains at Netherfield due only to the soaking he took on their behalf.

Four days returned to his company, and they had managed scarcely fifteen words. 'How is your sister?' 'More coffee?' Such an ill display of curiosity and intelligence. Why could she not speak in his presence?

Mr Darcy's few words had revealed nothing. She had seen nothing in his actions or countenance beyond a wish to stand by his friend—a friend who would have returned only on Mr Darcy's word.

Why did he not speak or seek her out? He was not shy, but he *was* taciturn and the company at Longbourn was not easy. Her father had occupied Mr Darcy's conversation during dinners, and he sat alone afterwards, looking out the window, clearly wishing himself away from the cacophony and congratulating himself on his escape.

No, again I am judging him too harshly. He had professed his love once, if poorly, and welcomed her and the Gardiners warmly to Pemberley. He had acted with gentle consideration towards her at the inn and done all he could for Lydia, conspiring with her uncle to do everything and take none of the credit for it. He was all that was good, the best man she had ever known. But was it mere civility and kindness, some sense of guilt, that drove him to remedy the situation with Lydia and Wickham?

It certainly did not seem as though it was anything to what Aunt Gardiner had suspected.

Love? Never that, but a sense of honour in remedying what he must feel was his own, earlier mistake.

A small sigh from Jane pulled Elizabeth from her thoughts and back to her duty. She dipped the cloth into the bowl of water and squeezed before returning it to her sister's forehead.

— ◦ ◦ ◦ —

Darcy, left without his greatcoat and clad in a wet jacket, was eager to change into dry clothing; he and Bingley returned to Netherfield at a fast clip that left each man to his own thoughts. While he dressed, Darcy was preoccupied with concern over Elizabeth, recalling the expression of shock and gratitude on her face as she watched him lay down her elder sister and cover her with his coat. As he had stood there, wet and shivering in the cold, only the thought of Elizabeth's condition had mattered; her sisters would be well—Miss Catherine was hardly damp and Miss Bennet was more in shock than in any danger. Or so he thought until he had seen the blood on her temple. Unfortunately, Bingley too had seen his 'angel' bleeding from a head wound; after seeing his stricken expression, Darcy accepted that he could not abandon his friend today. He penned a quick note to his cousin and another to his physician, and carried them downstairs to be sent express to London.

A footman directed him to the library, where he found Bingley's worries were on full display; the younger man was pacing, impatient and muttering by a table set with brandy, cold meats, rolls and cheese.

"Ah, there you are, finally! I thought you might need sustenance after all that happened."

"I am grateful, thank you." Darcy's eyes flickered over the selection as he poured a glass of brandy. "The library?"

Bingley gestured at the mostly empty bookshelves. "I thought to find some medical guidance in the volumes here. I did not," he replied to Darcy's questioning look before his emotions tipped over and he cried, "Blast, what a thing that was! What happened?"

Darcy shook his head. "You heard as I did. A dog chased a fox across the footbridge, startling Miss Bennet and Miss Catherine. One knocked the other into the water and then fell in herself."

Bingley pulled at his hair. "Poor Miss Bennet. I am wretched with worry. She was so pale."

"Mr Jones said she shall be well." Ignoring the small pang of hunger he felt, Darcy sank into a chair and prepared to provide Bingley a new set of reassurances.

"The country is a dangerous place."

"Nor more than is any town or—"

"I realise I sound like Caroline, but she referred to dangers of a social kind, which mean little to me. These are real," Bingley cried, warming to his subject. "The country hazards of nature, of flora and fauna! The water, and errant dogs and foxes! These are proven dangers! That bridge must be rebuilt with a railing."

"You and Mr Bennet can work that out between you as the bridge connects your estates. That is, if you plan to purchase Netherfield."

"I do, I shall! That is, if Miss Bennet—if she agrees to be Mrs Bingley—determines we should remain in Hertfordshire."

"It will be a decision for both of you when she awakens." Darcy, giving into his appetite, rose and inspected the table. He chose a roll and some cheese. "Come, sit and have something to eat."

Bingley ignored him. "She *shall* awaken."

"Of course. I am sure she will be lively enough tomorrow when you visit, and fully recovered when I return from London."

"You cannot leave Netherfield now." Bingley looked at him, alarmed. "You cannot leave me here, alone, to my thoughts and regrets. I was not there to assist. I dilly-dallied over my blasted beaver. Yours did not fly off, even as you rode willy-nilly after hearing the screams. I was occupied with giving chase to a ridiculous hat, when I have five just the same in my dressing room."

"*Five?*" Darcy nearly choked on the Stilton.

Bingley nodded sheepishly before saying mournfully, "I chose vanity over my heart."

The self-reproach in his friend's voice was an unwelcome reminder of days' past, when Darcy's confession of Miss Bennet's true feelings had led Bingley to fault himself for causing her pain. If this wallowing in needless guilt was a sign of maturity, Darcy resolved it must be banished. Only one of them deserved any blame in this situation; equally innocent was a neighbourhood dog, doing no more than following its instincts in pursuing a fox.

Had either of us followed our instincts last autumn and disregarded the opinions of others, at least one of us would already be married.

"You deserve no chastisement. You knew nothing of why I rode off. It was luck we both were there, for your coat was as needed as mine. The true heroics are those of Miss Elizabeth, who likely would have pulled both her sisters from any danger."

15

Bingley, looking pleased to find cause for praising someone, nodded eagerly. "Miss Elizabeth is an intrepid and fearless young lady. She acted as needed, with courage, as you did."

Darcy paused, his admiration for Elizabeth stirring the memory of her calming one sister as she held the other, trying to press her own warmth and life force into Miss Bennet.

"You would have acted the same, my friend, if the wind had instead played its tricks on me. As it is, both of us—and Miss Elizabeth—took part in the events."

He was pleased to see Bingley's expression soften. "Miss Bennet shall be well."

"She shall. Mr Jones has things in hand but I have sent word to my physician in town. There is no reason to think Miss Bennet will have any lasting injury, but thoroughness is always for the best."

"Ah, wise thinking. You are a good friend."

Bingley says that too often. I am a poor friend and rejected lover.

After a moment, Darcy overcame his maudlin thoughts. He wished one more chance to see Elizabeth. "I have informed my cousin of my delay, but I must leave at first light. Shall we send a note to Longbourn and ask after the ladies? If the news is as you hope, perhaps we could pay a short call later this afternoon."

CHAPTER
THREE

Longbourn had been quieter since Lydia's marriage, but having two daughters abed roused Mr and Mrs Bennet to livelier conversation than usual. His side of their exchanges was marked by amusement; hers by distress.

"My daughters are of the country, yet flee in terror from a fox and dog? It is rather shocking behaviour. At least Lizzy is surefooted."

"Mr Bennet!"

Elizabeth found escape in Jane's room from her father's droll observations and her mother's effusions, but occasionally she could still hear their voices. By late afternoon, she could see improvement in her sister. Grateful no fever had set in, she did as Mr Jones instructed and kept Jane warm—wrapped warmly enough to have made the patient uncomfortable. Elizabeth was standing by the west-facing window in Jane's room, her eyes resting on the silhouette of trees against the reddish-gold sky when she heard a small, weak voice.

"Mama? Lizzy?"

Quickly she turned, gasping with relief at the sight of her sister attempting to push off the heavy pile of blankets and quilts atop the counterpane.

"Jane!"

"So hot, Lizzy. Whelp me hith..." Jane managed to pull one arm free of the covers.

Elizabeth hurried to lay her hand on her sister's forehead, and discerning no fever, began peeling back the blankets. Jane's words were confused, but at least she spoke them! "Oh, how good it is to hear your voice."

"Why have I been shleping? Leaping? I mean, sleeping?" Jane said, blinking into the reddish glow. "'Tis early. Or late?" She began to sit up and winced, lifting a hand to her head. "Oh!"

Elizabeth sank onto the bed beside her. "I am sorry, dearest, if it pains you so dreadfully. Is your ankle hurting as well?"

Jane's brow creased in consternation, her eyes nearly crossing with effort as her legs shifted underneath the counterpane until she freed one. "Look, Lizzy! Mama says I have the wittiest...um, prettiest limbs!" She thrust her foot out. "Oh! My ankle! Ow!"

As Elizabeth did her best to replace Jane's foot upon its pillow, Mrs Bennet burst through the door and moved quickly to Jane's side. "Do I hear my dear Jane? Are you well? Let me get a look at you."

She peered closely at her eldest daughter; if Elizabeth had any question as to whether her inspection was more for Jane's welfare or to ascertain that her beauty had suffered no lasting damage, it was answered when Mrs Bennet leant back. "The bruising is hardly of notice; some powder surely will cover it. Do not fret, for I am certain any scars will heal."

She patted Jane's hand and gave her an indulgent smile. "Mr Bingley will not mind."

"Mr Bingley?" asked Jane, sounding more confused than tired. "Do I know him?"

"Jane?" Mary opened the door, stepping inside and allowing Mrs Hill to enter with a tray. "Oh, my sister...you look awful!"

To Elizabeth's surprise, Mrs Bennet suddenly took command of the room.

"Out, all of you," she said sharply, herding her daughters and the servant towards the door. "You are upsetting dear Jane!"

As she was pushed into the corridor, Elizabeth glanced back at her sister, who seemed preoccupied with waving her own fingers about in the air before her face. She certainly did not look upset, no; that emotion seemed reserved for Elizabeth herself, as she paced outside the door. Fortunately, she did not have to wait long.

"Mr Bingley has been quite worried. He sent a note a little while ago enquiring as to your health. We must reply to Netherfield with the good news!" Mrs Bennet bustled out the room with the same intensity with which she had entered, seemingly no longer concerned about visitors. "Mr Bennet!"

Hurriedly entering, closing the door behind her, Elizabeth blew out a breath—relieved to note that at least Jane's pallor was improved. "If you continue to perform so well in sipping your broth, you will have no further need to practise French or table-painting."

She was pleased to see a familiar expression of amusement on Jane's face. When her sister set down the spoon by the nearly empty bowl, Elizabeth moved the tray to the dresser.

"Lizzy, who is Mr Bingley?"

Elizabeth froze. "Jane, you jest nearly as well as Papa."

"Jesting. Jesters juggling jingles. Bingles. Bingley? Does he juggle?"

"You are confused." Elizabeth sat on the foot of the bed, careful to leave some room between herself and Jane's sore ankle; concerned as she was about exacerbating her sister's injuries, it was Jane's bewilderment she now found worrisome.

"My head hurts," Jane said plaintively. "Hurts, Lizzy."

"My poor sister. You hit your head quite hard." Elizabeth paused, holding back her own tears. "Do you remember today's events, and why you are abed at teatime?"

The question earned her a bemused look. "Ding, dong, bell, Pussy's in the well. Who put her in? Little Johnny Flynn. Who pulled her out? Little Tommy Stout....Kitty? Kitty in the water?" She spoke this last with frantic concern.

"She is well," Elizabeth said, gripping her sister's hand to reassure her. "Her hems were damp and her boots were sodden and her skirts suffered a jagged tear from a nail, but she is otherwise unharmed."

Jane laughed with apparent relief, and suddenly she sat straight up in bed. "Who pulled her out? Mr Darcy! It does not rhyme, Lizzy, but Mr Darcy pulled us out! Mr Darcy!"

It was both nonsensical and overloaded with meaning. The Bennet family had kept Mr Darcy well-occupied with saving its daughters. Elizabeth bit her lip, trying not to cry.

"He did, although Kitty was less in need of a saviour than of some common sense," she made herself say lightly.

"Who pulled her out? Mr Darcy Stout. But he is not, not really. Tall. Not stout. Tossed me over his strong shoulders. *'Dieu et mon droit!'* he cried!"

"No, that is not quite..." Elizabeth began hesitantly, uncertain how to navigate Jane's muddled thinking, which seemed to have confused her tumble with the Battle of Crecy. "He pulled you from the water. You had hit your head on the footbridge as you fell, I think. You collapsed into his arms."

"That is what I said." Wincing, Jane lifted her hand and touched the back of her head. "Would have lost the war. Wounded."

Mr Darcy always arrives when most needed. How I wish he was here now!

Her brow furrowed, Elizabeth forced a smile as she continued to press for a sensible memory. "But Mr Darcy was accompanied by Mr Bingley, who arrived moments later, and rushed off to fetch the carriage. He too was helpful. He rode beside the carriage, staring at you with such devoted concern, and dare I say—"

"Rescue, my lord Darcy, rescue, rescue! Darcy enacts more wonders than a man, daring an opposite to every danger!"

Richard III now? Elizabeth thought. *Dear Lord,* she wanted to cry, to pray aloud. *How long will Jane suffer these delusions?*

"He loves me, Lizzy," Jane sighed. "Mr Darcy loves me, loves me, would give his kingdom for me."

And as ridiculous as it was, even knowing Jane was not in her right mind...Elizabeth had a nearly desperate wish to set her straight on this score.

Even deluded, how could Jane think it? Mr Darcy had not looked at Jane once he had draped his greatcoat over her; he had looked at *her* and asked after *her* welfare, assured *her* that Jane would be well, and led Kitty over to their small circle.

He looked at me. For the first time since his return to Meryton, he looked at me and found my eyes.

When the carriage arrived, Mr Bennet and his man had lifted Jane and lay her across the seat while Mr Bingley had paced, staring worriedly at them. Mr Darcy had occupied himself with ensuring Kitty and Elizabeth were safely seated before he rode to Meryton to fetch Mr Jones. He had been occupied, managing things. Now, having done his duty and saved Jane, he was onto whatever the next item of business, which, Mr Bingley had said, was supposed to be saying his farewells at Longbourn. He might require only a change into dry clothes and be gone again. Gone without the two of them managing a word beyond how well they both were and how fine the coffee tasted.

But his gaze held more, she told herself. *There was more there than simple concern for me and my sisters.*

Elizabeth's prolonged pause to gather her thoughts allowed Jane more time to express hers—such as she was able. "Lavender's green, diddle, diddle, Lavender's blue. You must love me, Mr Darcy, cause I love you. When will he come, diddle, diddle, what will he say? When will he come, Lizzy, Lizzy? Be it today?"

Elizabeth made one more attempt. "You have never loved Mr Darcy, dearest. You love Mr Bingley. Cannot you try and remember?"

Jane looked up at her sleepily. "No such Bing...I mean, thing. Oh! Lizzy, do the people hereabouts know I am to be married to Mr Darcy? I am afraid they might not. Who knew the footbridge was the place to get husbands?"

Elizabeth startled. Her heart racing, she sought to assure

herself it was all nonsense, even find the humour in it. But Jane was not teasing her; Jane rarely teased and she certainly was not in any condition presently to do so. *Why, she is confusing Mr Darcy with Mr Bingley! Is the shock so great that she has mixed up their names, their identities?* She breathed in and out slowly, quelling her unease. *Jane will sleep, and in the morning, her thoughts will have settled. All will be well.*

It was only the sound of voices—voices Elizabeth identified quickly as belonging to Mr Darcy and Mr Bingley—that stirred her from the bewilderment created by her sister's shocking confusion. Jane's deep, even breaths allowed Elizabeth to escape the room without responding. Before she could fully think over her sister's meaning and state of mind, she would greet the gentlemen from Netherfield. It was an uncomfortable truth that she could not trust her parents to greet them with grace and gratitude. She could hear the conversation as she smoothed her hair and gown and descended the stairs.

"Miss Catherine had a cough prior to today's incident?"

Mr Bennet chuckled at Mr Darcy's enquiry. "We all look for a manner in which to distinguish ourselves. With four sisters and few talents to display, our Kitty determined a cough would occasion attention to her presence."

Oh no. She quickened her step and entered the sitting room.

"Miss Elizabeth!"

Mr Bingley sprang from his chair and took a step towards her eagerly; his usual friendly smile was in place, though overwritten with apprehension.

Behind him, Mr Darcy rose to his feet and bowed, as grave and distant as he had been a day earlier. "Miss Elizabeth, I hope you are well?"

She cloaked her dismay in a tight smile and nodded. Quickly, Mr Bingley began to speak, his worried mien showing the concern he clearly felt for Jane. "Miss Bennet, she is well? Your parents have assured us of her good health and Mr Jones anticipates a quick recovery, but you are her dearest sister and come from her bedside—"

"Bingley—" Mr Darcy's voice was nearly inaudible.

Despite her astonishment over the day's events and the melancholy in her heart, Elizabeth nearly smiled. Her uncertainty over Jane's state of mind was set aside by the kindly earnestness in Mr Bingley, plainly desperate for news of his angel's recovery.

She sat and did all she could to assure him, Mr Darcy, and her parents that Jane had awakened, eaten well, and expressed only minor discomfort. *After all,* Elizabeth thought, pausing as Hill carried in refreshments, *what are slippery rocks as a cause of injury when compared to Jane's state of mind?*

Gazing from one man to the other—one of whom deserved Jane's gratitude and the other, her own love and hand in marriage —she said, "On Jane's behalf, and mine, I must express thanks to you both for your quick thinking and assistance."

"If you must thank us, please allow Darcy the far greater share," replied a solemn Mr Bingley. "I was off chasing my flyaway hat when he heard cries of distress. Much as I would wish to have arrived sooner and lent greater aid to your sisters, I did the little I could. Darcy, and yourself, Miss Elizabeth, are the true heroes."

His friend demurred. "Had we not happened upon them, I am certain Miss Elizabeth would have had it well in hand."

"Indeed," chuckled Mr Bennet. "Our Lizzy is indeed an intrepid girl. Clearly too clever to be frightened of a wayward hound."

Mrs Bennet was roused to protest immediately about young Peter Goulding's vicious cur and the family's constant troubles in maintaining their household and livestock. As she concluded the tale of a hen who chased poor Lydia as a child and began another harangue about the troubles created by sheep, Mary entered.

"Mama, Kitty's cough has worsened. I have asked Cook to prepare her special tea."

Elizabeth rose, alarmed. She had seen Kitty only briefly, assured by Mr Jones that her younger sister had suffered only a brief shock.

Her parents showed less concern; Mr Bennet looked longingly at his library door while Mrs Bennet appeared embarrassed by any sign of her daughters' frailties. "Kitty did not fall into the water as did Jane. My girls are hardy stock," she reassured Mr Bingley. "Jane will be downstairs in a day or so, with no sign of the accident left upon her.

"I shall see to Kitty shortly," she added, giving Mary a dismissive look before turning to Elizabeth. "Do sit down, Lizzy."

Instead, she walked across the room to the window; it was cooler there and her cheeks were burning with indignation. She heard her father's dry chuckle, before Mr Darcy's deep voice filled the room.

"As was mentioned this morning, I have taken the liberty of sending for my physician in London. I was involved and bear witness to your daughters' potential injuries, and wish to ensure the good health of both Miss Bennet and Miss Catherine."

Elizabeth turned and stared at him; he was half-turned away, but his handsome profile seemed even more noble than a few hours ago.

"Such a kindness, Mr Darcy!"

Mr Bennet ignored his wife's effusive thanks. "Yours is a liberty we must suffer, sir, in order to reduce any suffering in our girls. I must say, you have taken a strong interest in their welfare since your timely return to Hertfordshire."

He raised his eyebrows and looked at Mr Bingley. "I cannot doubt your concern equals that of your heroic friend."

Embarrassed by her father's mocking tone, Elizabeth broke in. "Mr Bingley cares deeply for the welfare of all his friends, and has been most solicitous of Jane's health and happiness, be it last autumn at Netherfield or earlier today." She turned to Mr Darcy. "Thank you. We appreciate whatever guidance your physician can supply to us."

He looked startled by her direct address. *Is he amazed there is one Bennet showing him graciousness or is it simply that it is I who display it?*

Another few minutes passed as Mrs Bennet admired Mr Bingley's merits as a friend and neighbour and Mr Darcy's gifts of fortuitous timing and thoughtfulness in sending for his physician.

The effusive praise drove Mr Bennet to his book-room and appeared to discomfit Mr Bingley. Elizabeth saw Mr Darcy glancing impatiently at the clock and out of the window she had abandoned a few minutes earlier; dusk was settling.

Of course, he was to leave for London this morning and still wishes to be gone from Hertfordshire as soon as possible.

"Much as we appreciate your presence today at the stream, and all that you did to assist my sisters, I regret we delayed your journey to London, sir." Her words came out too clipped, without the warmth she intended, and clearly, that is how he heard them, for he turned to her, looking startled.

"I-I must go, to attend to family matters. It shall be a short visit."

"Miss Darcy is well, I hope." At his nod, Elizabeth smiled. "I enjoyed making her acquaintance."

It felt daring to mention his sister. Their meeting at Pemberley seemed to be from another time—the time before Lydia—before the distance and formality that had marked all but a few days of their acquaintance returned. He had encouraged Mr Bingley, and returned with him. And now he was leaving. Making wishes on flower petals had been a childhood whimsy; Elizabeth was too wise to believe she could turn back the calendar and too worn to hope Mr Darcy could understand her true regrets.

"We would not wish to keep her brother from her. Please give her my regards."

"I shall do so," he replied, looking as though he wished to say more.

But he did not, instead looking grateful when Hill entered with his dried and brushed greatcoat. The delay in its return only added to Elizabeth's mortification, and she was almost grateful when he and Mr Bingley left to return to Netherfield.

The door had no sooner closed than Mrs Bennet moved from espousing platitudes about Mr Darcy's kindness to venting her displeasure that it was he, rather than Mr Bingley, who had saved Jane.

"Would that Mr Darcy's hat had blown off and Mr Bingley's had fit his head! But no, he is a wealthy man with perfectly fitting hats. Poor Mr Bingley, losing his hat and his chance to rescue our Jane!"

CHAPTER
FOUR

E arly a riser as Elizabeth usually was, concern about Jane and regret over Mr Darcy's departure kept her from a peaceful sleep, and she found that she was not the first to hear Jane's thoughts on the daring and dear Mr Darcy. As she stepped into the hall after looking in on Kitty, Mary emerged from Jane's chamber.

"How is my sister?"

Mary, ever sombre, appeared troubled. "Jane has improved in health and spirit. She is grateful, perhaps too grateful, to Mr Darcy, and forgetful of Mr Bingley."

"She was the same yesterday. Hopefully it is a symptom of short duration."

After a moment of hesitation, Mary replied, "She asked whether Mr Darcy would visit today so that she could thank him for his aid. But...but she...she did so in a song."

Elizabeth breathed a sigh of relief. "That is all? No Shakespeare? No mentions of war?"

Mary frowned, and leant in close. "Jane did not respond to anything I said regarding Mr Bingley. She only wished to, um, sing about Mr Darcy. I am less than familiar with flirtations and courting," she whispered, "but is Mr Bingley's proposal not the one Jane and Mama have awaited?"

Elizabeth drew in an unsteady breath. "Obviously, our sister's confusion from yesterday's accident is of the greatest concern. We must allow her mind and body the rest it requires to fully recover. Pray keep whatever Jane says within the walls of her chamber."

"Best to speak to Kitty soon, before she hears something and writes to Lydia of it."

Of course, Elizabeth had not considered that Kitty's rooms shared a wall with Jane's! "I shall, but first I best try to speak to Jane."

Mary frowned, then reached to press Elizabeth's hand. "I shall speak to Kitty. You will have enough difficulty convincing Mama that whatever troubles Jane suffers will not result in our undoing."

After thanking Mary, relieved that at least one other Bennet had a bit of sense, Elizabeth took a deep breath. The idea that Jane's transfer of affections from one rich man to another even wealthier one could ruin them all was more perverse than distressing—and the least of Jane's problems. She nearly laughed at the irony in such agitations, but her concern for Jane and, selfishly, yes, her own pain over Mr Darcy's departure gnawed at her.

He has not abandoned us. He sent for his physician and promised he would return after completing family business. It was more than she had known he would do when he left her, still in tears, at the Lambton Inn. Then, he was off to find Lydia and fix the situation —without informing her. Now he was simply gone, unaware of the peculiar turn in Jane's mind. As were her parents and Mr Bingley.

Poor Mr Bingley! His heart would be battered by such an odd rejection!

She turned the knob and peered into her sister's chamber.

"Jane?"

"Lizzy!"

If asked, Elizabeth could report that Jane awoke with less pain in her ankle, a purple bruise on her temple, and a heart full of worry for Kitty and gratitude for the gentleman who had come to their rescue. Jane's mind, however, was still nonsensical, and definitely no clearer as to which of the gentlemen she owed her heart. She sat in her bed, one of Mrs Bennet's lace-trimmed pillows under her ankle and a soft blue blanket around her shoulders. Kitty had been without any such embellished comforts until Elizabeth draped her own prettiest shawl around her.

Jane smiled serenely and looked like a queen, but her voice was singsong.

"Old Doctor Foster went to Gloucester...why does he not come here? My head aches something queer."

"I believe Mr Darcy's own physician shall come today," Elizabeth reassured her. "Mr Bingley shall wish to know how you fare."

"Mr Bingley's a physician? I'd no idea his position... Kitty...is she well? I remember that she fell!"

Before Elizabeth could reply, Jane peered down at herself, looking somewhat alarmed as she considered her nightgown. She shrugged off the blanket. "Lizzy, I hate to be a pest, but I should like to get dressed."

"Oh, you need not. The doctor is accustomed to his patients in their nightclothes."

She did not appear to hear, moving out of the bed, landing softly on her feet. She grimaced and gingerly tried to stand. "Jane," Elizabeth scolded as she moved quickly to support her sister. Wrapping an arm around her, she led Jane to the soft chair by the window. "Dearest, Mr Jones wished you to stay in your bed. The physician will come in here to examine you."

Jane would not have it, and Elizabeth quickly saw that nothing would do for the patient but that she be dressed, and immediately. Not until she saw that Elizabeth was removing clothing from her wardrobe did she give any semblance of calm; however, she began singing *Scarborough Fair* once again—and her lyric was hardly anything for which Elizabeth could be thankful.

"Sober and grave grows merry in time! Mr Darcy shall be the true love of mine."

Mr Bingley would be so distressed if he were to hear it—if he thought Jane's smiles were for another. It hardly mattered what Mr Darcy would think; he would not be coming today. He had gone to London and Elizabeth thought it unlikely he would be returning any time soon, no matter his promise. He had been leaving, making his escape from Meryton—from her—when he spared the time to pull Jane and Kitty from the water. Nothing called him back here. Certainly not the lady he had once professed to love, and certainly not her ailing sister.

In the time it took her to grasp Jane's arms and help her to her dressing table, the dismal revelation that her sister's mind was unimproved from the prior's day's confusion had settled, unhappily, within Elizabeth. Jane's bizarre illness must be coped with, and most importantly she must be patient and understanding and —for now—say nothing of Mr Darcy's leave-taking.

"You shall stay in your gown and in your bed unless you can tell me this," Elizabeth said. She held up three fingers. "What do you see?"

Jane gave her an odd look. "One for sorrow, two for mirth, three for a funeral..." she gasped, grasping Elizabeth's hand and pulling it until she held up four fingers instead of three. "And four for birth," she finished, chin in the air. She looked at Elizabeth reproachfully.

Well, however insensible Jane's mind, there was nothing wrong with her vision.

This was not the Jane of yesterday morning. Her concern deepening, Elizabeth swallowed, uncertain of what next step to take with this changed creature. She stepped to the wardrobe.

"Blue is your favourite and brings out your eyes." She held up a gown she was certain Mr Bingley had admired her in, but Jane shook her head, a pout upon her lips.

"Mr Darcy loves yellow, I know. I recall him saying so."

Elizabeth stared at her in wonder. *Would she speak in nothing but rhyme henceforth? Would Mr Bingley believe her permanently damaged?*

Jane was fair and had no yellow gowns, but it seemed important to try and mollify her. Only Mary and Elizabeth, darker in hair and eye than their sisters, wore yellow; Mrs Bennet had made certain of it. "I see no yellow gowns, but green is always a favourite."

With a resolute smile, she took on the role of lady's maid and helped her sister dress and arrange her hair. Jane hummed of her true love—*Mr Darcy*—at the Scarborough Fair while Elizabeth was occupied with her own deliberations.

Jane had always been a sensible girl, the ideal eldest daughter, the perfect older sister and cousin to little ones. She had a maternal instinct that others of their acquaintance lacked, and in doing so had always put the concerns of others ahead of her own. She was a rational creature, albeit a sensitive, gentle one. Jane had never been a rambunctious girl; Elizabeth had relied on the Long and Lucas boys as her playmates in games of climbing and hoops. Jane was gentle and sweet, and her fall into the stream may have affected her far more greatly than it would have Lydia or Kitty or many other girls.

She was certainly not a coquette. Elizabeth's fears were not centred solely upon the unusual expression in rhyme and song— but that Jane would speak of *any* man, at all, in *any* way. She had grieved Mr Bingley's loss much more, Elizabeth knew, than she had ever confessed. Had the knock on the head released some sort of fear and need of Jane's? The fear of loneliness? The need to be loved?

Has Jane simply transposed the faces of Mr Bingley and Mr Darcy in her confusion? The two men could not be more dissimilar: one was handsome and light, always earnest and smiling; the other was tall and broad-shouldered, his hair and eyes dark, radiating intelligence and, she had learnt, repressed passion.

Where did that passion go? Did it slip away during the nights while he slept or did he set it aside to give to the next lady who catches his eye and heart?

If any remained for her, Mr Darcy had successfully concealed it. His eyes avoided hers; his conversation was with others. *As it has been for me,* Elizabeth admitted. She had not known how to approach the man and express her gratitude, let alone hold a conversation that was not centred on filling his coffee cup or asking after Miss Darcy. *We are all politeness.*

Stop it! she chided herself. *It is Jane's health which is our most important concern. She has spent months repressing her feelings for and about Mr Bingley. In her confusion, injured, she may indeed be referring to Mr Bingley, but giving him Darcy's name.*

"Lizzy! I would talk to you!" Mrs Bennet's shrill voice was heard in the hall.

Elizabeth persuaded Jane to sit and finish her tea until she could send in Mary or Kitty to help with her stockings and slippers. She slipped out the door, shutting it behind her, to find her mother standing just outside of it, looking more fretful than was her wont.

Mrs Bennet took Elizabeth's hand and pulled her down the stairs and into the morning room, where her father sat with her sisters. Kitty was curled up in the corner of the settee; Mary sat stiffly beside her, holding her hands in her lap and looking worried.

Mr Bennet glanced up from his newspaper as they entered the room and smirked. "Ah Lizzy. A report of a most alarming nature has reached us."

"Jane is singing about Mr Darcy," Mary said, eliciting a gasp from Mrs Bennet.

"Oh, this is worse than I imagined," she cried.

Elizabeth glared at Mary and made her way to a chair by the fire. Her mother followed and took the pillowed seat, her usual, beside her.

"Lizzy, tell us what Jane has said. What does she mean? Has she thrown over Mr Bingley for his friend?"

"Mr Hurst is already married," Mr Bennet assured her, winking at Kitty.

Kitty giggled. "Has Mama been reading Mrs Radcliffe's novels with Jane?"

Mrs Bennet drew a hand to her heart. "Mr Bennet, you know I

refer to that Mr Darcy! He stands about silently without a word to those who feed him a fine dinner and it is he who has plotted to steal away our Jane from poor Mr Bingley!"

"Mama, there is no plot—" Elizabeth began.

"Mr Bingley should have saved her! Mr Darcy had to get in the way and make himself the hero. And now look what he has done—muddling up Jane's happiness and Mr Bingley's proposal. Had dear Mr Bingley saved Jane and carried her home—*he* would not have bothered with a carriage—all would be well."

"Beyond a bruised head, ruined boots and a swollen ankle?" said an amused Mr Bennet.

"Fleeting injuries, no lasting damages!" Huffing, Mrs Bennet plopped in her chair. "Those awful Gouldings and their dogs! Longbourn shall never have a dog!"

Mr Bennet winked at Kitty. "I hope old Rex cannot hear you, Mrs Bennet."

"It is not such a terrible outcome. Mr Darcy does not smile as much as Mr Bingley, but he is taller and at least as handsome," offered Kitty, adding, "and his arms are very strong."

"Sister!"

Mary's indignation went unnoticed by Kitty, who appeared grateful—or greedy—for the attention. "Mr Darcy is very, very rich. Lydia says Wickham is quite jealous of Mr Darcy's wealth since they were raised as brothers and he has received nothing he is owed."

"Jealous, you say? Covetous is a better word," Mr Bennet said.

With the mention of Mr Darcy's wealth, it was as though the sun broke through churning storm clouds, and Mrs Bennet's confusion gave way to pragmatism. With a gleam in her eye, she looked at Kitty.

"Mr Darcy is the nephew of a peer, is he not? A duke?"

Kitty shrugged.

All eyes turned to Elizabeth, who was vexed that she had lost control of the conversation. Her patience with her family and their faith in Jane's feelings for Mr Bingley's hopes were faltering at an equal rate. How could they fix upon Jane's muddle between Mr

Darcy and Mr Bingley when she was not yet even in her right mind? Could they not see the importance of keeping either man as far away from her as possible for the moment?

"His uncle is the earl of Matlock, Mama," Kitty added.

Delight was a prettier emotion than greed, but Elizabeth saw them both in her mother's expression. "He has his own estate and house in town? No mother in the dowager house for Jane to contend with?"

Kitty answered eagerly. "Mr Darcy is orphaned, Mama, and guardian to his younger sister."

Elizabeth stared at Kitty, who shrugged and gave credit to Lydia for imparting valuable information on the family with whom her husband had once been connected.

Her eyes still alight, Mrs Bennet nodded. "Then he has need of a wife."

Finally, after too many minutes spent listening in amusement, Mr Bennet spoke—to Elizabeth's relief—with more reproach than sardonic pleasure. "Does Mr Darcy have need of the wife you wish? He is in no way obligated to marry our Jane, let alone have feeling for her. We must not be mercenary, Mrs Bennet. Mr Darcy pulled Jane from the raging torrents of our meagre stream. He may have left her to the aid of her sisters had he suspected the shackles of marriage awaited him."

"One of them must marry Jane, and if it is Mr Darcy she now wants, I will reconcile myself to it!" Mrs Bennet waved her fan, clearly satisfied that all had been settled.

"Mr Darcy does not wish to marry Jane!" Elizabeth cried, incredulous that it was necessary to speak such words aloud. "He is a friend to Mr Bingley and came here to encourage his suit! Jane is in no condition to want anything from either of them! She must be given time to heal."

Mr Bennet snorted his amusement. "You know a great deal about their intentions, Lizzy. Tell us, is Mr Darcy truly of heroic character? Will he honour Jane or stand aside for his friend, who appears to be in love with her but is incapable of making a proposal? He need not dampen the knees of his trousers by it or compose flowery prose—he simply must ask the question."

"Why should Mr Darcy not marry me?" cried Kitty. "He saved me as well and has sent for his London physician, for me!"

The shocked laughter which met her assertions soon led Kitty into a piteous coughing fit. Mrs Hill appeared and led her to the kitchens to sit near the steaming kettles.

Mr Bennet rose, tapping his newspaper on his leg as he often did when he wished to dismiss a problem without addressing it.

"You worry too much. Jane is a country lass, and a bump on the head shall not fell her." His smile held what he no doubt meant as a placating expression. "Love is a tricky business, eh, Lizzy? We must balance the hopeful truth with tenuous wishes, and hope that no one, including two gentlemen at Netherfield, are the wiser."

CHAPTER
FIVE

Not an hour later, visitors arrived at Longbourn. Hill's appearance in the drawing room brought Jane a look of anticipation, which turned quickly to disappointment when the callers were announced.

"Mr Bingley is here, ma'am, with another gentleman, a Mr Tilden."

Mr Bingley practically burst into the room, bowing deeply to all but his eyes intent on Jane as he introduced Mr Darcy's physician to the Bennets. Elizabeth waited with bated breath, hoping against hope that Jane would see Mr Bingley as the 'Mr Darcy' she spoke...er, sang of so lovingly. She was to be disappointed, however; Jane only slumped morosely in her chair.

Mr Tilden was an older man, stout and bespectacled; he was near in age to her own father, thought Elizabeth, with a kindly look about his eyes. He waved off tea, asserting that Mr Bingley had welcomed him a short while ago with refreshments, and indicated he would prefer to attend to his business at Longbourn and be on his way. His daughter, married to a vicar in Knebworth, neared her confinement, and wished his company.

As Jane and Kitty were present, he declared he would give them each a cursory examination right there in the drawing room. Mary gasped and Mrs Bennet tittered, but he explained he would be merely listening to hearts and looking at eyes while he asked questions.

"Jane's ankle!" cried Mrs Bennet.

"Of course." He nodded at Mr Bingley, who looked longingly at Jane as he was led off to Mr Bennet's book-room for the duration of the examination.

— ∘ ∘ ∘ —

Elizabeth liked Mr Tilden and the gentle manner in which he conducted himself with her sisters. He advised marjoram for Kitty's tea and a poultice spread if her cough worsened, and then peered closely at Jane's ankle. She winced only once as he examined it.

"This is healing well," he said, when Jane showed him how well it flexed. "I am pleased by the efforts of your Mr Jones. I see he did not rely on the country remedy of a cataplasm of cow dung on your bruises, but applied a poultice of bread, elder flower and camomile."

Mrs Bennet looked offended at the phrase 'country remedy' but her countenance soon turned proud. "Mr Jones has done right by us these twenty years. None at Longbourn has died."

"Did he prescribe anything else? Tonics or draughts?"

"No!" Mrs Bennet cried, too loudly. Elizabeth peered at her in some disapproval. "He ought to have, I am sure," she added more quietly.

Mr Tilden nodded gravely in appreciation and turned back to Jane. He examined the bump on her head and the small bruise on her temple before gently touching her scalp, ceasing his efforts when Jane cried out in pain. Then he asked her to follow his finger with her eyes, and look up and down.

"Miss Bennet, there is a swelling behind your ear. Unnoticeable to anyone's eye," he assured her and her mother and sisters, "but it should have had a cold compress placed there immediately. Better a day late than never, I suppose."

Mrs Bennet huffed and hurried off to find Hill.

"Is there any pain inside your head, when you move or even when still?"

"Jane fell down and broke her crown, and Kitty came tumbling after," Jane said serenely.

Mr Tilden raised a brow, his questioning more urgent. "Do you know who I am?"

"Doctor Foster?" she asked uncertainly.

To Elizabeth's surprise, he smiled gently at Jane. "Old Doctor Foster who went to Gloucester?" he asked.

She nodded tentatively and then, again to Elizabeth's surprise, she put her hand out towards Mr Tilden. "No...that is not right. Not Foster. Mr Darcy's doctor."

"Very good, Miss Bennet. Have your thoughts been in a bit of a scramble?"

Again, she nodded.

"Do things seem more clear this afternoon?"

"Yes," she said and he stood.

"All is well. I advise you to continue as you are. Since you are improving, I hesitate to prescribe anything unless you are beset by new symptoms."

"But what of the singing?" asked Kitty.

"And the rhymes," added Mary.

"I have seen far more unusual symptoms from a head injury in my day," said Mr Tilden. "And it appears she is getting past it. What she needs is time and rest, as Mr Jones has already prescribed."

"Mr Darcy is the bridegroom, and I shall be his bride. I shall like it above all things," Jane trilled in a singsong voice.

Elizabeth, Kitty and Mary all shook their heads at the doctor in a frantic display of denial.

He turned to Elizabeth. "If you could avail me of paper and pen and a cup of tea, I should like to write to Mr Darcy before I leave."

There was something in his gaze that alerted Elizabeth to a deeper meaning. After asking tea be sent, she led the man from the parlour to the small sitting room where she often wrote her letters.

"Will this do, sir?"

"It will." He looked about the room; it was rarely used by the rest of her family, and thus its furnishings were somewhat worn and the wall papers a little faded. Elizabeth found it charming—comfortable and with a good view of the woods—but hoped Mr Tilden would spare Mr Darcy a description of it.

"May I ask you a question?" Elizabeth waited for his nod before seating herself in a chair by the fire.

Mr Tilden settled into the chair at the writing desk. "I would be disappointed if you did not." At her look of surprise, he continued. "When Mr Darcy wrote to me, he mentioned your concern for your sisters' welfare. He also referred to you particularly as the person to whom I should discuss Miss Bennet's true condition."

At her gasp, he waved his hand. "She shall be fully well. In fact, your sisters are scarcely hurt by the incident. I would tell Mr Bennet that Miss Catherine would benefit from a trip to the sea to fully address her persistent cough, and as for Miss Bennet, her ankle will be back to its full strength, without pain, in another week or so if she rests it. However—"

He took off his spectacles and began cleaning them with his handkerchief. Elizabeth leant forward in anticipation of his next words. "Her head? She hit it harder than we realised?"

"Yes," he replied. "Your sister has suffered a concussion, resulting in some confusion. I have seen far worse, and her injury resulted in little blood or bruising and thus the impact was less than it could have been. Some folks suffer bumps to the head that render their memories unattainable. I have seen it in the cases of soldiers too near cannon fire."

The fear Elizabeth felt must have been reflected in her expression, for Mr Tilden continued quickly.

"Most, however, are like your sister, their memories jumbled and thoughts jagged for a few hours, days or weeks." He gave her a grave look. "She obviously believes Mr Darcy is more to her than simply a heroic neighbour."

"It is a rather delicate situation. My sister and Mr Darcy are not—"

"It is not my business to enquire, of course, but I thought it curious he asked me to come to Longbourn to see to her health and that of Miss Catherine. Knowing him as I do, I believe if he were betrothed or close to it, he would have remained in Hertfordshire as she recovered, rather than go off to London."

Was Mr Tilden criticising Mr Darcy? "He had reasons...family business, I believe."

The older man nodded as he inspected what had to be the most thoroughly cleaned spectacles in all of England before placing them in his pocket. "Yes, and as I said earlier, he was intent on my discussing the situation with you. 'Speak to Miss Elizabeth about her sisters' conditions', he wrote to me. 'She will wish to learn it from you, and she is best able to explain it to her family.'"

Elizabeth blushed. "He knows I am an inveterate inquisitor and will convince myself of my own facts if not informed of the truth."

"Perhaps, but it was *your* feelings that most concerned him."

Elizabeth, twisting her hands anxiously, could only wonder at his meaning.

"I must advise you," he continued, "that while your sister's condition will improve, it is best to keep her from any sort of surprise or shock. Keep her happy and content, ensure she is resting, and as the swelling is reduced, her clarity of mind should return as well."

"I see." She could not keep the doubt, the fear from her voice.

Mr Tilden's powers of observation proved strong as he could see Elizabeth was not truly reassured. "If she wishes only for pudding, give her only pudding," he said. "If she believes herself bewitched by Mr Darcy, allow her to believe it. It shall fade away soon enough."

"This is a cure? Accept her delusion and hope it is temporary?" Stunned, Elizabeth could not grasp such an idea. "What of the man whom she does love and whom we believe was ready to propose marriage? He will be hurt while we protect her."

Mr Tilden shrugged. "A veritable conundrum, indeed, but time is the true cure. You must contain her belief, and protect all of those involved. Keep your sister within her rooms, confine her misguided talk to this house. Only a few days, a week or two at most, I believe. She may be fine tomorrow. Time will tell."

Overly aware that time cured very little in one's heart, Elizabeth nodded.

The door, left ajar, opened fully, bringing Hill with tea, and with it, Mr Bennet. After Mr Tilden had taken a sip of the steaming brew, he told them about a widower whose head injury caused him to forget he had recently remarried, and thus he refused to allow his second wife into their home as anything beyond a governess to his children. Within weeks, being in close company in the home led to his interest in her and thus, the return of his memories of their still-short marriage.

Mr Bennet's interest was sparked and the two began discussing the origins of amnesia in Greek mythology. Elizabeth thanked the doctor and excused herself. Much as she was relieved to learn that Jane's muddled memories were likely to be short-lived, it was Mr Darcy's urgent words to his physician—and the man's decision to impart them to her—that consumed the next hour of her thoughts.

———— o o o ————

Jane did not know the blond man who had come to see to her health. Bingles? Was he the juggler, or yet another physician? He had come alone with Mr Darcy's physician, for reasons that made no sense. Besides, there was an earnestness in his voice and a warmth in his eyes that was too familiar, and too centred on her, rather than given equally to her mother and sisters. It made her uneasy. Mr Darcy was absent, Lizzy had disappeared, and this man was sitting too close, talking too much, and making far too many enquiries as to her comfort, her health, her thoughts, while her other sisters looked on, seeming...alarmed? She knew her words were not quite right, but making them behave seemed too difficult an effort for a stranger.

Mr Darcy will not like this man's behaviour. Shall I say something to him when he comes?

He smiled at her yet again, an overfriendly grin. "I hope for your health to return soon. There are still flowers blooming, and a walk in the gardens of Netherfield is a pleasure not to be missed."

Netherfield. Why does that sound familiar? Where is Mr Darcy? He had saved her. He would keep her safe. She could not explain it, but she just knew all would be well if he were here. *It might be worth the struggle to speak.* "Mr Darcy..." she began, smiling tightly over her cup, her head beginning to throb. "Mr Darcy..." she tried again.

Now why did her sisters suddenly appear so panicked?

———— o o o ————

Mrs Bennet bustled in, eager to boast of the estimable London physician in service to peers and the town's wealthiest families who would ensure the health of her most beautiful daughter. It was with some alarm that she noted Jane's bruising was more obvious than ever against her blonde hair and fair skin. Her mouth was looking rather pinched, her expression severe. And Mr Bingley...he appeared very unhappy. This was not acceptable.

"Dear Jane, you are so tired. Lizzy, there you are. You and Mary, help me get your sister back to bed. Mr Bingley, you will not mind if she rests now, will you?"

Mr Bingley rapidly agreed that Jane could do nothing, ever, that he would find disagreeable. But how long would he think it, if she persisted in appearing like a drooping bloom?

Her two sisters escorted Jane out of the room and down the corridor; Mrs Bennet followed, her eyes narrowed in dismay. Had

Jane been bleating about Mr Darcy in Bingley's hearing? She must discourage such talk!

Once they had her in bed, with the covers tucked carefully around her, she began her instruction. "Jane, Mr Darcy carried you from the water before Mr Bingley had his chance, but such actions mean nothing." She paced past the bed, peering at her daughter closely. "You are not beholden to him."

"Mama, now is not the time to speak to her about gentlemen," Elizabeth hissed.

Now, why was Lizzy in such a temper? She did not care anything for Mr Darcy, and surely could not wish for Jane to be blathering on about the disagreeable man! However, perhaps she was right about one thing—Jane needed a dose of Mr Jones's beauty potion more than she needed anything else at the moment!

A cough alerted them that Kitty had entered the room. "Oh Kitty, you will worsen Jane's condition! Go back to bed! You all are too noisy! She needs quiet!" Mrs Bennet pushed her daughters from the room, clucking at them about the need to entertain Mr Bingley.

As soon as the door shut behind them, she removed the bottle of tincture from a voluminous pocket. "It is time for your medicine, my dear Jane," she said, measuring out a healthy dose, as she had not remembered to give her any earlier in the morning. Such a difficulty, recalling details such as these, and now she could not even ask Mrs Hill to administer it! Someone would be sure to tell Mr Bennet or Lizzy, and *they* were sure to involve themselves with questions or protests. What did Mr Tilden know of preserving beauty? He likely only cared about fevers and such. "Open your mouth, dear! You will be back in your looks in a trice!"

——— o o o ———

"Poor Kitty, the lesser of two patients." Elizabeth rolled her eyes at Mr Bingley. "Keeping apart two sisters, one with a cough, the other with a bump on the head, is Mama's way of making both of them feel worse."

Finally he smiled at her little joke, but she was hard-pressed to find more idle chit-chat, and Mary was of even less use. What was Mama saying to Jane? The doctor had said she must not be upset —her mother's particular talent. But Jane *had* been more lucid while the doctor was speaking to her. She was improving! She must be.

"More tea?" Elizabeth leaned forward and refilled Mr Bingley's cup. "Please, have another biscuit."

He selected two and immediately took a bite of shortbread, while Elizabeth struggled to keep the flagging conversation going. It was hardly her fault that the only topics occurring to her had to do with Mr Darcy.

"Mr Darcy has been master of Pemberley for only a short time?"

"Yes, his father died some five years ago."

"That is very sad," Elizabeth said. "I am blessed to have both my parents, and Mr Darcy has neither."

Mr Bingley seemed not to notice the stupidity of her topic and nodded abstractedly. "Nor do I, as you know. When my own father died three years ago, Darcy was of great assistance to me."

Despite her concern over the lectures her mother doubtless was administering to Jane, Elizabeth had to admit some pleasure at the praise given to Mr Darcy; his friend seemed eager to impress upon her that Mr Darcy was the best of men.

"Mr Darcy is a gentleman who excels in helping others. My sisters were fortunate he was out riding yesterday and able to rescue us from danger."

"It haunts me, how but for chasing after my hat, I was late to arrive," said Mr Bingley. "Darcy was pulling your sister from the water when I got there. Miss Elizabeth, it is I who wished to have saved her, and carried her to safety."

She could hear the embarrassment in his voice and did her best to reassure him. How dearly this man cared for Jane, and how much she wished to preserve Jane's connexion to him! "You performed honourably, Mr Bingley. I thank you for your help. I understand it was your coat that kept my sister warm."

He only smiled at her rather sadly. "The thought of what could have occurred haunts me. I shall always be at her service. And you, and your sisters, of course."

Elizabeth shifted uncomfortably in her chair; it was torture hearing his pain. It was a relief when her mother emerged from Jane's chamber and joined them in the parlour.

"Lizzy, is Mr Tilden still here?"

"Yes, he is with my father now."

Mrs Bennet sat with them, relieving Elizabeth of the burden of conversation, and began asking Mr Bingley about his plans for Netherfield and whether he would make the library as impressive as that at Pemberley. She could see Mr Bingley warm to the topic and allowed her mind to drift away from the conversation. She thought it was a remarkable thing that a gentleman like Mr Darcy, the grandson of an earl, had befriended the son of a tradesman; they appeared to be so opposite in temperament and ability, as well. All of it spoke well of Mr Darcy—as if she needed *more* reasons to admire him.

"Netherfield is a fine estate, but of course, as Caroline likes to say, nothing can compare to Pemberley," said Mr Bingley.

"How many rooms are in Pemberley?" Mary asked, finally curious enough to take part in the conversation.

"How many ballrooms?" asked her mother.

Mr Bingley looked between them, clearly racking his memory for answers. "I believe there are some thirty guest chambers—"

Mrs Bennet gasped, and even Mary looked impressed. But in recalling that once upon a time, she had thought she might even one day be its mistress, Elizabeth could only wish they were talking about anything else in the world.

"Darcy is not one to throw balls, however, as his sister is but sixteen and not yet out. Until he has a wife to host for him, Pemberley's ballrooms are silent."

"There is more than one, then? Ballroom, I mean."

Mrs Bennet's question appeared to stump Mr Bingley, and

when the entrance of Mr Bennet and Mr Tilden spared him from overtaxing himself, Elizabeth found herself grateful. She wished for nothing more than to be alone.

Mrs Bennet delayed her escape. After Mr Tilden boarded his carriage for Knebworth, she turned to Mr Bingley. "Will you dine with us tonight? If you are alone at Netherfield, without company? We would be pleased to have you at our table until Mr Darcy returns."

He agreed happily, a notion which made Elizabeth wince. *We must ensure Jane takes a tray in her room.*

— ◦ ◦ ◦ —

Later that evening, after Mr Bingley had eaten his fill and returned to Netherfield, Elizabeth came to bid Jane a good-night. Thankfully her sister had stayed in her room, dozing and resting, rather than joining them at dinner. Without her presence, conversation had seemed almost ordinary; although Mr Bingley's concern for Jane had been obvious, he had been content with exchanging stories of their childhoods and discussing the families of the neighbourhood.

"Mr Bingley asked after you," she told Jane after bathing her forehead. "The poor man thinks his visit this afternoon exhausted you, and he fears returning tomorrow and affecting your recovery." Elizabeth said far less than she could have; disappointment and worry were now familiar on Mr Bingley's countenance. He, in fact, was beginning to resemble his friend Mr Darcy.

Seemingly uninterested, Jane examined her braid as if the answers to all the questions of the universe were plaited into it. "'O what can the matter be, and what can the matter be, O what can the matter be, Johnny bydes long at the fair.'"

Elizabeth's heart sank. Jane was back to insensible nursery rhymes. "It was a long day for you, dear Jane."

Jane took her hand, gripping it tightly. "Johnny bydes long at the fair. Where? Why does Johnny byde there?"

"Um." Elizabeth had no idea how to reply. It was the next thing to gibberish, and yet Jane gazed intently, plainly expecting an answer. "Who is Johnny?"

Jane closed her eyes, opened them again. Elizabeth noticed that they seemed almost to cross. Was she worsening?

"'Oh, where have you been all the day, my boy Willie? Oh, where have you been all the day? Bonny Willie, tell me!'"

Elizabeth listened in some horror as Jane went on, her brow creasing as she grew more agitated, repeating the folk refrain again and again.

"Do you mean...Jane, do you mean to ask where is Mr Darcy?"

Abruptly, Jane ceased repeating herself, looking at Lizzy expectantly.

"He has gone to London, dear, to be with his family. We do not know when he shall return."

Jane burst into noisy tears, crying piteously. Elizabeth did her best to be comforting, but it did little good, and on and on the sobbing continued. Just as she thought she must fetch...someone, anyone, for help, Jane stilled.

For a terrible moment, Elizabeth thought she had died.

Thankfully, she emitted a soft snore, and Elizabeth could breathe again. Jane had either swooned, or fallen asleep...perhaps both.

But her own tears were difficult to restrain. What could she do to help her most beloved sister?

CHAPTER
SIX

B reakfast saw the end of the previous year's gooseberry jam and the start of new arguments. Elizabeth had made the mistake of trying to explain both Mr Tilden's advice and Jane's confusion over Mr Darcy. It had not gone well.

"Why should he marry Jane? He saved me as well and you do not see me parading about talking about my wedding clothes!"

"Shush, Kitty," said Mary. "Jane is not 'parading about' but remains unwell."

Mrs Bennet paused, her fork mid-air. "And Mr Darcy shall marry neither you nor Jane! I should not have him as husband to my sweet girls. A singular good act by a man so proud? I am shocked he could stop staring down at his fine nose to see my girls were in trouble."

Elizabeth clenched the fabric of her skirt, breathing slowly in and out so that she would not worsen the situation with a display of anger. Righteous anger it would be, though. "Mama," she finally managed to say, "Mr Darcy has every right to be proud but he did not hesitate to act when he saw my sisters' distress."

"Do you suppose he has decided that Jane is for him, and

wished to thwart Mr Bingley? That nonsense about the flyaway hat? Perhaps it is Mr Darcy's fault the hat flew off!"

Mr Bennet's newspaper hit the table. "Oh yes, my dear, Mr Darcy commands all he sees. I am certain he conjured the wind, bellowing a gust from his fine, proud lungs, and chased the fox towards the bridge."

Seeing that his sarcasm was lost on his wife, Mr Bennet tried again. "The man saved both my girls and did all he could to maintain propriety. We owe him Jane's life but he does not owe us his own, nor will he offer to share his with Jane. Or Kitty," he said, raising his voice over the mumblings of his younger daughter.

"However, we must allow our Jane to come to this realisation in her own time. If we indulge her heart's misunderstanding, her head will right itself."

"But Mr Bennet—"

"No one shall tell Jane she is mistaken. The shock of such a thing could endanger her recovery."

What would Mr Darcy think if he returned here and Jane made clear her affections for him? Especially in her nonsensical way? He will be disgusted, affronted, repulsed! If only his family business would keep him away until Jane's mind could heal and she discover again that her heart belongs to Mr Bingley!

Weeks of wishing to see him again, and now she wished him far away. *Can there be a more exasperating creature than I?*

Besides, it was vital now that he return. Jane's hysteria of the night before was terrifying; she must at least see the man, and avoid any repetition of such a frenzy.

She knew he would; he had promised his friend. Elizabeth twisted and turned it over, examined it from every side over the course of two days. It both sickened her and filled her with dread, but she could see no other solution. Mr Darcy would have to pretend to love Jane, if only he would agree.

◦ ◦ ◦

Rare was the day when Mr Bennet requested Elizabeth accompany him on a walk outside, but shortly after breakfast he announced a wish to see the state of the footbridge before Mrs Bennet could set out traps for unruly dogs. Elizabeth had her own intentions, wishing to determine whether her father was Longbourn's only other sane creature.

As they set out on the half-mile journey to the stream, Mr Bennet slashed at the tall dead grasses with his walking stick, his eyes set straight ahead and his lips sealed. It made for a disturbing picture in Elizabeth's mind; never before had her father appeared similar to Mr Darcy.

The Mr Darcy I knew before Pemberley.

"I thank you for explaining the delicacy of the situation to your mother, Lizzy, but who will be Jane's husband? All my expectations for an easy son-in-law, unable to understand my drollery and jokes at his expense, are in the balance. Had only Mr Bingley spoken five days ago, all would be settled."

"Not in Jane's mind. Imagine if Mr Bingley had proposed! She would be engaged to a man she scarcely recognises instead of the great and heroic Mr Darcy." Elizabeth shuddered, still unable to understand how her sister's heart and memory had become so mottled.

"You would not have required a hero to pull you from the stream, would you? I think you would have pulled up your skirt and climbed out and up the bank. Then we would have only your mother wailing over muddy skirts and ruined boots. Even if you'd bumped your head as did Jane, when Mr Darcy arrived, you would have waved off his attempts to assist you. No fainting in his arms, not for you that 'hateful, odious man.'"

If her regrets were profound, Elizabeth's embarrassment was even deeper. Why had she spoken so carelessly, so stupidly and publicly about Mr Darcy? Her own feelings were so greatly changed, and no one, least of all Jane, knew how vast was the alteration in her thinking about Mr Darcy. No man could be hateful and odious and gaze at her as he had at Pemberley; no man could do what he had for Lydia and not boast the greatest, most decent heart in England.

One that seems to remain bruised by my words, and closed to mine.

She kicked at a pebble and missed, which elicited a chuckle from her father.

"You would be delusional only if you wished to marry Mr Darcy, eh, Lizzy?"

Turning away to hide her blush, Elizabeth huffed a loud sigh. "The problem is greater than that Jane wishes to marry Mr Darcy when in truth she loves Mr Bingley. The problem is there are expectations beyond yours and mine for such a happy ending."

"I have advised Mrs Bennet to be silent—"

Elizabeth rolled her eyes.

"—for all the good that will do."

"Papa, it is a great dilemma. Mr Bingley wishes to marry Jane, but Jane's confusion is such that both could end up unhappy—if he gives up and decides to leave, and she, when her brain rights itself and she remembers her heart belongs to a man she rejected."

"These are grave possibilities." After a dry laugh, Mr Bennet slowed his pace and turned to Elizabeth. "Time is not our friend, as it appears we must placate Mr Bingley and hope Mr Darcy's absence will turn our Jane against him."

"What shall we do about Jane? I have spoken to her as delicately as I can, tried to nudge her towards her previous state of mind, and it only upsets her."

Elizabeth watched a yellow leaf picked up by the wind, dancing along ahead of them; a few years earlier, she would have chased it, laughing as it rose out of reach and delighting in the random pattern of its journey. How often had she meandered along these paths, much like a leaf, with no particular destination beyond enjoying the sights, smells and sounds of the countryside. This past year their lives had proceeded with small steps forward on the expected path, and sudden deviations off of it, throwing their progress into worrying doubt. Mr Bingley would propose—he had left. Mr Darcy did propose—she had left. They met again and achieved greater understanding, and then Lydia had left with Wickham. And now they were returned, these two men who had loved and were loved by the Bennet sisters, and all was once again confused and doubtful.

They neared the stream and Mr Bennet walked onto the footbridge, tapping the boards with his stick and deeming it still sturdy enough after some fifteen years of use. "You girls ran across this bridge when you were in leading strings. As you undoubtedly remember, Lydia was a wild sort of child yet even when she ran ahead, she was surefooted."

"Unlike Kitty."

Mr Bennet chuckled. "Poor girl, always with a bruised knee and a scratch or two following after Lydia, and now she is playing second fiddle to Jane in our newest family spectacle."

"'Family spectacle' is an unkind way of putting it. It is Jane's present health and future happiness we must bear in mind."

"Yes, well, Mrs Bennet is in a muddle. On the verge of being celebrated by her neighbours for her eldest daughter's fortuitous engagement, she instead has been instructed to skimp on details of Jane's accident. Barring the chance meeting of a racing fox and a reckless dog, there would be an engagement to celebrate."

As they began the walk back to Longbourn, Mr Bennet turned serious. "Is Mr Darcy to return to Netherfield, or have we seen the last of the man your sister expects to marry?"

Her jaw clenched at his teasing words. "I recall he said his trip to London would be of short duration," she said slowly, imbuing her words with as little feeling as possible. "Mr Bingley would be the authority for such intelligence."

Mr Bennet gave her a studied look, a curious gleam in his eye. "Well then, my most curious daughter, please seek out the answer. I believe Mr Darcy's presence at Longbourn would do well for the return of Jane's romantic sensibilities."

CHAPTER
SEVEN

D arcy stalked up the steps to his town house, his only happiness that he had reached his home without interference or greeting from anyone on the walk from Matlock House.

"How can a man set to inherit his father's title be so unconscionably stupid?"

He had spent the past few hours at his uncle's bedside, where he had discovered a man suffering less from the sick headache than from the broken foot he had earned from his kicking his desk in fury after discovering the viscount's gambling debt and his own wife's upset over their younger son's affair with her friend.

The foot would heal but the violent action that broke it had, surprisingly, chastened the viscount, as had Darcy's quiet threat to withdraw his own backing for the viscount's investments in a racing stable. As for Fitzwilliam, he had been a fool to find himself entangled with a widow who had already enthralled another man, one who apparently was prone to jealousy and drink.

These were not Darcy's problems, nor were they troubles of his own making. No, he had made plenty of his own, and worsened them by coming to London.

For this I left Elizabeth, with two injured sisters and without even attempting to convey my hopes towards her? To assuage the anger of my uncle and repair his sons' reputations? How could this be solved with such ease in a mere afternoon whilst I have not been able to win Elizabeth's hand, let alone her heart, in a half year?

No, not a half year. Weeks, days… Their reunion at Pemberley was two months ago but he had been back in her company scarcely five days and able to summon up conversation only as her sister lay sodden and unconscious under his coat.

What must she think of me, leaving as I did?

While he had grown accustomed to knowing of her hatred and disdain, it was the memory of her shy smiles and blushes at Pemberley that had sustained him these past weeks. Disappointment and disinterest had marked her countenance since he and Bingley had called at Longbourn. Her eyes were dull, not that he could glimpse them as she averted them from his when in his company. All that was obvious was her disappointment in him for his lack of effort to rein in Wickham, and thus her youngest sister's future tied to such a man…

He had waited for some sign of encouragement from her, and seeing nothing, set his attentions to Bingley's success with Miss Bennet. That engagement would bring Elizabeth happiness and, he dared hope, soften her heart towards him. Months of soaring hope and plummeting spirits were concluding now. Bingley should have his joy, even if his own window for happiness appeared to be closing.

Darcy glanced at the day's post and was surprised to see missives from Bingley and Tilden. Both, he hoped, held happy news. He reached first for his friend's letter, smiling at the sloppiness of the writing, but excusing it for the haste and happiness he assumed afflicted him.

He sank into a chair and opened it, noting the letter itself was written just as ill. Bingley wrote much as he did everything, quickly and somewhat thoughtlessly. In other words, it was illegible to the average eye; Darcy had grown accustomed to deciphering his friend's penmanship, and although some words were blotted or smeared, he could read most of them. It was their meaning that remained unclear as he stared at the note.

Darcy,

I hope for your swift return to Netherfield. I have been daily to Long-bourn. Miss Bennet suffers from some pain in her ankle, a bruised head, and a cut or two. Although her beauty is untouched, her mind evidently retains some bewilderment. Miss Elizabeth maintains that she is confused about the events of the day of the accident, and that perhaps a more complete recovery is possible if she were to see us together. I shall not despair, even though she can apparently withstand only the briefest of visits—I have not seen her half an hour total since your departure. She says so little before one of her sisters seems to steal her away. If I have lost her respect and affection—

Darcy rose, shaking his head in disbelief, and read the words a second time. A large ink blot obscured whatever Bingley had next written. He stepped to the sunlit window and held up the paper, peering closely at the scribbled words.

Miss Elizabeth is quite—

The words were illegible, as if Bingley had spilt water on the ink. *What about Elizabeth? Does he mean she wishes me to come?*

Netherfield is open—more terrible blotting obscured the words—*can stay and—.*

CB

P.S. Miss Catherine also is recovered.

Darcy read the letter a third time but had no better luck in deciphering Bingley's words. He folded it and held it in one hand, tapping it on the desk blotter as he considered what he had read and what he had interpreted.

Was Miss Bennet more grievously injured than he had supposed?

Lost her respect and affection? Is Miss Bennet confused or has Bingley spent too many hours alone in a large house, pacing and worrying over her? He was a notoriously impatient man, his attention quickly diverted from one shiny object to the next. Bingley had spent less than a week back at Netherfield—only the past two of them by himself. Was he truly unable to hold still long enough to allow the lady time to recover and accept his attentions? Darcy suspected that his friend, so easily led away from Miss Bennet ten months earlier, was again in need of firm counsel. A shove to the back was more likely.

Unless Miss Bennet truly has had a change of heart. Does she lack the courage to turn away Bingley? And yet, I was certain of her feelings for him—unlike Elizabeth's for me. It makes no sense.

He reached for Tilden's letter; the man was a fine physician and he knew whereof he spoke.

Mr Darcy,

I have seen to the Miss Bennets. Much to her regret for the lost attention, the younger is recovered. Miss Jane Bennet requires more time to fully heal. She shall walk easily enough in a few days, but I prescribed rest as the best restorative for her head injury. She has a dizziness in her thinking, a confusion of fact that can only be ascribed to a concussion.

Darcy knew something of concussions. He recalled a classmate at school, a boy made ungainly by his rapid growth, hit in the head by a cricket ball and unable to recall the name of his headmaster, house, or home county for at least a day or two. All turned out well for Waffley, that was his name; his head had stopped a wicket, after all, and he was considered the hero of the hour for sacrificing his pale blond head for the victory. Miss Bennet would recover just as easily, and Bingley would be on one knee within the hour of her sentience returning.

I spoke to Miss Elizabeth as you requested; she has a full comprehension of how her elder sister is afflicted and how it may affect you. It seems Miss Bennet's affections are at least temporarily misplaced, directed away from one man and towards the one whose face she saw first after her accident.

Aghast, Darcy struggled to control the direction of his thoughts. *Misplaced? Towards myself?* If this was true, as Tilden and possibly Elizabeth asserted, the sister of the woman he loved now thought herself in love with him? Was this Mrs Bennet's machination? If so, it was an odd scheme; it would not have surprised him had it been concocted by one of the *ton's* desperate matchmaking mothers. But this was Jane Bennet; in her sister's words, she was 'all that was good' and loved Bingley, and Darcy had seen nothing to contradict Elizabeth's avowal. She must be genuinely addled, like Waffley.

I returned to Netherfield to encourage Bingley in his proposal and make my own attempt with Elizabeth. Instead, his efforts have been hindered, Elizabeth and I scarcely spoke, and her sister now awaits my attentions? The poor girl. And worse—poor Bingley! Much as Darcy could be affected by Miss Bennet's temporary misunderstanding, Bingley would be the true victim. His letter had revealed the Bennets' efforts to suppress the eldest daughter's confusion. Nevertheless, his concern was clear and justified. *I have only to be patient and heed Tilden's advice that time is their ally. Bingley must be protected from his angel's momentarily cooled affections.*

As Darcy picked up a pen to write a reply to Bingley's note, the larger question hit him like the crack of a whip.

Elizabeth! How is she affected by this? Whatever her feelings for me, her embarrassment must be great. She has borne enough mortification for her family. Would she believe me to be irate at the supposition I am under some obligation to her sister?

The perversity of it would have made him laugh but Darcy's concern for Elizabeth, and for whatever anger, unease and bewilderment she might be feeling, swept through him. He stood and strode to the door. He would visit his sister, ensure she was well, and return to Netherfield in the morning.

———— o o o ————

It was midday when Hill alerted Elizabeth that Jane's hopeful suitor had called at Longbourn. Elizabeth slipped into the morning parlour where the patients reclined. Kitty was curled up in a chair, paging through a fashion magazine, while Jane reclined on the sofa, her injured leg resting on a cushion, plucking the petals of a flower from a bouquet sent by none other than the suitor himself and muttering 'he loves me, he loves me not' whilst systematically stripping the bloom.

"Mr Bingley has come."

Jane looked up expectantly. "He loves me? Charming Willie?"

Elizabeth briefly closed her eyes. There was no question as to the identity of whom she referred. "No..."

Jane's bright expression fell. "He loves me not, he loves me not, he loves me not." She tossed the denuded bloom to the floor—where it joined several others.

"Jane..." Elizabeth said cautiously.

"Loves me not, loves me not, loves me not!" Her tone increased in both volume and frantic intensity.

"Perhaps he would rather have a less fickle lover," cried Kitty. "'Tis not fair. *She* does not want him."

Elizabeth sent her a quelling glance. "Jane, Mr Bingley wishes only to see that you are well." She sat carefully on the sofa beside her, feeling all the anxiety of wanting to protect Mr Bingley's feelings, and hide Jane's. They had hurried her away quickly on the previous two visits; how long could they cover for her? But steps sounded in the corridor; and then Mr Bingley was at the door, bowing his greetings. Before he could say a word, Jane opened her mouth.

"'Your vows you've broken, like my heart,

'Oh, why did you so enrapture me?

'Now I remain in a world apart,

'But my heart remains in captivity,'" Jane sang.

To the amazement of her sisters, their least dramatic sister proceeded to croon a long, heart-melting song of unrequited love, loss, and rejection, her voice low and sultry. Mr Bingley stood, entranced, his mouth slightly open.

"'Greensleeves now farewell adieu,

'God I pray to prosper thee:

'For I am still thy lover true,

'Come once again and love me.'"

When she finished, her head drooped, as if a light extinguished.

"Oh Jane." Elizabeth went to her, hugging her sister, and trying to hold back her tears. Whatever love Jane's muddled mind attributed to Mr Darcy, the pain and heartache in that tune all belonged to Mr Bingley. "Let me take you to bed. If you will excuse us, Mr Bingley, my sister seems to have overexerted herself this afternoon."

He only nodded dumbly, his eyes fixed upon Jane's bent head.

After putting a docile Jane to bed, Elizabeth returned to the parlour; as she neared the door, she could hear Mrs Bennet's shrill voice, insisting to Mr Bingley that Jane would be well shortly.

"We despise that she is confined to her rooms, but she needs her rest and her sisters are of little help. Mary, pounding on the pianoforte, and Kitty, storming about...the poor girl misses dear Lydia, who never would have fallen from the fright of a dog! Sure-footed is my youngest! Not that Jane is not graceful, she was pushed by Kitty when the heathen dog chased the fox, so—"

Elizabeth rushed into the room, throwing a meaningful look at the settee, where Mary sat, clutching a book and frowning. Mr Bingley stood, looking nearly as unhappy.

"Mama," Elizabeth said breathlessly, "my sister asks for you." It was safe enough, she thought; Jane had fallen asleep as soon as her head found the pillow.

"Oh, dear girl!" Mrs Bennet excused herself quickly, a look of relief on her features.

Elizabeth closed the door and took the seat across from Mr Bingley. His brow was creased with worry.

"I am sorry." She gave him an earnest smile. "Jane was in company for too long before you arrived and became fatigued. She is resting now."

Mr Bingley's expression matched her own. "She is well, though?"

"Better, although she continues to tire easily. She is improving. We must remember it has been only two days since she struck her head."

"Miss Elizabeth," he said in a halting voice. "I am not known for my frankness, but...that song. It is an anthem to a lover rejected. She would not even look at me. I must ask you: Is your sister unable to forgive me for leaving her those many months ago?"

She little knew how to respond; Mr Bingley knew something was dreadfully wrong, and he must be told something...but what?

"No, but it is a situation of some delicacy. I am sorry." Elizabeth looked away from him—Mr Bingley was staring at her imploringly, his hands gripping his knees tightly—as she tried to explain. "Things are not as they should be. Although Jane is confused and her memories muddled, Mr Darcy's physician believes it is of short duration. From what she has said to me, I sense Jane has lost some of her...most recent memories."

"She does not know me?"

"It is a temporary condition, we are certain."

He looked away and blew out a breath. "It is as I suspected. Much as I despise the situation and any suffering for Miss Bennet, I deserve her hatred."

"No!" Elizabeth cried. "Her heart is engaged, I am certain. That song...even if she is confused, it was for you, I know it. I will not lie to you—she has suffered. But her happiness when you returned... she was overjoyed."

"And so soon, she has forgotten me."

Oh, the absurdity of the past few days!

"No. She is injured."

"Your father—"

"He feels as I do, as Jane will feel when she comes to her senses. When the swelling lessens, all will return to its normal state of being, I am sure of it."

The door opened and Mr Bennet stepped inside; his attention was directed towards a book left lying on a table but he ignored it and sat down as Mr Bingley began attempting an explanation for meeting alone with Elizabeth. Apparently even he could forget Mary's presence in a room.

The older man directed a small smile at the younger man, which only served to further discomfit Mr Bingley. "I suppose you have been seeking some reassurance as to our Jane's recovery of her senses."

Mr Bingley nodded eagerly. "Yes, sir, I wish only for Miss Bennet's return to full health."

Mr Bennet looked at him doubtfully. "That is all of your wishes for my eldest daughter? 'Full health?'"

"Er, no—"

"Are you returned to the country to hunt and fish, or did you have other plans in mind besides your own leisure?"

Before Mr Bingley, who even in the fullest of health and mind was less than equal to parrying Mr Bennet's japes, could stammer his response, Elizabeth quickly interjected. "While there is much to enjoy in the country, I believe the chief reason you returned to Hertfordshire was to see my sister."

"Yes, yes," Mr Bingley cried, displaying earnest chagrin in his voice and expression. "I learnt only recently that Miss Bennet had called on my sisters in London. When I learnt too that she had been wounded by my absence here, I hurried to Netherfield." He looked at Mr Bennet. "I had hoped to propose to her the very morning of the...the accident. I would have been her rescuer but for my hat blowing off. I went to fetch it, in order to appear as I should at Longbourn, and Darcy heard cries and rode off."

Mr Bennet sighed. "Mr Bingley—"

"I wished I had been the man to rescue her."

"And you would have, but for circumstance," Elizabeth said.

Mr Bingley still looked angry at himself, so she dared further comment. "However it was, the fact remains that Mr Darcy was the first man who was standing before my sister after she hit her head. I wonder if she might recognise him. You could, possibly, do her a great service, and ask him to return. It is possible that his presence might jog her memory."

"Agreed," Mr Bennet said.

Mr Bingley nodded soberly, paced a few steps away, and then turned. "I understand, and I have written to him. But can you tell me...would she have been agreeable to my proposal?"

"Oh indeed," Elizabeth assured him. "Very much so."

A look of relief swept his face. "I am glad, for I do—"

"No, no, no, sir," called Mr Bennet, holding his finger in the air. "Do not speak the words to Jane's sisters or myself before you speak them to her."

"Yes, of course. I hope to do so soon, and be welcomed someday as her suitor." Mr Bingley looked apologetically at Mr Bennet. "I apologise for any slight to propriety, sir. I ought to have sought your permission."

"Jane is of age. She shall have my blessing."

Bingley smiled, clearly pleased that at least one obstacle to his happiness was conquered, before his expression clouded. "You are certain about Miss Bennet's injured memory...it should heal soon?"

"Mr Darcy's physician, and our own Mr Jones, believe all Jane requires is rest," supplied Mr Bennet. He rose from his chair and picked up the book he had been glancing at impatiently during his five minutes of paternal concern. He turned when he reached the door. "You will ask Mr Darcy to return?"

"I have. I shall again."

Mr Bennet nodded and disappeared through the door. Elizabeth was grateful for the respite; she had felt herself blush and her heartbeat quicken at the assurance of Mr Darcy's return, and required a moment to collect her wits. When she looked up from her lap, she found Mr Bingley watching her in some distress.

"Mr Darcy's presence would be welcome," she said a little awkwardly, her own anticipation adding conviction to her reassurances. "It would be helpful, I think, to easing Jane's impairment. It truly is farcical, and you know a farce always has a happy ending."

Mr Bingley gave her a relieved smile. "I do hope you are correct, Miss Elizabeth! I am impatient for your sister to be well... We were parted for so long, and to have our happiness put off due to the chance of a dog and a fox and a hat is vexing."

Elizabeth was grateful her father had left the room, else Mr Bingley would have found himself thoroughly ridiculed for such a stupid pronouncement. If her own expression betrayed her thoughts, Mr Bingley did not see it, for he went blithely on with his concerns.

"I have more than one hat. That is not to say it was not my best hat, for a better beaver I have never owned! But I was too preoccupied with possessing it, and lost the prize thereby."

"I...see?" Elizabeth said, holding back incredulity.

"Still," continued Mr Bingley, in a voice more certain of itself than it had been earlier. "A good hat is not so easy to come by as you might think—and for your sister, why, she deserves the most respectable appearance in a man—and I wished to retain it for my wedding day. I bought it, you see, for a special occasion—when I believed Darcy himself was to be wed."

"You did?" she could not prevent asking in amazement. "Did he say he was?"

"Oh, no, not exactly—although he never speaks of it, well, there is some previous arrangement with his cousin."

No there is not—or there was not!

"Often, when one does not speak of something, it is because it is untrue," Elizabeth suggested. "And rarely have I been acquainted with a gentleman as honest as Mr Darcy."

"Something made me think things were progressing in his personal affairs and he might be headed for the altar. But it was probably another thing entirely, some business or another." Mr Bingley shrugged. "You likely have the right of it!" Nodding vigorously, he avowed, "Darcy is extremely clever but he is not one for duplicity or surprise in his dealings—especially with his family."

After Elizabeth considered all that Mr Bingley had imparted—including his wary acceptance of Jane's memory loss—and showed him to the door, she wondered anew whether the man was clever enough to marry Jane, after all.

Mr Darcy led him back here. We must hope Jane will take the reins when, and if, they marry.

CHAPTER
EIGHT

"You have a lady with a bruised noggin, a friend with a bruised heart, and me, with a bruised bit of everything in need of diversion."

Colonel Fitzwilliam rubbed his chin and stared across the table at his cousin. "Let me understand this. Bingley's angel hit her head, woke up in your arms, and now considers you her knight in shining armour. A knight she is in love with, for he has all the qualities she admired in Bingley," he said, "as well as a man of action and owner of a pair of fine, muscular arms."

Opening the door to his cousin always meant opening a bottle or two of his finest wine, which invariably led to his opening his mouth—and his heart. It was little wonder Darcy had avoided his company in the months after their visit to Rosings. But here he was, trapped within his own drawing room, only a night's sleep away from removing himself from London, and he was sharing too much with Fitzwilliam. Again.

"Something like that, although—"

The colonel held up a finger to delay Darcy's response, and, took a long sip of wine. "Furthermore, all of this occurred just as you and Bingley were riding over so that he could propose to said angel. Result being you have a lady mistakenly admiring you—the stalwart friend—as well as a despondent suitor. Either this is the oddest marrying scheme of all time—"

Darcy shook his head. "Miss Bennet is not a schemer."

"If you say so." Fitzwilliam looked at him sceptically. "Then I suppose we must await the straightening of the angel's halo until she remembers she loves Bingley so he can propose and trumpets sound and happiness is returned to all."

He threw his head back, laughing. "This is the stuff of Shakespeare."

Darcy stared at his red-faced cousin. *Leave it to him to enjoy the perversity of this situation. His face still bears the marks of his own romantic farce.*

He raised an eyebrow and replied disdainfully. "You, a man set upon outside a widow's house by a drunken, jealous paramour arriving to woo the lady you had just left, and suffering from a blackened eye, dare to speak of my life as Shakespearean? Comedy, I assume. I am overcome with joy that you find such levity in the morass in which I find myself."

Fitzwilliam guffawed. "Yourself? That is the least of it. Your heart is not engaged—only your pride."

Not for the first time, Darcy wondered whether he should have confided in his cousin after Hunsford rather than sink into reticent despair. "My honour, you mean, and that of Miss Bennet."

The whisk waved his infernal hand again, making Darcy feel as though an inexperienced soldier dismissed for confusing the French with the Italians.

"Yes, it is a ridiculous muddle," Fitzwilliam announced. "Had you only lost your hat as well, or ensured Bingley's was pinned to his head, he might have reached the damsels before you and himself been happily—and officially—engaged."

He had told the story over dinner, but apparently his cousin's head-knocking had dulled the clarity of mind which Darcy had long relied upon, and he had forgotten the gist of the problem. "I shall assist him and the Bennets in any way possible."

"Take care for your honour. While I admire your steadfastness as a friend, and willingness to return there for Bingley's sake, it could be a compromising situation, or one that poses opportunity."

Darcy shifted in his chair. "I fail to catch your meaning."

"If your only concern was for Bingley, you would have left, he would have followed, and whatever happened there would be none of your concern. After all, you have business elsewhere, with Georgiana and Pemberley, that demands your time. But you are far too honourable, and too good a friend for that. And of course," Fitzwilliam said, putting his feet up on one of the room's finest tables, "Bingley's heart is not the only one involved with a lady."

Darcy startled. "I told you I have no feelings for Miss Bennet, nor does she have sincere feeling for me!"

"I do not refer to the ailing and lovelorn Jane Bennet, you goggin, but to her sister." He stared at Darcy, all humour gone for the moment. "You have been in love with Elizabeth Bennet for a very long time, I think."

It was a statement of fact, not a question, and there was no manner of reply he could make that would in any way sum up the depth of love and longing he had for Elizabeth. His feelings were so tender, so ready for the understanding of mutual regard and attachment; this past week had brought him no satisfaction, no resolution, no hope. Darcy could hardly think how to explain the circumstances of the position in which he now found himself without revealing to his cousin all that he felt, *had felt*, for nearly all of the past year. Closing his eyes briefly, he exhaled and turned away from Fitzwilliam's determined study and stared mindlessly across the room at the portrait of his great-grandfather Darcy; his was an austere countenance that mercifully was not reproduced in any of his descendants, although Elizabeth's remarks about his own severity made him wonder how like the man he might be. 'He means to be severe on us.' She was teasing him, as he was teasing her. She must realise that now; she was all kindness at Pemberley —yet she was solemn and withdrawn just days ago. Had all that occurred to her sister Lydia destroyed any softening of her feeling towards him?

"Yes."

He could not look at his cousin and see the mirth or the pity such a confession would evoke. Fitzwilliam's voice, all humour washed away by his admission, broke through his thoughts.

"You have said nothing of it, and I respect you too much to press you on what you might not wish to disclose, or even understand yourself. But I have suspected it since the spring. You would not speak of it but something was off with you—has been off—for months now."

Darcy nodded slightly, which seemed to encourage Fitzwilliam, who leant forward and rested his elbows on his knees. His grave expression of concern nearly broke Darcy's reserve.

"I wear the wounds of misbegotten love and lust on my fists and face, but my heart has not been touched as yours has. You have sealed your wounds inside. Will you talk to me now?"

Sighing, Darcy realised he welcomed the chance to speak of it, to speak of her.

"Last autumn, at Bingley's estate in Hertfordshire, I fell in love with Elizabeth and fought it off. My 'victory' was short-lived, for I realised at Rosings that I had to have her as my wife—and was refused, rather vehemently." Darcy ignored Fitzwilliam's startled expression. "I was humbled, rightly so. I had behaved poorly in company, as I believe she said to you, and cruelly advised my friend against her sister."

"Bingley, who is now chomping at the bit to propose to the same sister?"

Darcy nodded.

"I have a dim recollection that I may have played a part in this calamity by carelessly speaking to the lady of your advice to him." Fitzwilliam looked aghast. "You said nothing to me of it, of my actions or of your feelings for Elizabeth Bennet."

Darcy shrugged helplessly. "It matters little now. Despite the current complications, Bingley and Miss Bennet are in love."

"And your hopes?

"Last month, Elizabeth and I met again and every hope I had returned."

"You felt she returned your affections?"

"I thought so, until last week, when Bingley and I called at Longbourn and she spoke not a word to me. She could not even look at me." Unable to hold himself in check, Darcy leapt from his chair and stalked to the mantel.

"Darcy—"

"I have been a fool. I returned to Meryton thinking I had a chance, again."

"Again," the colonel repeated, shaking his head. "And nary a word to me, who introduced you to the first girl you kissed."

Darcy managed a chuckle as the memory of that awkward encounter when he was a green fifteen-year-old boy.

"Aye, there's a laugh. I should haul you back to Hertfordshire by the collar and teach you how to woo a woman properly. Alas, until the bruising lessens and my natural good looks return, the ladies of London must tend to their needlework and letters."

"There is no need to 'haul' me there. I leave in the morning."

"Ah then!" Fitzwilliam stood, grabbed the half-full bottle of wine, and ambled over to the door. He turned to Darcy with an expectant look. "Shall we go upstairs and finish this tale? The hour is late, my boots are tight, and it is best we have this conversation near our beds."

Chuckling, Darcy rose and led their way to the stairs. "When I leave, should I fear you will take command of my house and servants?"

"Already done, old man. Your house and your theatre tickets. You know my brother is loath to share his."

He joined in Fitzwilliam's laughter, already feeling lighter than he had in weeks.

CHAPTER
NINE

Cook was considering the two pounds of dirt-covered parsnips sitting in a bucket when Longbourn's groom sidled into the kitchen. He knelt by the bin of apples and began rooting for any old or rotted ones to feed to the horses.

Turning back to the stove to stir her soup, Cook called out, "What say you, Samuel? Will it rain today?"

"Aye, in the night." Palming two apples, he stepped closer to the stout, grey-haired woman. "More important to some in this house, I hear Mr Bingley's friend has returned to Netherfield."

"Mr Darcy?"

"The hero of the day himself."

Cook set aside her spoon and patted her hands on her apron. "Suppose I should start my baking. Once the mistress hears of it, we'll be setting two extra seats at the table for every meal."

"One of 'em sweet on Miss Jane?"

"Both, I hear. The wooing was easy but the choosing is hard."

A few times per day, Mrs Bennet insisted on a private word with Jane with no one else present, to 'encourage the return of her vigour and beauty'.

"Mama, I do not believe your lectures are doing anything to restore her health," Elizabeth said worriedly, as she was allowed to enter her sister's room at last. "Your pontificating does her no good."

Mindful though Mrs Bennet was of Mr Tilden's warning to coddle Jane's feelings, Elizabeth found herself worried that in her impatience for her sister to return to herself and be the Jane familiar to them all, her mother might actually be hurting her progress. Granted, Mrs Bennet did not stay long, and her voice was never shrill as she spoke and she swore her words were gentle ones, but by the second visit, the signs of Jane's alteration always seemed to have worsened. She had refused her usual baked egg for breakfast and instead insisted on ham and spice bread. As with her preferences in dining, her sister's spirits remained newly unpredictable. They sat in Jane's room, enjoying the afternoon sun. Jane rested against the pillows, yawning, staring at the ceiling, as Elizabeth mended a shirt.

"We should expect company again today," she began. Jane's sudden hopeful expression compelled Elizabeth to quickly elaborate that Mr Bingley was likely to call again. Jane only shrugged. In some despair, she wondered if they had perhaps been *too* tentative.

"Sister, I hope you will believe me when I remind you that you cared for Mr Bingley for months. Not a week ago, you were achingly happy to hear of his impending return to Netherfield. You—all of us— anticipated he returned to propose marriage to you."

Jane responded by pulling her pillow over her head.

Elizabeth felt the teacup in her hand shaking, her grip too tight on its handle. Quickly she set it down, rattling the saucer as she did so.

Can you recall none of your feelings? she wanted to ask. *Are you trying to remember?* But she clenched her teeth against the impulse. Jane was ill, confused, and must be allowed to heal. It was unfortunate, in some ways, that Mr Bingley persisted in visiting so often while Jane was unwell, but she understood that only the strongest of feelings would cause his frequent presence. If it put pressure upon Elizabeth and her family to protect her and attempt to minimise any damage to her future happiness, well, they owed Jane that, and much more.

— ⚬ ⚬ ⚬ —

In their decade of friendship, Darcy had seen Bingley in every sort of mood the man could muster—and none ever verged too far from his essential good-heartedness. Even Caroline could not truly pique his temper. But upon his arrival at Netherfield, the change in his friend was obvious. Bingley was distressed. Darcy was wary, wondering whether Bingley truly wished him to accompany him to Longbourn. It had seemed wise—allow Miss Bennet to see the two men, standing side by side, and—perhaps—begin to recognise and remember. Of course, Bingley did not understand the fullest extent of Miss Bennet's confusion, especially concerning her supposed feelings for Darcy. They might be walking into an exceedingly fraught situation.

He assumed Bingley had had too many drinks the previous night, alone in the house and at ends when his concern over Miss Bennet's health turned into horror over her amnesia. When he was in his cups, Bingley was impetuous and emotional. When paired with silliness, it made for amusing hours. Darcy had never seen him as he was now, in a mix of fear, sorrow, and hope.

Bingley's relieved expression upon seeing him sank like an anchor in Darcy's gut. "Thank goodness you have arrived. Perhaps you shall be the key to unlocking my angel's memory, as you were the hero who saved her in the first place."

"I am no hero. Ask Stirling, who spent hours cleaning my finest Hessians." Indeed, Darcy's man had not been amused by the damage done to the fine leather boots.

"I have been of even less help. She will not speak to me."

"Miss Bennet is confused, temporarily," Darcy assured him.

"The pain of her total disinterest in me is excruciating."

"You wish to dwell upon your own losses when she is the one suffering with confusion?"

Bingley nodded vigorously and fell into a chair. He held his head in his hands and took a deep breath. "I must tell someone, for I have too often been a man incapable of action and decision-making. To have no place at all in her mind is more than I can bear."

"Bear it you must, for only a few days more, a week or two at most. Is that not what Tilden told Mr Bennet?" Darcy took the seat next to Bingley and patted his shoulder. "Patience, my friend."

"I am ever patient, but the thing of it is that Miss Bennet has forgotten me. How I wish I were you."

Did he suspect Jane's feelings centred on Darcy? "You do not," Darcy said firmly. "I am sorry—"

"—No, I am the sorry one. That cursed hat. It should have been I who saved her."

The hat again, the stupid hat. Darcy held onto his patience. "Truly, neither Miss Bennet nor her sister were at risk."

"I have burnt it, did I tell you? Stomped it to tatters as well." Bingley looked up from the carpet and glanced at Darcy, who could barely believe this obsession with millinery.

"You burnt the hat you went to such difficulty to save? Or burnt something else? A letter from Caroline, perhaps?"

"No! A letter is not the source of my sorrow," Bingley growled. "The cursed hat, of course, that blew off and led me on a merry chase while my Jane nearly drowned. Would that it had been a mere letter, for parchment might be easily destroyed, whilst beaver skin required my boots to crush, my poker to spear! It has been destroyed, as it deserved to be."

As Darcy took in the entirety of Bingley's admission, pictures of his friend's tantrum formed in his mind and he quickly found himself struggling to restrain a chuckle. Even a man as even-tempered as Bingley occasionally revealed glimpses of a family disposition more easily discernible in his sister. Most of what Darcy knew of Miss Bingley's tantrums emerged in half-drunken rants from Bingley or Hurst, but he had heard her vitriol against the Bennets in Hertfordshire and countered her petty swipes against Elizabeth at Pemberley; of course Bingley should rise to anger when his heart's best hopes were imperilled.

"Miss Bennet was in no danger of drowning."

"Because you were there!"

"As were you, if only a moment later. And she was standing in shallow water, in no immediate peril. I should have waited for you to arrive. I am sorry for my unthinking haste."

Bingley remained disconsolate. Darcy rubbed his face, speaking to him as he would a child.

"She and Miss Catherine were startled and stumbled. Miss Catherine was in danger only of dampening her skirts, and I lent a hand to lift her back to firmer ground. Miss Bennet stood in shallow water, her shoes ruined and her head knocked. She appeared in distress, and as Miss Elizabeth was about to descend the embankment, I wished to spare her and moved more quickly, and from an easier direction."

"You *held* her. You had the privilege of rescue."

"I pulled her, and lifted her up onto the ground." Darcy exhaled loudly, now rather disgusted by Bingley's self-pity. "Would you rather I have allowed Miss Elizabeth to receive a dunking as well?"

"I only wish it had been me. If she never again recalls my face, it might have been my last chance to hold her in my arms."

What god of irony had created such a situation? This cannot be so bad as he thinks. Nearly groaning with the effort of restraining his frustration, Darcy stood and approached his friend. He clapped Bingley on the back.

"Whatever her current confusion, it is fleeting, a passing bewilderment created by the concussion. My cousin has told me of men who lie wounded and talk to nurses as if they are fellow soldiers or younger brothers. He has never told me of such a condition as one that endured."

"And if it is? If Miss Bennet does not come to her senses?"

Bingley gave a quick gasp. "Or she does, but neither does her warm regard for me return."

"Calm yourself," Darcy urged him. "Be rational. Think of what the doctor says, what a seasoned colonel says."

With a slow nod, Bingley sat back in his chair. "I am impatient with being a patient lover."

As am I, Darcy thought. *As am I.*

Bingley smiled, if a bit grimly. "Perhaps Miss Bennet will set eyes on you, and her sensibilities shall return."

Darcy could believe Miss Bennet's quicksilver change of mind upon seeing him as easily as he could that waving a magic wand would change a man into a toad.

"I am dubious as to whether the sight of me will help anything." He gestured at Bingley's waistcoat. "But at least I will not offend her eyesight with such a shade of purple."

"Bah, this is no time for you to grow a sense of humour."

Hating to further injure his friend, Darcy apologised. "Perverse as it may be, I prefer pragmatism and patience. It would be ideal for all of us if Miss Bennet shakes off this dream, but it could take time. Recall that a mere leg wound needs time to heal, but one to the head has injuries less obvious to the eye."

Come, Bingley, he wanted to say. *Be a man and win her heart all over again. Wretched indecision got us here and will only further drag us into the mire.*

Instead, he said only, "Your future awaits."

Bingley practically growled in response, his frustration over-riding his manners. "Let us be off then, to Longbourn. We have a hypothesis to test."

CHAPTER
TEN

"He has come."

Mary said aloud the exact words Elizabeth was thinking with some apprehension; before another thought or wish could form, she realised Mary was still speaking.

"Mr Darcy is here, Lizzy. Do you believe he has come to begin courting Jane?"

"Of course not," said Elizabeth, peering out of the drawing room window to see the two men dismounting their horses. "He sent us his own physician, but he is a man who manages his own business and comes to see with his own eyes how Jane and Kitty fare. And see, Mr Bingley is with him."

Yes, and he appeared anxious, while Mr Darcy looked serious and intent. Suddenly he turned and gazed directly at her. Dropping the curtain, Elizabeth cursed her impetuosity and moved back to her seat beside Jane. *He has returned. What does he know? Will he stand with Mr Bingley and endure what has happened with Jane?*

Jane herself did not look up from her apparent fascination with the colourful threads in the blanket covering her knees.

Elizabeth half-feared her father would request the gentlemen attend him in his book-room before allowing the ladies of Longbourn to besiege them. When he remained seated with his book, she felt some relief. She greatly desired that, somehow, the sight of Mr Darcy might provoke Jane's memory. On the other hand, if it did not, there would be the ordeal of trying to shield Mr Bingley from the truth and from her mother's loudly given opinions.

"Sit up, Mary!" Mrs Bennet cried. "Kitty, do not interrupt your sister or the gentlemen. They are calling on Jane, and it is to her their conversation must go. After all, two suitors!"

"Mama, Jane has but one suitor—"

"A choice of two!"

Mired in her own misery, dreading whatever depths of disgust Mr Darcy might now hold the Bennets, Elizabeth could only shrink from whatever else her mother might impart with her usual enthusiasm.

Does he realise the reception that awaits him?

⸻ ◦ ◦ ⸻

"Mr Darcy!" called Jane from her seat on the settee.

And there went his first hopes, that her memories might undergo a sudden restoration at the sight of the man who had rescued her...or at least that she might fail to recognise him at all.

Darcy stood beside Bingley, awaiting a greeting for his friend. None came from the lady herself, but her sister—the ever watchful, ever caring Elizabeth—stepped in quickly to alleviate the awkwardness.

"A good morning to you both," she said with what Darcy perceived as forced cheerfulness. Still, her eyes were bright and full of something that could be mistaken for mischief—or desperation. How could he worry over Jane Bennet and Bingley's hopes when Elizabeth was living with such madness?

"On a fine day such as this, sir, I am certain you would prefer a ride through the fields to a visit to the Bennet sickroom."

"Why, Lizzy! What a thing to say!" cried Mrs Bennet, cutting a sharp, mortified glance at him. "Pray, forgive the remark, sir. She is so thoughtless sometimes—"

"Not at all, madam," he replied, appalled as ever by the woman. "Miss Elizabeth's words are apt. It is indeed a fine day, and after a succession of rain, it bears appreciation."

"But—"

"Truly, far more careless words have been uttered that give me far greater offence."

"Oh, dear—not by my Lizzy, I hope."

"Indeed not," Darcy said firmly. He chanced a look at Elizabeth, who stood stonily, her cheeks flushed with what he recognised as more anger than embarrassment. "Miss Elizabeth and I have always enjoyed spirited conversation."

Her eyes darted to his, startled but relieved. He dared a smile and earned a small one in return before Mrs Bennet again made her thoughts heard.

"That is a relief, indeed," she said, ignoring Mr Bennet's chuckle. "How very good you are, Mr Darcy. And how you honour us with your visit. We have much anticipated your return." She looked pointedly from him to her eldest daughter, whose greeting he had yet to reciprocate.

He bowed and took a chair near the door, a deliberate choice that would keep him safely apart from the centre of conversation. He watched as Bingley took the empty seat nearest Miss Bennet, who paid him no heed whatsoever. It was as if the man were invisible.

Miss Bennet looked well; only her elevated foot and a bruise on her forehead, artfully concealed but still visible on her fair skin, indicated she was not in full health. If anyone looked ill, it was Bingley. His customary joyful animation, already subdued, had disappeared when Miss Bennet made obvious her recognition of the wrong man. The two younger daughters—the wan Miss Catherine and the vexed-looking Miss Mary—appeared as confused as he by the situation.

On second glance, however, he could see the difference in Bingley's beloved—it was in her eyes, he thought. She did not recognise Bingley, it was plain, and her gaze wandered to himself far too often for his comfort. But there was something unfocused and lacking in the formerly amiable young lady. The very fact that she looked so often at him was odd; he recalled the way she had paid more attention to her stitchery than to Bingley back when Elizabeth had been so certain her sister was in love. It was peculiar indeed that her eyes should seek him out in such an unusually pointed fashion.

Elizabeth remained quiet and ill at ease, not as she had a few days earlier, when his presence seemed to disturb her; now she wore a pained expression that showed her to be suffering under the weight of her sister's alteration and her mother's inanity.

"My parents have thanked you, sir, but let me express my gratitude and appreciation for all that you did to rescue Jane, and my sister Kitty. It was a great kindness you and Mr Bingley showed."

When Elizabeth finished speaking, Miss Bennet smiled, nay beamed, at him with a beatific expression Darcy had never seen on her.

He could sense Bingley's distress at her attention and endeavoured to keep his own eyes upon Elizabeth. "You need not thank me. As you say, Mr Bingley was at the ready to assist, and you hardly needed my aid."

Miss Catherine put her hand on her heart. "It was truly heroic, as you rode up, dashed through the water and saved us both."

Miss Bennet actually clapped, bouncing a little in her chair as if in appreciation of her younger sister's hyperbolic words.

He shifted in his seat, deeply uncomfortable, as Miss Catherine continued to convey her appreciation. He had never heard the girl speak so many words with such a forceful nature, and it seemed as if Miss Bennet was actually encouraging her platitudes. Such behaviour was unrecognisable in the quiet, polite lady he had known. Elizabeth looked aghast at her sisters, as if she suspected they conspired between them to embarrass her, whilst their silly mother smiled benignly as if all was as it should be. It was excruciating to witness, let alone be the centre of it. When Miss Catherine paused her speech, Darcy took advantage to end it.

"I am happy to find you and Miss Bennet returning to good health. You were pleased with Mr Tilden's advice?" After addressing his question in the general direction of Mr and Mrs Bennet, Darcy stiffened slightly when he felt Miss Bennet still staring at him. Gazing down at the carpet, he willed away the flush he felt rising under his collar as Mrs Bennet continued to praise him, her daughters, Mr Tilden, and Mr Jones, and abuse her thoughtless neighbours and the rogue pup she likened to the devil's spawn.

"...the Gouldings have not even thought to send a note or to call on poor Jane and Kitty!"

Darcy had long felt contempt for Mrs Bennet and her abhorrent lack of perception and grace; it incited in him the same behaviour—a conscious display of cold civility—as would that of officious strangers. Now she swam in waters she had never foreseen; her favourite daughter at home, the one she considered a prized beauty, seemingly tossing aside the man who loved her in favour of a man who would never see her as any more than Elizabeth's much-loved sister.

"The Gouldings have a new granddaughter and two small grandsons to worry over, Mama. We should send a note and a basket to them!"

Elizabeth's observation pleased him. It displayed her generosity towards their neighbours, and long-practised maternal management. And now, with good humour and tact, she was managing not only her mother but yet another sister as well; her kind heart was over-burdened, and he ached with the wish to comfort her.

She continued to distract the others with an enquiry about his journey from London, preventing her mother from expressing further violence. Darcy provided lengthy—and he feared, dull— answers about the roads, prompting Mr Bennet to remark on a fallen tree on the lane behind Netherfield. Bingley began to speak eagerly, enquiring as to how his servants and horses could be of service; he glanced at Miss Bennet, clearly hoping to impress her.

The object of his attentions smiled—she had always smiled too much, Darcy thought, but *these* smiles were newly pointed towards himself—and ignored Bingley as if he had not spoken, which rudeness set off Mrs Bennet upon another soliloquy about thoughtless neighbours until refreshments arrived.

"Did you say you came from your house in town, Mr Darcy? Is it near that of your uncle, the earl?" Mrs Bennet went on breathlessly, looking at him and then at Bingley. "I have always said my Jane's beauty should not be kept confined to country society. Although ours is more than adequate, Jane has a delicate beauty that would charm London."

Darcy missed his formerly civil but perfunctory acquaintance with Mrs Bennet. A week ago, he knew she reviled him for his hauteur and the thoughtless insult he had given to Elizabeth; she rarely spoke to him unless to insult him indirectly as 'Mr Bingley's friend'. He had been otherwise ignored, which suited him perfectly well. Now, it seemed the lady was playing her two hands, as if uncertain which of the two men would be her future son, and determined to keep them both on the leash.

You have no idea who holds my leash, madam.

He watched as Elizabeth's face reddened, her mortification at her mother's enthusiasm for a match between her eldest daughter and the wealthier more prestigious visitor at Netherfield grew in decibels.

She would shield me from the vulgarity of her family as I should have done for her at Rosings. A misguided fool in love as I was could hardly guard her from Lady Catherine, let alone propose properly.

Darcy took a breath to dispel the awful memories and turned his attention back to the performers in Longbourn's drawing room. Immediately Miss Bennet smiled at him; he nodded politely. Practised as he was at ignoring the fluttering lashes of ladies bidding for his notice, he was uneasy evading this lady's gaze, for while Bingley sought it, her eyes were fixed instead on him. It was disconcerting that the lady of his prior acquaintance had been demure and shy, happy to follow others' conversation and always ready to agree on a point. Now, although not leading the conversation—for who could do so when Mrs Bennet was in the same room?—her attentions remained fixed upon the wrong man.

"How are your family?" Elizabeth said, plainly trying to turn the conversation. "I hope they will forgive you for leaving them so quickly. They must have been disappointed at such a brief visit."

"Oh you must stay, for at least a month, Mr Darcy," her mother interjected. "Of all horrid things, leave-taking is the worst, and you have done it twice from us already. It is not good for one's constitution to move about from town to country to town so frequently. And to think of the horses!"

As Mr Bennet coughed and appeared to be readying some sharp retort to his wife's inanities, Darcy saw Elizabeth struggle to remain calm.

"Yes," he said to his hostess. "My business in London is not yet finished, but I shall remain here with my friend." Smiles and nods of agreement came his way, but it was only Elizabeth's he sought; when his reward came, he returned her smile before sobering at the gratingly familiar sound of Mrs Bennet's voice.

"We are justly pleased then. Will your sister join you here? Netherfield requires a hostess so that Mr Bingley can entertain."

Bingley quickly saved him and began to speak about his own sisters' busy schedules. As the conversation grew lively, Mr Bennet slipped out the door without an offer of rescue to the other men. Darcy glanced at Miss Bennet. Serene though she was, there was an odd unsteadiness about her stare that reminded him of a cross-eyed scullery maid who had worked at Pemberley when he was a boy.

Darcy wondered again at the mysteries of the mind and heart. How had the lady confused his basic human impulse to pull her from danger with Bingley's ardent affections for her? If he had initially considered that she could merely be play-acting, perhaps at her mother's behest to catch a wealthier prospect, he now knew better; Elizabeth's sister was no pretender. She was as pure of heart as any woman he had met, genuine and kind-hearted. Even Miss Bingley, who deemed her 'not good enough' for her brother, had admitted the lady's virtue and comportment while blaming the mother for any scheming and duplicity. That too now seemed shaken.

"We hope you will call again tomorrow, gentlemen," he heard Elizabeth say. Darcy looked up and saw her gazing at him, her head bent towards that of her clearly fatigued sister. In her eyes, which so often conveyed mirth and joy, he saw only worry and humiliation. He could scarcely imagine Elizabeth's mortified feelings; wishing to erase the pained smile she wore, he did the little he could and rose to his feet.

"Of course, we shall return tomorrow," he said quietly, in words meant only for her.

"Yes, we shall," cried Bingley, standing up and going to Miss Bennet. "I hope you shall be in full health tomorrow."

She gazed up blankly at him and turned away. One glance at the despair on Bingley's face made clear it would be a long night at Netherfield. *I had best lock up the guns and the better brandy.*

CHAPTER
ELEVEN

The following morning, Mr Bingley appeared to be as tired as Elizabeth, and more exasperated than she had imagined him capable.

He and Mr Darcy had arrived quite early, promptly after breakfast, a meal in which Mrs Bennet had continued the discourse she had begun shortly after the gentlemen had left the prior day and Jane had gone to bed. Elizabeth had answered none of her questions about whether Mr Darcy would reciprocate Jane's interest or whether some form of mediation—a duel, Mrs Bennet proposed—could help settle Jane's mind.

Such notions were put down by Mr Bennet, who showed less amusement at his wife's inanities than was usual. Elizabeth could only be grateful and go early to her own bed, where she lay awake for too many hours remembering the glances she had exchanged with Mr Darcy, and how his eyes had settled on hers with an appearance of sympathy. It was better than disgust and likely all she could anticipate. *How I would have preferred warmth and understanding!*

But they had scarcely exchanged a word.

Now he sat once again in Longbourn's drawing room, trapped

by her mother and to a lesser extent, Jane, while Mr Bingley—who had spent mere moments in his seat, staring at Jane while she did likewise at Mr Darcy before Elizabeth took pity and asked his assistance elsewhere—paced in the music room. He looked mournfully at her, all vestige of his cheerful demeanour erased. "I never knew her feelings—she was kind and pleasant but the effort to converse weighed on me. I was happy to have the burden," he quickly assured her, "but she has forgotten me utterly."

Sighing, Elizabeth sank into a chair and wondered whether humour had any place here at all. She had always enjoyed Mr Bingley's company, and believed he would be a wonderful husband to Jane and brother to her and her sisters. But he was a man who had been led away from Jane by *his* sisters and Darcy, and persuaded to return to her by Darcy; his faith in himself and in Jane was flagging.

"I begin to be sorry that Darcy returned here at all," Bingley said. "I could bear it if your sister could look upon him with perfect indifference, but it seems almost as if she does not."

Poor Mr Bingley! Such a dear heart. Only Jane is near happiness, and that will fade when she learns of the hurt she has caused him!

"She has few words for anyone at all, I remind you. She remains quite ill, although her physical appearance is improved. As to her memory, I wish I could find any words to comfort you, but it is wholly out of my power," replied Elizabeth. "The usual satisfaction of preaching patience to a sufferer is denied me, because you have shown so much."

"Patience?" Mr Bingley scoffed. "Had I the patience you honour me with, I should have ignored my sisters and returned to Netherfield last autumn."

Alarmed, Elizabeth leant closer to him. "You will not leave now? Not when progress is made every day?"

"Progress that you see, but I do not." He ran a hand through his already tousled hair and gave her an imploring look. "I love your sister, yet I have never said those words to her. I was not on hand to save her as was Darcy, but I am a man of action and it is a struggle to sit idly by, whilst she ignores me."

"She is not *trying* to ignore you. You cannot believe she is yet unaffected by her accident; you must see that she is not herself." His concern was not baseless, Elizabeth conceded inwardly. If Jane did not speak much, her attention *was* rather obviously fixed upon his friend—even though Mr Darcy was very careful to show as little interest in her as was possible. "Perhaps you could take some action? Have you any ideas?"

She watched as Mr Bingley straightened in his seat; he took a deep breath and seemed to regain some small bit of his usual liveliness.

"Her very first smile, when I returned, was a story I told her about a Netherfield tenant who broke his leg and had to be carried home on a door. His wife saw him coming, and in her fearful run to meet the procession, she tripped over the dog and broke *her* arm." He grinned in remembered hilarity. "Your sister suggested the couple ought to attend morning *and* evening church services," he chuckled. "Perhaps she would like it if I regaled her with some of the many such drolleries I possess."

It took all of Elizabeth's restraint to find an answer both patient and polite. If this was an example of Mr Bingley's wit, everyone would be much better off if he kept it to himself— whether or not Jane herself enjoyed such tales. "Possibly, since her mind is still muddled, you would do better to read to her? She loves poetry, and even if she cannot follow every word, she might find her favourites comforting. By tomorrow, I will have some selections awaiting you. For today, I would simply...well, not ignore her, precisely, but pay no heed to her behaviour. Mr Tilden said recovery would take time, and we must give it to her."

Her suggestion succeeded in giving him hope and purpose, and they returned to the drawing room, where Mr Bingley seemed pleased to see a tray of cakes. He glanced quickly at Jane and took a seat closer to Mary and Kitty. Elizabeth, relieved to have offered him some advice, turned her attention on the rest of the room and arrived at a quick conclusion: not since the Wickhams' post-wedding visit had there been such an uncomfortable gathering at Longbourn. Her head ached. Once Mr Bennet had deserted them, her mother seemed increasingly perplexed over which gentleman to favour with praise and whether it was best to ignore the proverbial elephant in the room: Jane's fickle attention. Elizabeth watched both men shift in their chairs as one looked embarrassed by praise, the other mortified by its presentation.

Her own mortification was nearly complete. *Why cannot Jane recover her wits?*

Elizabeth knew that *she* had lost Mr Darcy's esteem—if her own words to him had not broken him free of her charms, Lydia's actions certainly had, and his quiet, successful efforts to fix that seemingly hopeless situation must have disgusted him. Ignorant though they were of what Mr Darcy had done, her family's lack of grace towards him was a painful thing to watch. And now, she must make an effort to speak to him of the last thing on earth she wished to say.

Elizabeth forced a smile and rose from her chair; intent as she was, she failed to notice how quickly Mr Darcy followed her actions. She gestured at the window and looked around the room, surprised to see Mr Darcy too had stood up—and he spoke before she could. "There seemed to be a prettyish kind of a little wilderness on one side of your lawn. I should be glad to take a turn in it, if any would like to accompany me?"

Mrs Bennet looked at him rather sourly.

"Of course, you know that Jane cannot go." She gestured, rather dramatically in Elizabeth's opinion, at Jane's ankle. But it could not be said Mrs Bennet did not think quickly when it came to arranging people. "Jane shall remain inside. Mr Bingley, you and Mary can keep her company. Lizzy, you and Kitty may show Mr Darcy about the different walks. I think he will be pleased with the hermitage."

Mr Bingley looked happy, probably that Jane would not be able to stare at Mr Darcy for a time, and Mary never stirred out of doors if she could help it. Elizabeth was relieved to escape, but worried what Jane might say in her absence, if she would manage to hurt Mr Bingley with words of her bizarre attachment. She could only hope her mother would not allow it. After pelisses, coats, hats and gloves were collected, the small party set out to enjoy Longbourn's gardens. Elizabeth took a deep breath, wondering how to manage Kitty. She could say what she had to before her sister, but the whole affair was embarrassing enough without worrying how Kitty might add to it.

"The last of the lavender should be cut before the next storm," she said, gesturing towards the small cutting garden some thirty yards away. "I shall gather some for the still room."

"Oh, pooh, Lizzy. Do you never think of anything except chores?" Kitty hated anything to do with gardens, as she was excessively afraid of even the most innocent of the creeping, crawling things of the earth.

"Perhaps you would go fetch my herb basket from the stillroom for me," Elizabeth suggested. She knew her sister well; Kitty would dawdle as long as humanly possible in returning from her errand.

When she was gone, Elizabeth breathed a sigh of relief; she truly did need a walk in the fresh air. Worrying about Mr Bingley and Jane's awkwardness was exhausting. Despite the difficult conversation sure to follow, she nevertheless was pleased as Mr Darcy fell into step beside her.

She glanced up at him. "My mother and sister have said it repeatedly, sir, but I do thank you for returning, and so quickly, to a place from which you thought yourself free."

"I wished to see to the health of your sisters, and to um...keep my friend company here."

The gentleman clearly was uncomfortable, but so was she, and through no fault of their own.

"I am certain Mr Bingley appreciates it. As you see, things are rather unsettled." When he only nodded, Elizabeth wondered how exactly she could broach her request; there seemed no polite way to manage it. "Mr Tilden wrote to you and explained Jane's...delusion?"

"Yes. I had hoped there would be more of a recovery at the sight of me. She cannot truly believe in any attachment to me, based upon so little an act as lifting her from the water."

Elizabeth heard a sigh that sounded of both regret and shame, but she was wrestling with her own and said nothing before Mr Darcy again spoke.

"First Bingley thought your sister indifferent to him. He was convinced, wrongfully and regrettably, of this by his sisters and myself, as you remember," he added, looking at her ruefully.

Sadly, Elizabeth admired his expression, thinking he wore chagrin well, and wondering if her own was equally apparent. "And, again on your word and bolstered by the smiles Jane gave him on his two calls to Longbourn, his hopes and my family's expectations were raised. They appeared on the cusp of happiness together..." She sighed, steeling herself to lay her last, tiny bit of hope to rest. Surely her next request would kill whatsoever final crumb of affection he possessed, and she could not help delaying it for a few more moments.

"Please tell me that you understand no one at Longbourn with any sense believes you under the slightest obligation to my sister. My father has spoken to me on that subject," she said instead, wishing he had told the same to the gentleman instead of escaping to his book-room. "Lifting my sister, or truly any lady, from the water is not a declaration of affection or intent, and only my mother would think it signalled anything except a debt of gratitude. Ours, not yours."

Elizabeth still found Mr Darcy's expressions difficult to read, but he appeared somewhat astonished. "If I may speak frankly, this is a most unusual situation. I am sorry for your sister, and for Bingley. I will do all I can to support his suit until Miss Bennet returns to herself. He should disregard any advice I offer in the future, but I will convey any you can provide to him."

"Thank you." They stopped in front of the lavender shrub, where only a few blooms remained. Pulling her small shears from her pocket, she crouched down and clipped the branches.

However misguided his advice, he is a thoughtful friend. I reacted no better to Charlotte's decision to marry Mr Collins. She reminded me of her pragmatism, that she did not think herself a romantic but a realist. Now I must be realistic as well, and cease delaying the inevitable.

Standing, she took a breath and looked at him fully. His dark eyes were fixed on hers so intently she felt herself sway. Her cheeks flushed. "Would that you could extend that support...I realise I ask too much of you—of your time and patience—but my sister..." She trailed off, swallowing down the lump of regret and embarrassment. "She is much more...ill than she has appeared to you thus far. Her bruises are fading but it is almost miraculous that she has not betrayed some of her more agitated behaviour. Your presence today pleased her, but also quieted her. I know it is too much to ask, but if you might continue to visit her, just until the effects of the concussion fade..."

His brows drew together. "You wish me to step beyond mere tolerance, and to *encourage* her delusion? Do I understand you correctly?"

"Yes," she replied, her cheeks flaming. How had everything fallen apart, so close to happy resolution? "If you would only agree, I swear to you that no one would imply it meant anything...least of all myself."

He blinked and looked as if he wished to say more, but instead rubbed a finger under his chin.

Their own association had no satisfactory resolution—in her mind, if not his—and now she was asking him to involve himself in the romantic affairs of her sister and his friend. The very thing of which she had so angrily accused him in April!

"I know this," she said, waving her hand, "must be the last place you wish to visit." She swallowed down the lump in her throat that came with the acknowledgement.

Behind them they heard Kitty's voice calling out "Lizzy, where are you?"

Exhaling slowly, trying to prevent tears, Elizabeth turned and saw her sister heading in their direction. "Mama wishes Mr Darcy to return to Jane," she called loudly.

Elizabeth, who had believed she could not possibly be further embarrassed, rather wished she might be anywhere else in the world. She stared at her feet.

"Your mother is expressive in her care of her family," Mr Darcy observed in a kindlier voice than she expected.

Elizabeth tried to steady her own. "You are all that is polite, sir. My mother is far more than that—she is always effusive but Jane's condition has made her overbearing."

"She is a mother, concerned for her daughters' futures."

"And her own," said Elizabeth, more sharply than she intended.

"In that she is no different from any mother, be she the wife of a shopkeeper or that of a peer."

Mr Darcy's voice was soft, as if he were reassuring her that Mrs Bennet was not an embarrassing harridan. *Reassuring me about my own mother!* Her mother's worries, so loudly proclaimed after the Netherfield party had left, were behind her.

"You have met Lady Catherine." His expression was chagrined. "She is the daughter of an earl. And that fact, her birth-right and the privilege it entails, is in every expression of how she views the world and her daughter's future in it."

"How similar that is to how my father views the world—this *neighbourhood*—from his own lofty perch."

She felt Mr Darcy's intent gaze. "Your father is unconcerned with the circumstances? Some would claim your sister's honour was at stake."

"He despises society for forcing such sentences on men and women so poorly suited for each other." It was vital for him to understand that the Bennets did not intend to force Jane upon him, but Elizabeth wondered whether he would also understand the allusion to her parents' marriage and moved to lighten the conversation. "Although I believe he also fears a challenge from you. You are rather intimidating, Mr Darcy."

"Stern intimidation and disinterest are of great help in society," he admitted. "Does your mother feel as your father does?"

"She is rather frightened by you, which works in Mr Bingley's favour. My mother would prefer an amiable son-in-law for her most gentle of daughters. She is not a patient woman, however, and is overly concerned with Jane's reputation. Her ideas hold no sway with my father."

"Lizzy!" Kitty called again impatiently.

Elizabeth quickened their pace before Kitty said anything else mortifying.

"Miss Elizabeth, neither of us is pleased by what has happened to your sister and my friend. May I be honest in speaking with you?"

"Of course."

In a low voice he said, "There is no time. Tomorrow, early, I shall be walking by the footbridge."

"I shall be out before sunrise," she replied, wishing with all her heart she would fall into the stream when she arrived, and that her memories of this awful day might somehow be erased.

CHAPTER
TWELVE

That evening, while Elizabeth plaited Jane's hair, her sister crooned contentedly her own version of the old folk song, *Johnny Bydes Long at the Fair*.

"He bought me a twopenny whistle, He bought me a three-penny fair, He bought me a bunch o' blue ribbons, To tye up my bonny brown hair. I saw him coming, And I saw him coming, I saw him coming, Home frae the Newcastle fair.'"

Elizabeth soothed Jane's blonde locks away from her forehead. Whatever else one wanted to say, Mr Darcy's presence had given Jane an ease not experienced since the accident—an exact opposite of Elizabeth's own wrenching feelings. It gave her the wherewithal to bear whatever harsh sentiments he might choose to express to her upon the morrow. Would she sleep at all this night? It was unlikely.

Jane's brow furrowed. "My bonny brown hair?" She fiddled with one of her own golden tresses, but then suddenly snatched at one of Elizabeth's.

"Ouch! Jane!"

"You have bonny brown hair!" she cried. "Johnny wants the bonny brown hair!"

"No, dearest," Elizabeth tried. "All is well. Your hair is lovely."

But Jane had begun to sob, showing signs of another tantrum. "'Tis only yellow, ugly yellow."

"Jane, dear, Mr Darcy came home, do you remember? Mr Darcy came home from the fair, so to speak, and do you know his own sister has hair of the same golden colour? He loves his sister, and must therefore be fond of the colour of your hair as well."

Any hope that she might be forgetting her 'delusions', as Mr Darcy had so aptly named them, faded when Jane calmed immediately.

"Lizzy, go to bed. You are looking peaked," Mrs Bennet announced, entering Jane's chamber. "You are kind to have borne Mr Darcy for an afternoon for I know you so abhor his company, but I hope you will continue to tolerate him for Jane's sake. I suppose walking out with him was disagreeable, but he must at times be got out of the way of Mr Bingley. He is still the likelier prospect."

Elizabeth was unsure of what she could say in Jane's hearing. Her sister was currently wrapping one of her plaits around her hand and unwinding it again with intense interest. "Mama, there is only *one* prospect."

"Lizzy, there are things even you and your nimble mind cannot understand. Jane grows more beautiful daily, and is bound to be of interest to any gentleman who sets his eyes—and his heart—upon her. But you can be of use to her. You ought to leave her alone with each of them at one time or the other whenever they call."

"You wish to foster a courtship whilst Jane is so ill? Mama, you cannot be serious."

"It is what the men wish, not merely myself."

Elizabeth felt ill at Mrs Bennet's confidence. *Mr Bingley is despondent, Mr Darcy appalled, and Jane will soon feel more foolish than Lydia or Kitty ever have. What mischief is at work in the world!*

"I shall do all I can to ensure your happiness and comfort." Elizabeth's assurances echoed those she had ever heard Mr Bennet give to her mother: not empty of sentiment, but marked with deliberate sarcasm.

With her sister settled under her counterpane, Elizabeth went to her own room and curled up on her own bed to consider how she would answer Mr Darcy. *Forgive us, please. Give Jane more time to recover. Tell me you do not hate me, nor despise my family.*

It took real effort to keep her mind on creating a plan; being in his presence had distracted her. He had followed her out, perhaps eager for some conversation of sense; and he had consoled her over her mother's nerves. He plainly felt some responsibility for Jane's recovery. But enough to continue with the humiliation of having to see her daily for another week or two, whilst having to listen to Mrs Bennet and her inappropriate speculation?

Elizabeth swallowed back her emotion as she recognised Mr Darcy, whom she could scarcely look at a week earlier, had become the first person with whom she felt she could speak freely —of Jane's heart, at least, if not her own.

A situation of my own making. Had I not refused him...had he spoken with more respect...had I not listened to Wickham....

It was if she had lived on a precipice since the gentlemen had returned to the neighbourhood; the perversity of events and Jane's strange connexion to Mr Darcy rather than Mr Bingley ought to have been amusing. Yet it was not, not when she was not a disinterested observer to the happiness of either party. Her father might find it amusing, but he assumed she would be returned to normal with every rising sun, and he seemed to have no fear of the illness's permanence whilst her mother simply ignored it. Jane's calm temperament had entered rough seas, and only she seemed available to steer her sister through these waters until she—hopefully—returned to her senses.

After twisting and turning it over, examining the situation from every side over the course of two days, Elizabeth's conclusion remained unchanged. It sickened her and filled her with dread, but she must use every argument she could think of to convince a man—a man for whom deceit of any sort was abhorrent—to participate in a distasteful deception.

The sky was a deep purple when Elizabeth slipped out of Longbourn's kitchen door. Rex immediately approached from the barn and trotted by her heels. She slipped a piece of ham to him, and urged the old dog to remain silent on their walk.

Within ten minutes they had reached the footbridge, where a tall, familiar figure paced. She knew him so well, recognising gestures and pauses in his conversation, and yet understood so little of him. *He is too good to leave his friend in such an awkward state, as I have left him.*

Mr Darcy bowed as she approached him, his eyes clear and his jaw shaven, even in these early hours. She hid her surprise—not having seen him this early since that fateful morning in Kent—and nodded her own greeting before speaking.

"I suggest we walk near the orchard to escape public view." She winced at the awkward request especially when he, back in the laconic form she recalled from Rosings, only shrugged. Rex, apparently agreeing with Mr Darcy in enthusiasm, did not follow. They began strolling towards the edge of the old apple grove and she determined to satisfy her curiosity on at least one subject.

Sensing Elizabeth's inattention, Darcy stole a glance at her. The hesitant, shy expression he had seen when they encountered each other was no longer there; instead, he glimpsed the desolation and worry he remembered from the inn at Lambton. If he had wished to never again witness the anger and disgust he had seen at Hunsford, this—this guilt and anguish—was far worse.

"I hope your sister does not suffer any effects from our visit yesterday. I do not believe Mr Tilden would discourage fresh air, if your mother would permit her to be taken out of doors."

"Not at all. The garden might be a refreshing change," she replied. "Mr Tilden's orders are enforced by my mother, and will keep Jane from the joy of walking into Meryton or visiting our neighbours. It is a blessing. Time and immobility mean ears that do not hear the jibes from my father and the talk among our neighbours."

Darcy slowed, shocked by her words. "Mr Bennet is amused by your sister's...by the situation?"

"Oh, my father is not one to show his concern to the world. Although he has expressed some worry to me, he does not dare show it to my mother. She would fret even more than his joking provokes."

Darcy watched as the ribbon from her bonnet fluttered in the wind before tapping her cheek, prompting Elizabeth to smile. "It appears cruel but it is how he has managed their marriage for twenty-three years."

"A wise husband, indeed," he said, allowing some generosity into his words. Little as Mr Bennet deserved it, his daughter, so lovely and earnest in trying to manage her family, deserved all of *his* respect and assistance.

○ ○ ○

Elizabeth made no reply as they walked side by side, a respectable distance between them. Taking a deep breath, she inhaled the sweet smell of apples mouldering on the ground. "Mr Darcy, may I clarify the status of things?"

"The status..." His gaze fell, and although he appeared more concerned than eager at her request, he quickly nodded his agreement.

"You told Mr Bingley to return here, that you were mistaken about Jane?"

With heightened colour, he nodded, his gaze yet away from her. "I apologised last week."

"Last week!" Startled, Elizabeth tried to make sense of the timing. She had thrown her words at Mr Darcy in April. Whether he believed her then mattered little; her anger alone would have put him off, furthering his belief that she was from a family of vulgarians.

No, it did not! He wrote me the letter, anger and regret underlying his words, and did all he could to point to Jane and myself as exemplary young ladies.

"So recently, then."

With an intent look, Mr Darcy explained. "Come May, Bingley was with his sisters visiting their relations in Scarborough, and then off to a house party with friends for much of the summer, until he and his sisters joined us at Pemberley."

His voice trailed off, and Elizabeth was mortified to recognise their memories had settled on the same events, those few days of bated possibility they had shared at Pemberley, and the terrible way it had ended. *Lydia.* She could never fault him for his delay in telling Bingley about Jane's feelings! He had been much occupied repairing the Bennet family's reputation!

"I apologise for the delay. I have been much engaged with family matters. I wrote to him, hoping we could meet, but he is an unreliable correspondent at best."

She smiled knowingly. "And an unreadable one at worst, I have heard it said."

He returned her smile and continued. "Despite your assurances that Miss Bennet cared deeply for Bingley, enough time had passed that I could not risk telling him of my mistake until I knew—that it was clear—her feelings for him remained. I saw it within minutes of our first visit to Longbourn last week. Thanks to you, I recognised first the reserve, and in ensuing days, the joy and love in her expression as she spoke to my friend."

The last, and only time, Elizabeth had heard Mr Darcy speak so many words, it had been during his proposal. His horrible, poorly presented proposal. That April day he had said so much wrong, and five months later, he was here explaining the thought he had put into addressing his errors, and complimenting her for informing him!

"I apologised to him for my officiousness and explained my mistake the day before the accident. He was coming to propose—"

"You encouraged him, and yet you were leaving? Did you not wish to be there with him to celebrate his success? His engagement to my sister?"

CHAPTER
THIRTEEN

Of course I was going to leave! His mind screamed. *I had no encouragement. You would not look at me, could barely speak in my presence. It is only now, now that you have an interest in my aid towards your sister, that we speak so easily.* He had no reason, Darcy reminded himself, to expect anything else.

"Business, with my family. My uncle has been ill."

It would go unsaid that Lord Matlock was ill with worry over one son's gambling and another's entanglement with a notorious widow. *Lady Catherine is but one of my difficult relations. Hypocrisy is thy name, Darcy.*

"I see. May I ask, all is well with him? Will you soon be called back again?"

He shook his head. "My cousin—you will remember Colonel Fitzwilliam?—will write to me if my presence is needed. My responsibility now is here, ensuring your sister regains her...um, faculties, and accepts Bingley's hand."

"In between those events would come recognising Mr Bingley, acknowledging his ardour, and returning it." Elizabeth stopped beside him and sighed. "Jane must also realise you are but Mr Bingley's friend and guest at Netherfield."

Darcy held back from stating he was a friend to her as well, and satisfied himself with listening to her thoughts.

"Do you know, I have never truly considered how chance and timing play into the major twists and turns of our lives. Had we dawdled longer at the Lucases, or had I been on the bridge beside my sisters rather than walking ahead of them, it is likely neither of them would have fallen."

"You will not take blame for all that has happened," he said sharply—likely too sharply. She looked at him, clearly taken aback.

"I am sorry, but an untethered dog chased a fox, at just the wrong moment. Life can change in a heartbeat," he said, "for good or ill. Bingley faults himself for Miss Bennet's injuries, and excoriates himself for his failure to save her."

Clearly stricken, Elizabeth protested that he was blameless. "He was of service as soon as he appeared!"

"Indeed, but when another man is first to rescue the woman you love? It is difficult." As the wind picked up, Elizabeth reached for the ribbons securing her bonnet. Darcy glimpsed the smooth pale skin of her neck and sighed inwardly before he continued.

"Had Bingley arrived at the scene with me, I am uncertain what action he might have taken. He is uncomfortable in the water and my haste in the face of his hesitation might have worsened the situation."

When Elizabeth looked at him with interest, Darcy related the story of Bingley, as a small boy, falling into a stream near his home. "He was pulled by the current and trapped against a log for close to an hour before his father found him. He was quite ill afterward. Years later, when he finally ventured again into the water, at Cambridge, he was overwhelmed by the splashing and rough play."

"At Cambridge? Was it you who saved him there, as you seem to do so well?" When he winced, she immediately began to apologise.

"No, no," he insisted. "You meant no insult and I deserve your censure. Bingley's attachment to your sister is not imprudent. I have seen him fall in and out of love since he was eighteen years old, but what he called love was merely flirtation. It was different with your sister and I failed to recognise it."

She lifted her chin and in a mirthless voice said, "He failed to fight for it, for her."

Because he listens to his sisters and me.

"He cares deeply for your sister, and while he may have been uncertain whether her affections matched his, it was clear she enjoyed his company. If we had allowed them more time..." Cursing himself yet again for his own imprudent advice to Bingley, he said firmly, "If your sister truly shared his feelings—as you told me she did—it would have been a fortuitous alliance for both of them. It still can be so."

"I would like to believe that."

"Now Bingley is in misery of the acutest kind." Darcy sighed.

"Poor Mr Bingley! Pray, do not think Jane is unfeeling! She loves him. When this...illness...passes and her sense returns, she will be in agony for the hurt she has given to him."

Agony and hurt; are these not overly familiar to the two of us? Briefly Darcy wondered whether Elizabeth had told her sister about his proposal. He watched as she lifted her face and gazed at the sun rising over the tops of the distant wood. He ached with yearning to enfold her in his arms and beg her to forgive him and marry him. Instead, he gathered himself and spoke, all of his unsteadiness concentrated in the fingers he tapped against his leg.

"You asked for my help in resolving the problem, and have intimated that encouraging her...um, feelings towards myself might be part of it. Can you tell me why?"

She blushed, and her expression of misery returned. "Yes, although it may be uncomfortable for you."

"Uncomfortable?" He gave her an earnest look. "Though it qualifies as further interference in their affairs, I shall do everything in my power to unite my friend and your sister." He looked at her warily. "However, you cannot ask me to be her suitor. I cannot give credence to her delusion. That is a dangerous game of hearts and minds and reputations."

"I do not wish her heart to be broken! Just eased away from thinking of you as the man who holds it."

Elizabeth looked pained, albeit too briefly for his own vanity, before she continued. "You shall not be a true suitor, of course, but perhaps you can give her more courtesy than you do to others in our household, without truly paying her attention. Come to Longbourn so she thinks you are calling on her, to see to her health, until the bruises on her head have gone and her senses returned. So that she does not worsen, as she did while you were in London."

If Darcy was surprised to find himself asked by the woman he loved to feign a romantic interest with her sister, he knew she was equally surprised to find herself doing the asking. Every step in his romantic pursuit of Elizabeth Bennet had been fraught with misunderstanding and stupidity—now it had progressed to absurdity. He could not form a reply. The bitter irony of her request was too much.

"Perhaps, if you could allow her fantasy...or at least, if you did not openly refute it, all of us might be better off."

"A charade? You wish me to pretend affections for your sister?"

She looked at him miserably. "Not affections, just kindness and attention?"

"I do not wish to hurt your sister but—"

"You cannot risk your name and reputation. I understand. You have been asked too much." Elizabeth stared at her feet. "I have put great faith in the doctor's advice, and asking you to place faith in it as well is unfair. It would require a few days, a week. A fortnight even. I would never have anticipated any longer than that, and you would have been quite free to leave at any time—" Her words ground to a halt.

She had wanted him to remain for a week or two, and be free to go. That was all? With his heart suddenly heavy, Darcy's next words were more plaintive than he intended.

"I have not Bingley's charm and friendliness and your sister is in no danger of truly preferring me to him. I do not *wish* to encourage her, or pain either of them."

"Mr Bingley is a pleasant man," she said. "But I cannot imagine him being truly comfortable with any open expression of kindness or attention on your part. I would have had to distract him whenever possible. You are correct, sir. It would have been a difficult ruse."

Darcy looked away, feeling unequal to a reply; Elizabeth's ire at his former persuasions against her sister clearly remained ardent.

Elizabeth's voice softened to a barely audible pitch. "The amity between my sister and your friend came in an instant, and it will return soon. I must cling to that belief."

He wished she would argue that he had his own charms, but Elizabeth's love centred on her sister. His love was for Elizabeth; in that they were equal, although he was the poorer for it. He would take part in this charade if there was any chance at all it could make her think better of him.

"Yes, I shall help best as I can with this ruse," he said. "Worthy as your sister is, I could not love her. I hate to cause Bingley pain."

"Of course," she said quickly, looking more pleased with his willingness than he could appreciate. "We cannot have him made jealous. I will obtain the help of my sisters in distracting him from noticing any of your efforts."

What of yours, Elizabeth? You worry more for your sister's heart and Bingley's jealousy than your own.

Darcy felt sick at the conversation, wishing to do nothing else but claim the hand and heart of the lady asking him to pretend to love her sister. *How could I berate Bingley for hesitating to propose when I could not manage to begin a conversation with Elizabeth a week ago?*

———— ⊙ ∘ ∘ ————

Mr Darcy's troubled expression pained Elizabeth; she understood his thinking far better than she did that of any other acquaintance

—on every subject but herself, of course. *Does he think I wish him to prefer Jane's company to mine, and to leave as soon as all here is well? Shall we never speak to one another with clear minds and open hearts?*

She hurried to reassure him of the temporary nature of her request. "Both Mr Jones and Mr Tilden believe Jane will return to herself as the swelling is reduced. The only remedy, unfortunately, is rest, cool cloths, and time. The doctor emphasised that keeping her quiet and calm was of the utmost importance."

Elizabeth groaned, recognising that the morass of confusion Jane was experiencing was shared as well by Mr Darcy and Mr Bingley, and it was only deepening in its hold over everyone's actions and wishes. Stooping, she picked up a rock and tossed it in the stream, watching it splash and create a spreading circle of ripples.

"What I *mean* to say, sir, is that your prolonged absence from Longbourn could shock my sister. I believe it is best if you and Mr Bingley remain in Jane's company for the hopefully brief time her convalescence may require. Seeing the two of you, together, may hasten the return of her discernment."

"That makes sense." Mr Darcy chuckled briefly. "How anyone could ever confuse me for Bingley is such an odd notion."

"It is bewildering. I believe all you have in common in your appearance is the same fine tailor." Elizabeth blushed as soon as she said the words, but she saw he was not offended but seemingly amused by her observation.

"And yet he indulges an affection for purple waistcoats. It is not in my character to slight a friend. Bingley loves your sister and it is painful to me to see the pain this causes him."

Her cheeks flamed. Of course he was doing this to help Bingley; it was as well that he had reminded her, for her heart had soared at his agreement to be of assistance.

"I...I do understand. Again, I apologise for asking it of you." The circle of ripples from her carelessly thrown stone widened and faded into nothingness, just as her own foolish actions would, in time. She must not, metaphorically at least, jump in after it, chasing a foolish dream.

———— o o o ————

"It shall not happen, not again," Darcy muttered as he watched her teasing words fade into embarrassment, as her gaze again returned to her feet.

She glanced up. "What was that, sir?"

He could not let the unease linger, no matter any risk to Miss Bennet's recovery, no matter the silliness of her family. Besides, one could not witness the silliness without also witnessing the genuine affection they held for each other.

These people shaped Elizabeth. Caroline Bingley mocked them, despised all she saw here And I behaved as if I agreed.

How he loathed his behaviour of a year earlier. Darcy hoped he could show them improvement in his manner, but his only real care was for Elizabeth. Did she *see* any improvement? Had she forgiven him for his previous mistakes and failings? They were friends now, as her visit to Pemberley had shown them both. She had now asked him to become her ally, her partner. Clearly, it had deeply discomfited her to do so; the request was not a simple one. And yet, she had trusted his friendship enough to do it.

As he looked at her beneath the felted sky, every repressed feeling within him thrummed and pulsed. She peered up at him with something else besides embarrassment in her gaze, and Darcy had to stop and take a breath lest he seize her in a desperate kiss. Elizabeth reached out, as if to touch him, then dropped her hand.

"I promise I am not encouraging your, um, interest in my sister."

"I could have no interest in her, as I told you." He swallowed, thinking how ridiculous his words sounded.

"You are a true friend to Mr Bingley."

"To you as well, I hope," Darcy replied, unable to repress all of his frustration at this circular conversation. "I am glad to help Miss Bennet and Bingley, but you have to realise…you must know that I do not think only of them."

Her lips parted, as she looked at him with a mix of confusion and wonderment. "I...I thank you, whatever your reasons, from the bottom of my heart."

Darcy gazed at her, noticing the shadows under her eyes and wondering whether Elizabeth had any notion of how truly beautiful she was, compared to her sister or to anyone. If she thought she in any way was not the handsomest woman of his acquaintance.

"Elizabeth, you have expressed gratitude to me. I wish to express a similar sentiment to you. I owe you thanks for more than you will know."

Her eyes widened, and he quickly continued.

"I have not expressed myself well on any occasion in your presence, but I wish to do so now, if you will permit me. Before I met you last autumn, I had no notion of what it meant to please a woman worthy of being pleased. You taught me that much-needed, much-deserved lesson in the spring." He smiled with all the earnest warmth he could muster, determined to dispel any lingering concern Elizabeth had over her just refusal of his proposal.

"I owe you thanks for the words you expressed to me then," he continued, "and since we have met again, my gratitude for your friendship and generosity in allowing me to once again be in your company and appreciate the singular Miss Elizabeth Bennet who draws smiles, and instils happiness and confidence in others."

———o o o———

Mr Darcy's words washed over her, absorbed yet barely understood. Elizabeth found herself lost as she admired the handsome intensity of his expression. *I saw it before, in April as he opened his heart to me only to have me stomp on it.*

His countenance softened while also growing more animated, but still he kept his hands firmly clasped behind his back. When he finished speaking his heartfelt praise of her and their gazes met, he seemed uncertain of her reception of them and she saw the conscientious shift he made to regain some control; there was a brief look away, before he cleared his throat, and looked back at her with a gentle expression.

"I would do nothing to ruin any camaraderie we have built, but I must tell you—"

Her nerves alive and fraying, Elizabeth placed a hand upon his chest, desperate to gather her own composure and courage. Mr Darcy broke off in surprise, but remained still as she formed her anxious resolution and turned to him. She thought he looked puzzled, and perhaps a little alarmed.

"Mr Darcy, I stand here as a sister who is grateful, and as a friend who is appreciative but who has nothing to lose."

She closed her eyes, unable to look at his expression, hearing the quick intake of his breath before she opened her mouth to continue.

"I think only of you," he blurted, before she could speak. He smiled—a little nervously, she thought—and Elizabeth saw his eyes alight.

Her heart was beating so fast she was certain it caused her voice to shake, but with her courage rising, she returned his smile —and opened her heart. "Yes, well then, although you have not asked, I will tell you how I admire you."

Admire? That was the least of her feelings. 'Ardently love and admire you' had crossed her mind, but she did not wish him to think she was mocking him. She gazed at him, but Mr Darcy remained immobile; Elizabeth, certain he was blushing, began what seemed a nonsensical explanation of her feelings.

"The things I once believed about you—the things I felt about you—well, I can only recall them with painful regret. You, Mr Darcy, are the best man I have ever known, and I love you."

For one long moment nothing moved amidst the trees—not a bird nor a branch. Mr Darcy appeared dazed. His eyes seemed almost blank, and Elizabeth felt her heart fall.

I misunderstood! I thought he would wish to hear my confession, that he would reciprocate quickly with his own admission and—

All other thought disappeared as she found herself in his arms, crushed tight, his mouth on hers.

CHAPTER
FOURTEEN

D arcy kissed her with breathless ardour, every brush of his lips eager and tender in equal measure. Elizabeth responded with such feeling as could not but encourage him. His hat toppled from his head and lay disregarded on the ground as he traced her cheek and kissed her temple before drawing away to gaze at her.

"I love you, Elizabeth Bennet. With all that is in my heart, I love you."

He gathered her close again, traced his finger in the loose hair peeking around the edge of her bonnet, and whispered endearments which made her blush. He kissed her tenderly before regaining himself; as he drew back, Darcy said earnestly, "I beg your pardon. As you see, I am not a patient man. Hearing your words to me, and telling you how deeply I return them does not grant me such liberties, but I must tell you my affections and wishes are unchanged."

He swallowed and in a hushed, reverent voice, said, "I have long wished to earn your love and respect, and call you my wife. I wish to marry you, if you will have me."

Elizabeth stopped smiling long enough to agree, and accomplished other means that assured him of her joyful acceptance.

Moments later, breathing heavily and in near disbelief that they had finally—and so rapturously—expressed their mutual feeling, Darcy leant his head against hers. Tightening his hold on the lady who fit so perfectly within his arms and within his heart, he murmured, "When first we met, I realised you were the handsomest woman of my acquaintance, but you are even more beautiful now."

"And you, sir," she breathed, "have improved greatly in your manner."

◦ ◦ ◦

It was startling to Elizabeth how quickly time could pass when one was completely happy and completely in thrall to the person mere inches away. One of her hands rested in Darcy's, and with the other, she reached up to touch his lapel, his neck, his cheek. *How did we so quickly achieve this artless joy?*

It was neither quick nor artless, she reminded herself, but half a year since they had angered and insulted each other with their opinions; her own had been misguided, misinformed, wrong, cruel...

"What is wrong?" Darcy's worried voice matched his expression. "I apologise if I have been remiss as a lover, jumping from admitting my feelings to marriage and neglecting to court you. I am—"

"Do not apologise." Elizabeth smiled and shook her head. "Not a thing is wrong and I believe you have courted me far longer than is usual or indeed necessary. I am as impatient a lover as you. I-I am so happy, and realising how horribly wrong I was, how badly I misjudged you and then was cruel enough to say such terrible things."

"You said nothing I did not deserve, but I hope you no longer believe... I hope that my letter helped."

"Your letter and my own late-to-arrive common sense."

"I was awful."

"You were not. You are all things wonderful."

Elizabeth rolled her eyes. "Your words and actions provide further evidence that you and your heart are all things stubborn. Such faith is a wondrous thing." Her fingers grazed his cuff. "When did you know your feelings for me?" she asked shyly.

"They have been in my heart for well over a year now, and I returned here with Bingley with hope that what I had seen in your expression at Pemberley would return."

"I did not know. I was pleased you brought Mr Bingley back to Netherfield, but in your expression I saw nothing that revealed your own pleasure in being here."

He grimaced and, lifting her hand, laced their fingers together. "I saw none in yours, my love. I could scarce look to you for fear of further discouragement. I wished for anything but your gratitude. Bingley's discouragement was my doing in the first place, and it was only right that I attempt to put things right."

"You looked so fierce," she said, biting her lip. "So distant and proper, I thought your disgust of Lydia and Mr...her husband...had severed any hope of a future connexion between us."

"And I thought all the disgust to be on your side," he said, sighing.

With her free hand, Elizabeth touched his jaw and compelled him to meet her eyes. "There is none on my side."

"Nor mine. He gave her an endearing smile, and she thought she had never seen such ease and contentment in such a handsome man. She stepped closer and laid her head on his chest.

"We can discuss our memories and plan for our future, but first we must address the present." Her arms wrapped around his neck, she looked up into his eyes. "We must hide what there is between us."

———— o o o ————

Darcy was long-skilled at hiding his thoughts and concealing his emotions, especially the ardour he had had felt for Elizabeth. It was simple to withhold one's frustration and melancholy; he was unschooled in repressing that rarest of feeling: joy. He wished to throw his hat in the air and peal the church bells with the news that she loved him.

His hesitation must have shown in his expression. She touched his check and began explaining quickly. "I have no desire for secrets between us. I mean we cannot *yet* share our happy news. Nothing at Longbourn has changed. At times Jane grows hysterical, and often speaks nonsensically. I do not know why, but somehow within her muddled brain, she is clinging to you, or the idea of you or perhaps the idea of rescue."

Darcy kissed her hair, inhaling deeply before saying, simply, "I understand."

"I am sorry. No matter that the request for silence regarding our future could come from you and my father, my mother would never keep it to herself, and I cannot tell how much Jane understands. And if she were to have some sort of an outburst of befuddled jealousy, Mr Bingley would be deeply hurt. I wish to avoid such an outcome at all costs—if you can possibly bear with me."

He relished the confidence she had in him—revealing these private details of her sister's illness, sharing her fears, relying on him as her partner in managing the situation—even as he despised the shackles on his ability to shout her acceptance of his suit to the world. They were conspirators, joined together in a scheme. If he could play the role she assigned, it would give them the time Miss Bennet needed, and then their betrothal could be announced.

"I would bear anything for you, for as long as you require me to do it, and thank the heavens for the privilege," he said.

Elizabeth could have basked in the contentment of this moment for a hundred years, and resented the circumstance that made it a stolen one. Darcy's patience with the restrictions she had just named were but more evidence of his good heart.

"I hate that we must hide this, *us*," she said, frowning.

"I do as well. It will, hopefully, be a wait of a short duration. As I said, I have no desire to hurt your sister's heart or her good name and future prospects. Your plan is a good one. We are all of us friends, and spending time together, within company, over the next days or weeks may provide the time needed for Miss Bennet to heal."

Elizabeth smiled before glancing anxiously at the brightening sky. How long had they been together? Had anyone noticed her absence?

"How does Mr Bingley do?"

"Weary, lovesick, and likely in need of yet another hat."

She looked at him curiously. "Another? I thought he retrieved the one that blew off his head."

"I am slightly appalled at myself for revealing the fate of Bingley's beaver. I trust you, however, with my life as well as my friend's hats."

Elizabeth smiled at his mischievous expression, marvelling that it was for her within their close conversation. "I am sworn to secrecy."

"I should not tell the story, but it will amuse you in its poignancy. It was lost, then found. Alas, it soon was seen as the object most responsible for preventing Bingley from playing your sister's hero, and it was eliminated from his sight."

"Eliminated?"

"Stomped and burnt."

Her hands flew to her mouth and she could not quell her laughter as he looked upon her with tenderness.

"Poor Mr Bingley! My family is quite fond of him and all wish for him to be Jane's husband, as he wishes to be the hero of our tale," she said slowly, thinking aloud. "Do you suppose if you acted the part of a difficult paramour, or at least a less than ideal one, while Mr Bingley remains close by an example of what a young man should be, that it might help nudge her memory?"

"'A difficult paramour?'" He chuckled. "The cool detachment of which I am often accused may indeed assist us. I shall do my all and act as a bored and disinterested suitor."

She gave him an arch look. "With perhaps a touch of officiousness?"

"I believe I am well-practised in exhibiting boredom and disinterest."

"I have some memory of it," Elizabeth said, laughing in delight. When she saw the intensity of his expression and the exact moments of those memories came to her, she blushed and quickly returned to their subject. "Revisiting those places where Jane and Mr Bingley spent time together may help as well. Despite her illness, Jane spent many happy hours at Netherfield in conversation with Mr Bingley."

"We have no hostess there. I, um, do not believe Bingley's sisters are aware he is here."

"Oh. Well, that is likely to everyone's benefit. Miss Bingley is unlikely to be pleased, let alone assist. And if Jane spoke some sort of nonsense in her presence, it might add fuel to her disapproval."

"You are correct, I believe, and in fact she would act counter to our scheme."

"It is our scheme, then? We act together?" Elizabeth held out her gloved hand and looked at him expectantly. He took her hand and pressed it; then he sealed his actions with a kiss.

"I would be pleased to share ownership in this scheme, my love. Very well pleased indeed."

———— o o o ————

We are engaged to be married and we are accomplices in a marriage scheme. Ours and Bingley's.

As he walked back to Netherfield, Darcy nearly laughed out

loud at the insanity of it. *I, who have done all I can to avoid entangling myself with the daughters of scheming society mothers and fathers, and debutantes, have joined forces with the loveliest, cleverest woman of my acquaintance to ensure an understanding and engagement between two persons besides ourselves. Whilst concealing our own newfound understanding.*

Together they would manage the affairs of others to ensure felicity between Bingley and Jane Bennet. That couple had their hearts and minds out of alignment and in steering them back to what had been a deep and true attachment, Darcy recognised his own best chance to prove his devotion, to care for Elizabeth's heart and mind as his own.

Only yards from Netherfield's front doors, he could still feel the imprint of her lips on his; the memory of her expression of nervous mischief as she extended her hand and asked for his agreement flooded through him. *A few days of patronising Miss Bennet's feelings, and all will be well.*

Darcy entered the house with a smile and, suddenly ravenous, strolled into the breakfast room. A quick glance at Bingley's plate told Darcy all he needed about the man's state of mind. It had been filled and left untouched but for one muffin, shredded and made inedible as its crumbs floated in runny egg yolk.

"Good morning," said Darcy, wishing he could make it so for his friend. He poured himself coffee and eyed the breakfast foods arrayed on the sideboard. After choosing ham, rolls and fruit, he turned and asked, "May I bring you anything?"

Bingley looked up at him, his face pale, eyes red from lack of sleep, and shook his head. Darcy took the seat across from him and quietly began to eat. There was no point in asking whether Bingley was well; clearly he was not. He would speak when he wished to, and better Darcy have some sustenance for what might prove to be a long conversation.

"I do not wish to give up, Darcy. I feel as though I should be examined by a physician."

"What?" Darcy lifted his serviette to his lips. "It is more than a poor night's sleep that ails you?"

"It is not me she loves. You told me you were mistaken about her feelings, that she does in fact care for me, but you were wrong."

"No, I was not wrong. Her head is addled...her memories confused," he added quickly when Bingley glared at him.

"Yes, her confusion was established days ago. You were wrong about her feelings last year, and—"

"But I was corrected. I was told my mistake—"

"You were corrected. I have never asked you, how is it you found yourself to be wrong? Who corrected you? To whom did you apply for the truth?" His voice shifted from plaintive to something approaching mocking. "Did you intercept letters or rely on spies? Pray you did not pay them, for they were gravely off base."

It occurred to Darcy then that if he and Bingley were to continue as mates in romantic pursuit, the very least he could do was to confess his personal early disappointment. He did not, as yet, have the right to inform Bingley of his own happiness, and indeed, it might seem too much like gloating at this point. But it seemed proper to let Bingley know that he too had suffered, Darcy reasoned, and it might distract him from his hurt over Miss Bennet's inattention. It most certainly could not hurt anything, beyond his own pride.

"Shall we go to the study? I should like to tell you a story, in utmost privacy."

Bingley, his eyebrows raised, sprang to his feet, led them to the study, and informed a footman to follow with coffee and rolls, and then leave them undisturbed.

Blowing out a breath, Darcy sank down into the cushions of what he considered the only comfortable chair in Netherfield's library. It was an ugly purplish velvet but it sat at a good height with well-padded arms for reading, and had served as his only refuge the previous autumn from the dual onslaught of Miss Bingley's relentless conversation and Elizabeth's confusingly enchanting presence. Much as he wished the humiliating but needed rejection he had received from her to remain private, he would share his tale with Bingley. If anyone deserved to hear it, it was his friend—a good man now fearing the loss of his newly regained love. *If I have not previously been considerate of his feelings, I must be now.*

"Sit down. I wish to tell you what you ask, and in doing so, I will beg your pardon for concealing the workings of my own romantic sentiments and ask you to keep my confidences."

With an expression of sudden wariness, Bingley took the seat across from him. He leant forward, a new tension and overindulgence in brandy clear in his posture, or lack thereof. Through clenched teeth, he asked, "Your unexpected candidness is alarming me. Just tell me you are not taken with my angel."

With a laugh, Darcy shook his head. "No, it is not your Jane whom I love. It is her sister. Elizabeth."

CHAPTER
FIFTEEN

When he had finished an abbreviated telling of his history with Elizabeth, punctuated by Bingley's frequent interruptions and gasps, Darcy felt prone to hysterical laughter. He, a man known to be reserved and steady, had now laid out his sad tale to two men as unlike him as possible—one whose heart was often affected, the other whose remained determinedly untouched —and neither of whom could know of his happy ending.

"This is astonishing. You proposed to Miss Elizabeth? The two of you argued endlessly last autumn! Of course she refused you!"

Darcy shrugged at his friend's lack of perception, purposely ignoring how much Bingley's understanding matched Elizabeth's view of their time spent in company.

Bingley smiled grimly. "The first half of this story would please my sisters. Jane has thrown me off, and all would be restored to Caroline's plans for my felicity with one of her friends."

His tone, morose yet mocking, surprised Darcy. But again, this was Bingley, whose impetuousness and good humour had always marked him as reasonable. "And the second half?"

"Why, you, in love with a Bennet sister—the one Caroline truly envies and dislikes. Truly astonishing! Tossed over by the clever one!"

"Elizabeth is as pretty as she is clever," Darcy replied with some indignance—and a bit of guilt for not revealing that he had, in fact, not been *tossed* anywhere.

"Not clever enough to love you, my friend. With the luxury of time, you may get past your little infatuation." His appetite apparently returned with the news of his friend's heartache, Bingley reached for a roll and began slathering butter on it. "I apologise if being in company with Miss Elizabeth is a hardship for you, and hope you can greet her with indifference. She is a cheerful girl, after all."

Infatuation? Darcy growled under his breath as his guilt disappeared beneath a litany of grievances with Bingley's paucity of understanding. "That is not exactly—"

His friend's plaintive voice stirred him back to a more sympathetic attitude.

"Has Jane in fact thrown me over too? I cannot make it out, Darcy! She looks at me as if I am a common stranger!"

Darcy busied himself pouring a cup of coffee as he reflected on his own months of anguish, followed by a few days of joy and rising hope, and more weeks of despair and waning hope. Their amity, achieved only this morning, was too new to grasp fully or boast of, a single bloom of tender bud, only scarcely opened.

I made her smile and laugh. She kissed me. I held her in my arms, and she held me.

"Darcy?"

Shaking himself from the mists of tenderness threatening to enfold him, Darcy again sought to reassure his friend. "Yesterday, when Miss Elizabeth and I were speaking in the garden, Miss Bennet was our subject. Miss Elizabeth knows her sister better than anyone, and she was adamant that Miss Bennet loves you."

"Perhaps that has changed."

"In a handful of days? She was clearly attached to you when we called at Longbourn on Monday and Tuesday. Had she not fallen and hit her head in the morning, she would have happily agreed to your proposal on Wednesday afternoon."

Gazing at Bingley, Darcy mused on how slow were some days and weeks when a man's heart was aching, and how quickly they passed when one was in love and wished to move on to mutual happiness. Darcy recalled that sensation when he thought on his nearly three days in Elizabeth's company at Pemberley. It passed in a flash yet was well remembered to the minute. The weeks afterwards were a blur of Wickham, Lydia, Mr Gardiner's study, and of stumbling hopes until he had arrived five days ago to support Bingley. To seek his own answers. Well, he had found them, had he not?

If it were up to him, he would tell Bingley all of it—but Elizabeth deeply feared such candour. Miss Bennet, she said, was far more muddled than Bingley knew. She was clinging to hope in Tilden's prognosis, that her sister would heal quickly without him ever knowing the extent of her confusion, her infirmity, her false attachment to Darcy. Some would shun such weakness, thinking it a failing of the mind *and* character. Could he guarantee Bingley's passion for Miss Bennet would survive such a revelation? He thought it would; nevertheless, if it was only a matter of a few days, why put it to the test? He certainly could not add his own intentions to the fraught situation. Miss Bennet's and Bingley's feelings must both be protected until Miss Bennet healed.

"You are certain about Miss Bennet's feelings for me? Miss Elizabeth is certain?"

"Miss Bennet is for you," he assured Bingley. "In fact, not only is Miss Elizabeth quite certain of her sister's heart, she is doing everything in her power to speed along her regaining such a realisation."

Bingley's face lit up. "Miss Elizabeth is such a clever person. If anyone can help to unravel this mess, it is she."

"Miss Bennet cannot go out in company yet, but our visits *have* been helpful, she says. We are to continue to provide such careful companionship as might gently assist in her recovery. Do not you see? Miss Elizabeth trusts us and our discretion as she does no other. She even hopes that, somehow, a visit to Netherfield might be arranged, to further jog her sister's memory."

Bingley looked doubtful.

"Miss Elizabeth is acting on the advice of my physician, and is certain time is all that is needed for her sister's memory to return in full. Are you questioning the word of the finest doctor in London?"

"Of course not," Bingley cried around a mouthful of bread. He swallowed and took a large gulp of coffee. "It is...well, I fear that whatever love she had for me may have been knocked out of her head and heart when she fell."

Darcy brushed aside the image of Cupid and his arrows lying squashed underneath Miss Bennet and stirred his coffee.

"Those who love simply and fully, as I believe Miss Bennet did, do not simply erase it from their hearts, Bingley."

"You truly believe that seeing me helps? It has not thus far. And why must you come too? She looks at you far more than me."

"Miss Elizabeth believes it is for the best. Her sister only recalls my rescue, which makes me a familiar point within her confusion." Darcy's reassurances appeared to have stimulated Bingley's appetite; he reached for another roll and began slathering it with jam.

"Spend time with her so when her head clears, she remembers. Besides, you are laden with far more charm than I, Bingley. I shall withhold my paltry share of it whilst you expend all that you have."

He clapped Bingley on the shoulder. "Your Miss Bennet is worth the earning."

"She is, indeed. Please make sure we remind Caroline of my angel's worth."

"Caroline?"

"Netherfield will need a hostess if we are to have the Bennet ladies here."

— o o o —

If Darcy could find relief from his concerns by a fast ride through the park, and Elizabeth by taking a long walk through the countryside, others more inclined towards sedentary pursuits had no such outlet.

Mrs Bennet could flutter a handkerchief only so many times or take her salts so often before her nerves would again overtake her. In the case of her most beautiful, most marriageable, and closest to the shelf daughter finding herself lacking an engagement to either of the two rich, handsome gentlemen constantly in Longbourn's parlour, her vexation and her lifelong fear were cresting.

While she would not credit herself as a reader of minds, she certainly understood how to tell when and if a gentleman was interested in one of her daughters, and whether one of her daughters was sweet on a gentleman. She did not get her deserved credit for Lydia's marriage to the fine Mr Wickham, but she was certain she would be celebrated when dear, beautiful Jane wed kind Mr Bingley and his five-thousand a year.

Or if she does. Nothing is as it should be!

None of her hopes for a quick denouement, of Jane's heart recognising what was supposed to be, had come to fruition. Mr Bingley, fair and genial, was the perfect husband for Jane, and yet the girl's attentions had not gone back to him when the dark and brooding Mr Darcy entered Longbourn.

No, she practically fixated on the man!

Yet not only did the sight of Mr Darcy *not* heal Jane of her confusion, he made no great show of politeness towards her nor concern for his wounded friend.

Of all the things to be made insensible of—how could her dear Jane forget who she loved and ruin all that Mrs Bennet had anticipated? Worse, while she stared at Mr Darcy, the man himself remained as proud and aloof as ever. Jane's warm gazes went unanswered, her smiles unreturned. He would not know the part and lines of a lover if Shakespeare himself thrust the script at him!

Poor Mr Bingley reminded her of a neglected pony, what with his beseeching eyes and large teeth. Those eyes had been set on Jane nearly since they had met a year prior, and certainly he had gazed at her steadily since his return. Yet something was different the day prior, when rather than staring at Jane, Mr Bingley appeared content to take a chair by her, or by Elizabeth or Kitty or Mary, and allow them to steer the conversation towards whichever topic most interested them.

Far too many questions flooded her mind: *Is Mr Bingley stepping aside? Has he lost interest in Jane? Is he ceding the field to Mr Darcy? Can Jane end up with neither a suitor nor a husband?*

She would need her salts, after all.

There is only one answer, she decided. *Dear Jane needs more of the beauty juice prescribed by Mr Jones, more doses, more often. One of those fine fellows is bound to notice!*

◦ ◦ ◦

After a lifetime in a house as fraught with sisterly squabbles, maternal indulgences, and marital tension as Longbourn, Elizabeth easily anticipated the signs of her mother's distress; even before Mrs Bennet began to spew inanities and insults, Elizabeth could recognise it in her eyes, or hear it in her tone or in a shift in her breathing. Especially now, when Mrs Bennet's expectations were sorely tested.

Although Elizabeth had felt dull the past months, the connexion she had to Mr Darcy had increased her awareness of everything around her that might hint at *him*. Now, when he was near and their mutual affections proven and declared, her attentions strained to centre on his conversation or his movements; when he was absent, her every thought was of him, regardless of the cacophony of music, voices, and action around her. Hearing her mother speak his name set off her senses, and she flew into the morning room.

"Who shall marry our Jane? Mr Bingley has gone adrift! His friend has scared him off and yet *he* seems not to want her either!" Even as she wailed, Mrs Bennet's voice took on a mocking tone.

"Not good enough for him? Not handsome enough or in society! Mr Bingley admired everything about her and yet steps back!"

"Mr Darcy?"

"He is too proud. Jane may suffer from confusion, but her heart is suffering at his indifference. If he is now her choice, it is time he proposed."

"Mama!" Elizabeth shut the door behind her and quickly ascertained that the other door and the windows were closed. She cringed as she saw her mother's audience was not Kitty or Mary or even Mrs Hill, but Mrs Philips.

She greeted her aunt and took a seat beside her. She enquired as to the health of her uncle and Kitty's expectations of a card party, an entertainment for which the Philipses were especially renowned. Her aunt preened while Mrs Bennet eyed Elizabeth suspiciously.

"My sister tells me poor Jane remains unwell, but as a happy outcome of her accident, now suffers from a surfeit of suitors."

Elizabeth glared at her mother, who returned it with an indignant cry. "Do not give me that look, Lizzy! Your father may be amused but we are faced with a quandary. If Mr Bingley has lost his chance with Jane, *she* cannot lose her chance with Mr Darcy! He was seen with his arms wrapped around her, draping his coat over her. Little more is needed for him to act honourably and marry your sister."

"But first he was seen in much the same situation with Kitty, and gave *her* his jacket," Elizabeth asserted, glancing at her aunt. "If justice is what you seek, then by all rights, it is Kitty who shall be Mrs Darcy."

Mrs Philips gasped, which quickly led to a short coughing fit. When it was concluded, she turned to Mrs Bennet, whose face had turned even redder, and then back to her niece. "Can it be true? The man could be promised to two of your sisters?"

Elizabeth smiled at her aunt, a kind-hearted lady of sharper intellect than her sister but, with neither sons nor daughters of her own, somewhat innocent of the travails of motherhood suffered so publicly by Mrs Bennet.

"Mr Darcy is obliged to neither of my sisters. If such a threat had hung over his head, I do not believe he, or many men, would have ruined a pair of good boots jumping into a shallow stream to pull out two girls frightened by a dog.

"In fact," she continued, "think of those heroic gentlemen we would not know today had every one of them had to parse whether the lady in need of rescuing was marriage-minded, not to mention handsome, pleasant, fertile, and of good character."

Mrs Philips tittered. "Oh, you are a sensible girl, Lizzy."

"Lizzy is a champion of Mr Bingley, who all of us prefer as a husband, son or brother to the puffed-up Mr Darcy. But his chances have been harmed by his own indolence and hesitation. Jane no longer looks kindly on him. Or so I believe."

"Aunt, we wish not to announce this complicated dilemma to our neighbours. Jane has suffered a concussion," Elizabeth said in a measured voice. "We have been assured by two physicians that her memory and her feelings for Mr Bingley shall return in time."

Mrs Bennet made a small noise. "In time. As I said."

"Have patience, Sister. Apparently Mr Bingley has it, but it has ever been a lack in your character. In Lydia's as well, although her impatience secured her a handsome husband."

Elizabeth slipped out the door, unnoticed, as a conversation—centred on Mr Wickham's many wonderful qualities and Lydia's great fortune in wedding him—grew louder.

CHAPTER
SIXTEEN

Jane opened her eyes to see the late morning sun shining through the open drapes. She glanced over to see which sister was sitting beside her, and was vaguely surprised to see the chair empty. She pondered over this for some time, finally recalling Lizzy saying last night that they would be attending church today; they must have left without her!

She sat up, and the room whirled in a most irregular manner. Nevertheless, she persisted. She felt a bit more wakeful than usual, although her head ached. Mama was not here to give her more tonic; it took away the megrim, but it did make her *so* tired.

Where *was* Lizzy? Oh yes, at the service. She missed Lizzy, who helped her so gently and kindly. But Lizzy was at church. 'Six days shalt thou labour, and do all thy work.' Jane must help herself.

Perhaps she had not always been the most pious of her sisters, but Jane had always taken pleasure in the songs, in the shared moments in prayer with her own quiet devotion. Hadn't she? But her current malady possibly pointed to a judgment of some sort. Mayhap in the past she had been too concerned about her appearance and the opinions of her neighbours. Mr Bather certainly had preached often enough on the subject. Slowly, carefully, she made her way to the wardrobe, and began opening its drawers and cupboards.

"Too pretty," she muttered. "All anyone cares for. Too good. Must wear something horrid." She pulled out a large apron she wore when working in her stillroom. It had faded to a dismal grey, and Lydia said it made her look like a great dull mushroom. She decided to put it on, but then noticed the prettiness of the embroidery on her night rail. No! It would not do. She tore it off, pulling it over her head and tossing it on the floor—which caused a bout of dizziness that nearly felled her.

When her vision settled, the mirror showed her unkempt self, hair escaping her braids, standing in her shift. She scrutinised the image carefully. Her shift was a plain cotton thing, ending just above her knees. Briefly she considered a petticoat, but all of hers were so pretty, usually meant to be seen. It would not do, not when she was trying so hard to be devout. Stockings were out of the question; not only were they all lovely silk ones, but the notion of attempting to tie her garters seemed...impossible.

Much more carefully, she fitted the thick strap of the apron over her head and let it drop. As expected, she immediately appeared lumpish and dreary. The ties were beyond her ability to fasten, but all anyone ever saw was the front of one's person when one was confined to sitting in the parlour all day. With satisfaction at her drab, shapeless appearance, she turned away from the mirror and carefully moved to the door. Her ankle hurt less than it had but her toes grew cold as soon as she left the comfort of her cosy bedroom rug. Fetching her slippers was beyond her ability.

Cautiously, she crept down the stairs, an inch at a time. She met no one; everyone must be at church. At last she arrived at the big front parlour, where thankfully a fire was snugly burning. With a sigh of relief she sat decorously on the settee nearest it, but after a few minutes, she drew up her toes to tuck them beneath the apron's hem, as even with the fire, it was chilly. The apron, perhaps, was not so warm as the dresses she usually wore.

But suffering for piety's sake was something the martyrs of old would do, would they not? Mary, at least, would approve.

A wave of fatigue passed through her. "When the bough breaks, the cradle will fall," she hummed. It seemed rather awful, though, for the baby's bed to fall from a tree. Perhaps they swaddled them in first?

She closed her eyes. "Only for a moment," she told herself. "'For in six days the Lord made heaven and earth … and rested the seventh day.'" She gave way to her fatigue then, closed her eyes and was snoring within moments.

———— o o o ————

Mr Bennet had stirred himself from his comfortable chair. Having used Jane's need for company as his excuse to miss church services, he belatedly realised he had not bothered to spend a moment with her. Guilt was not a familiar companion, but it was Sunday; if there was a day to turn an excuse into a fulfilled promise, then he would indeed go and sit with Jane.

He usually enjoyed her company, although she was extremely dull of late. Jane was a kind, thoughtful girl; an ideal daughter, if he needed to be effusive about it. Her paternal attentions, before her injury, were much better performed than those of Mary, who never failed to include an admonition about some failing or sin, or Kitty, who often looked confused throughout the whole of any conversation. He would miss Jane when she married, of course, but he was happily anticipating her removal to Netherfield for more than just her own marital felicity. The three miles between Longbourn and Netherfield were nothing to Mrs Bennet; he would gladly purchase her a phaeton if it would provide her an easier way to ride over every day to visit the new Mrs Bingley.

Bingley was a nice fellow; his amiability and abundance of patience for difficult relations would make him a perfect husband for Jane if Jane could see her way back to him from her temporary admiration for Mr Darcy. The gentleman from Derbyshire was wealthy, intelligent, and ridiculously ill at ease at Longbourn; if

Jane was not making him uncomfortable with her staring, Mrs Bennet did by yammering on about the neighbours.

While Mr Bennet could be grateful for Darcy's actions a week ago, he had seen the bridge and therefore had scepticism that any heroics had been needed. Could Lizzy have been as effective a saviour to Jane? She might at least have been able to drag her out of the stream. Had it *been* Lizzy, at least Jane would not have fainted with the vision of Darcy's face imprinted in her mind. Had Darcy not acted as he did, all would have been well and Mrs Bennet would have been planning a wedding.

It was a conundrum, and rather a dull one at that.

Vexed by these troubling considerations, Bennet sat back in his chair, leaned his feet against the window seat and closed his eyes. *I should not trouble Jane right now. I am poor company indeed.*

———— ◦ ◦ ◦ ————

Sunday was a daunting day for Elizabeth. The whispers she heard in the pews behind her were little different from those she recalled from a year prior, when questions and eyebrows were raised at the Netherfield party's departure and Mr Bingley's continued—soon determined permanent—absence from Longbourn. Jane's wounded heart had been made plain thanks to Mrs Bennet's loud and indiscreet conjectures on her eldest daughter's guarantee of future happiness as Netherfield's mistress. Now gossip was centred on Jane's lack of church attendance as a sign of either deep physical injury or a moral implacability towards a genial rake.

Services brought their travails to the attention of those who had not already called at Longbourn to satisfy their curiosity and assure themselves of Jane's health. It was with no small amount of trepidation that she watched old Mr Goulding and his wife step towards Mrs Bennet. While her own better angel—or Jane of only a week ago—might have joined them to temper her mother's display of cool forbearance, Elizabeth wished only for a breath of cool, fresh air. Her mind had been awhirl since the day prior, and she could not expect a change any time soon.

Although the Bennet pew was very near the front, the seating for the current possessors of Netherfield Park—which did not have its own chapel—was closer still. Thus, the current tenants were set on display, the jewels of the humble congregation. Elizabeth had divided her time between staring at the back of Darcy's head and attempting *not* to stare.

Of course, the entire congregation was staring, so perhaps it made her more conspicuous if she did *not* look? Was she wearing her besottedness for all to see? It was so unfair that he had no one before him except Mr Bather, the rector, in whose myopic vision he was only a fuzzy silhouette. At least Papa had stayed home with Jane, and thus could not tease her.

What had Darcy said? *I think only of you. With all that is in my heart, I love you.*

She felt her cheeks grow warm.

Last night, like those before it, she had slept poorly, her wonder and curiosity taking fire once her body was still and her mind ready to rest. This time, of course, the fire of her curiosity had wandered in entirely different directions. The effect, however, was the same. Glancing in the mirror that morning, Elizabeth had seen her own fatigue; she hoped her fellow parishioners would follow the spirit of the Sabbath and refrain from comment on her appearance.

As the service ended and the congregation dispersed, Mr Darcy and Mr Bingley stood slightly apart. Suspicion about their return to Meryton, and disbelief as to how the less likable of the pair had served as hero to the Bennet sisters, hung about them like a mantle.

Not wishing to allow the gentlemen to appear ostracised, Elizabeth took Mary's hand and pulled her over to them. After greetings were exchanged, Mr Bingley made quick work of canvassing the sisters for news of Jane; a slight nudge to Mary's side prompted her to lead the conversation. Elizabeth gratefully stepped back to stand by Mr Darcy.

"You are bearing up well sir, under the scrutiny of our mutual neighbours."

"I wonder, were there no intrigues or scandals of high fascination here whilst we were gone or is the potency of recent events simply as enthralling as the novels I suspect my sister hides from me."

Mr Darcy, like Elizabeth, kept his eyes on the conversation between their companions as he replied. His expression betrayed nothing of humour, but she could hear the mirthful challenge in his voice.

"Ah, Kitty too hides such books," she confided gaily. "As to scandals, I have heard nothing of spirited dogs nipping at treacherous lovers or cantankerous cows upsetting an elopement," she said quietly, nodding at elderly Mrs Merkin and her two solemn-faced daughters. "In July, there was a to-do when a chamber-pot fell from a window ledge onto Meryton's main street and narrowly missed Sir William Lucas, and last month, I understand a mug of ale was thrown during a dispute over the fence between the Moores and the Oldhams. Our headlines are not fit for London's illustrious papers."

"No, they are far more interesting and likely less injurious, and you are so beautiful this morning I can hardly breathe," he said, all in a low undertone and with the same impassive expression with which he used to comment idly upon the weather.

Astonished, Elizabeth could only stare at him, wide-eyed.

"Lizzy?"

Reluctantly she moved her attention back to Mary; she was gesturing uncomfortably towards a red-faced Mrs Bennet, standing between Mrs Philips and Kitty. The few people still standing in the churchyard were staring as the Gouldings stormed towards their carriage, their grandson looking back angrily at Mrs Bennet.

"Oh no," Elizabeth murmured. She heard Mr Darcy mutter Mr Bingley's name as she moved towards the unhappy trio. "Mama, what did you say?"

Mrs Bennet was not finished with her glaring so Kitty

answered for her. "She said 'better that the dog had fallen in and drowned than poor Jane have her life upended'."

"Mama!"

"It is a mongrel!" cried Mrs Bennet. "It was seen near our barn yesterday!"

"Undoubtedly to visit Rex!" Sighing, Elizabeth watched the Gouldings' carriage drive away.

"Mrs Bennet, may I have the honour of driving you back to Longbourn?"

Mr Bingley stood in front of them, smiling, his arm extended to the lady. Mrs Philips pushed her sister towards him and hurried away to her husband. Mrs Bennet's expression brightened as she took the young man's arm. "This is how it should be," she cried. "You are the perfect gentleman, Mr Bingley."

At Elizabeth's nod, Kitty followed. Mr Darcy offered his arm to Mary and looked hopefully at Elizabeth. As she took his other arm and they followed in the curricle's wake, Mary said quietly, "That was most kind of Mr Bingley."

"Yes, quite gallant indeed," Elizabeth murmured. "Nicely done, Mr Darcy."

○ ○ ○

Mrs Bennet bustled into Longbourn as Bingley helped Miss Catherine down from his curricle. She leant heavily on his arm; he had not noticed a limp before she boarded the vehicle, but then again, he had forgotten that she too was injured in the incident at the footbridge. Perhaps her pain came and went? The poor girl had been overlooked. He should likely ask if she was well but his mind was too focused on the satisfaction of being at Longbourn, in more intimate company, for at least a few minutes. *Without Darcy's distracting presence!*

Bingley had no complaint against his friend—or against Miss Elizabeth or Miss Mary, of course. It was simply his desperate desire to be the sole recipient of Miss Bennet's attention—*if* he was even permitted to see her. Nothing was as it should be and nothing as he wished it. But he would be pleasant and optimistic of everything sorting itself, the sooner the better.

Widening his ever-present smile, Bingley followed Miss Catherine through Longbourn's door. He was handing off his hat and gloves to Mrs Hill when he heard a scream.

"No, no, no, no...!" Mrs Bennet shrieked.

Miss Catherine, her limp forgotten, raced towards her mother's voice. Recognising that he now had *his* chance to be the Bennets' hero, Bingley quickly followed her into Longbourn's large front parlour, where he found Mrs Bennet gasping and gesturing frantically by the fire. Alarmed, and somewhat dreading that he might encounter a large spider, Bingley stepped closer. There, curled up on the settee and half-asleep, was Miss Bennet.

Curled up, half-asleep, and nearly naked! Her toes, her limbs, her arms—all uncovered and exposed! Her creamy skin, so soft and enticing, peeked out—nay cried for attention!—under some odd, sheer grey fabric. There was more flesh than fabric. He stood in shock, unable to move let alone think, as his manners were forgotten. Mrs Bennet was still shouting, Miss Catherine was gasping, and suddenly Mrs Hill rushed past him, blocking his view and tossing a blanket over the drowsy Miss Bennet.

"Jane!" he heard Mrs Bennet cry. "You must go to your room! Mr Bingley, you must get out!"

Startled, he began backing quickly out of the room, bumping into a chair before righting himself and tearing his eyes away from the sight of his angel, bewildered and barely dressed, staring at him in wonder.

As he threw open the front door and drew in a breath of cool air, he could hear her lovely voice, singing, "Do you know the muffin man?"

CHAPTER
SEVENTEEN

"I cannot return to Longbourn," Bingley said hopelessly. "It was the shock of it all. I thought it was a spider. I meant only to help, to provide rescue to my angel. Instead, I can never see her again."

Darcy purposely turned away on the guise of refilling his glass to disguise the mirth upon his face. In fits and starts, Bingley had finally gotten out the story of his rather infamous latest visit to Miss Bennet, and it was imperative that he not add to the poor fellow's mortification by bursting into laughter. But it was a near thing.

He cleared his throat, fixing his mind upon the memory of his last conversation with Lady Catherine in order to quell all hilarity. When he was finally certain of his control, he faced his friend.

"That is the opposite of what you must do," he said. "Everyone knows it was an accident. Everyone knows Miss Bennet is ill, and not responsible for her choice of, er, dresses. If you stay away, they will believe you blame *her* for the error. It will be a slap in the face to them all."

"I would never!" Bingley cried. "But how could I face them again? They know what I saw. My angel, clothed only in afternoon sunlight, as fair as a glistening mermaid with translucent grey scales, swimming upon a lake of blue velvet." He paused, seeming rather taken with his descriptive prowess. "The settee, you know. I will never be able to look at it in the same way again."

Darcy was forced to turn away once more, the image of a scaly Miss Bennet paddling away upon the front parlour settee almost overpowering his ability to focus on his longstanding fury with Lady Catherine. "You have a choice, Bingley," he said, after regaining his composure. "Either you give up entirely on your pursuit of Miss Bennet, including relinquishing this lease and never coming again to Hertfordshire, else do the gentlemanly thing."

"I *am* a gentleman! How dare you imply otherwise!" Bingley's cheeks reddened blotchily, plainly recalling his ungentlemanlike fit of shock-induced staring earlier that day.

"If you are a gentleman, act like one," Darcy said severely. It was no time to tiptoe around the matter; Elizabeth would be horribly disappointed if her sister's suitor disappeared in a torrent of bashful awkwardness. He could not permit it. "We accepted an invitation to dine Tuesday evening. We shall proceed with our plans, and you, especially, shall act as though you never saw anything at all. A gentleman never sees nor remembers anything which his host does not wish him to see or remember. He never references it by word, action, or deed. It did not happen. That is, unless now that you have, er, viewed Miss Bennet *en déshabillé*, you did not care for what you accidentally beheld, and no longer wish her to be your wife. In that case, you must regard it as a close call, and be thankful that you were appropriately warned away. Let some other fellow loyally nurse her through her brief illness, and be forced to deal with the spectacle nightly."

Bingley's eyes widened, his mouth gaping at the recollection of what it would mean to be wed to Miss Bennet. A thin line of drool emerged from his lips, and Darcy was required to make his way to the fireplace to tend a perfectly healthy blaze before he either burst out laughing or hit the younger man over the head with his poker. But dash it, Bingley must be brought to reason, and the sooner the better. He had been entranced with Miss Bennet for months, and could be forgiven for accidentally failing to flee as quickly as he might have done.

It was Bingley's turn to clear his throat. "I have decided you are correct, Darcy," he announced solemnly. "I shall behave as if nothing ever happened. I saw nothing, and told you nothing of the incident I did not see."

"Of course," Darcy said, equally solemn, poking the log. "I have no idea to what you refer."

"I *will* marry Miss Bennet, and no other fellow will *ever* have the privilege of seeing what I did *not* see," Bingley added impetuously.

"Perhaps, then, we should call tomorrow as per our usual habit. Keeping everything the same." Darcy had no intention of staying away from Longbourn for a minute more than necessary. Besides, if he had to spend the day with Bingley brooding, he would probably be obliged to hit his friend with the poker after all.

———— o o o ————

Longbourn's Sunday dinner was more of an ordeal than usual. There were no guests to leaven Mrs Bennet's soliloquies, of course, and after Lizzy had heard of what happened upon Mr Bingley's earlier arrival, she had to wonder whether the gentlemen might ever visit again. She blamed herself; she ought never to have left her sister alone, and all because she had selfishly wanted a few minutes with Darcy.

"You must stay away from Mr Darcy, Lizzy," Mrs Bennet proclaimed as if she had heard her daughter's thoughts. She speared a parsnip to emphasise her point. "He is for Jane if she does not want Mr Bingley. Two in the hand she has now, and it is nearing October. A choice must be made!"

Elizabeth looked around the table to see her family, with expressions expectant or amused, awaiting her reply. "It is not a choice, Mama. One man wishes to marry Jane—or he did, before we all abandoned her to her illness today—and the other is attempting to help right her memory of loving Mr Bingley. Mr Darcy owes Jane nothing."

"We have kept all of this a great secret, but it cannot hold forever." Mr Bennet glanced at Kitty, prompting the rest of the family to do the same.

"No!" she cried, "I have not written to Lydia nor breathed a word to Maria." Then Kitty turned to her mother. "It is not fair that Jane has two suitors and Lizzy and I have none—nor does Mary, of course," she added. "I do hope Jane soon sees Mr Bingley as she should see him. He gazed at her today in such pained adoration. Handsome though he is, Mr Darcy's expression holds only discomfort."

Such an opinion immediately piqued Mary's concern. "Perhaps Mr Darcy's physician should examine him. Perhaps his head or stomach bother him."

"He did not finish the soup or take any cake here two nights ago," said Mrs Bennet, her attention now firmly fixed on Mr Darcy's medical issues. "I did not inform Cook, who would of course take the insult, but it was peculiar. He has said in the past that I set quite a fine table."

Mr Bennet looked up from his plate. "You have hit on the answer, Mrs Bennet. Perhaps it is the bloat rather than arrogance that plagues him."

Mortified on Mr Darcy's behalf, Elizabeth held on to her temper long enough to swallow the bit of bread that had gone dry in her throat. That her father—who had, plainly, not looked in on Jane even once whilst they were at the service—should exercise his wit upon them now was especially infuriating.

"Mr Darcy has proven himself quite patient and kind to this family, aiding my sisters first when they fell and now supporting Jane whilst she recovers. Do you truly think he wishes to be here, in Hertfordshire, when he should be with his sister or friends in London or at his own estate? But no, he is here, in company with Mr Bingley as a friend to encourage and assist him in his hopes for

Jane's hand. Nothing could have compelled his return here but that he is a better man than any of us could have imagined."

Flushed at knowing she had revealed her own violent emotions, if not Darcy's true motivations, Elizabeth reached for her water glass and took a long drink.

A moment or two later, Mr Bennet filled the silence that followed Elizabeth's declaration as well as her expectations of him.

"Next to being married, a girl likes to be crossed a little in love now and then," he said, chuckling. "It is something to think of, and it gives her a sort of distinction among her companions. How would it be any different for a man?" He sipped his wine and looked cheerfully at the three daughters sitting at the table.

"Once Jane's future is settled with Mr Bingley or Mr Darcy, I expect great romantic dramas for the rest of you. She and Lydia have set a high standard."

———— o o o ————

A plan made is not a plan in action. Not after Darcy had seen the light in Elizabeth's eyes, heard the softness in her voice, and kissed the blushes on her cheeks. Seeing her affection for him only made him long for a recovery for her sister.

By Monday afternoon, Darcy struggled to stay awake whilst Jane Bennet hummed something about daffodils. Or was it coneflowers? Why did she continually pluck the petals off, sometimes happy with the outcome, other times growing sad, frowning at the bared result? In his role of dull suitor, he had recited all the Latin names of roses he could remember, even telling her of the ones that grew wild in the east garden at Pemberley. She had seemed pleased to listen, then gone back to denuding blooms.

Only days in, this charade was testing his patience. Beautiful and ladylike, dazed and uncommunicative—unless she was singing —poor Miss Bennet seemed no closer to recovery than when she'd fainted in his arms. He liked her, or at least liked the young woman she had once been; he liked many people and enjoyed time in company with a handful of them outside of family.

But Elizabeth, most of all. So joyful and clever and witty—how she delighted him. She had looked to him for reassurance when they had appeared upon Longbourn's doorstep in the early afternoon. Of course, they were allowed nothing more private than a long shared look. As he had suspected, the Bennets pretended the incident with Bingley had never occurred, and only in Elizabeth's expressive countenance had he seen dismay and embarrassment—and, most of all, a fear that her sister was worsening, not improving.

"Jane spends many hours in the stillroom. Soon, when she is full well, she will return there," Miss Mary paused in her perusal of a book to thus inform him.

Darcy nodded, and stifled a yawn. Yes, this corner of the room was decidedly dull.

He could extend courtesy but earning his interest was a far greater undertaking. There was no one to ask his opinion of books or of news from the Continent, or jest about an ugly lamp or make him laugh at a tale of sisterly hijinks. Nobody to challenge him with her opinions—of anything. Darcy yearned to argue, to provoke. It was an art, the ability to reason and debate with wit and charm in a crowded room, or in a one-to-one conversation. No, the one lady capable of that was seated across the room, speaking to Bingley. Politely, warmly, with mutual interest.

She is as good an actor as I, but her partner is far more interesting.

Bingley was the man fortunate enough to listen to whatever story she was telling. It was humorous, no doubt, as her expression of merriment and the chuckles she was eliciting from Bingley and Miss Catherine apprised him. Bingley smiled more than he ought, making clear how much he enjoyed Elizabeth's company. Was he beginning to prefer her companionship over that of his angel?

No. Of course, only a fool could not be drawn to Elizabeth, but her wit and intelligence daunted Bingley in the past. What was it he had said? That she was 'far too clever for him and enjoyed arguing too much'? She is opposite of her sisters, then.

Darcy glanced at Miss Bennet and wondered rather shame-lessly how it was that Bingley could be so in love with her. If she was the opposite of her sister, she was also the opposite of Bing-ley's sisters, and thus shared Bingley's pleasant, contented disposi-tion. Yet he was more than that. Did the accident steal more than Miss Bennet's singular memory, also erasing depths and under-standing? The blue of the velvet settee she sat upon brought Bing-ley's poetic efforts to mind, and he nearly snorted.

"Mr Darcy? Jane is speaking to you," Miss Mary said helpfully.

Blast. What could she be asking me? She has not yet spoken a coherent thought today!

Darcy turned his head and found Miss Bennet gazing at him, her finger resting on a dead iris.

"Um. It is tolerably dried, I suppose, but not fine enough for Pemberley."

She smiled serenely and began to sing.

"'Mistress Mary, Quite contrary,
How does your garden grow?
With Silver Bells, and Cockle Shells,
Sing cuckolds all in a row.'"

Elizabeth glanced over at Jane as she beamed at Mr Darcy peering down at her collection of dried flowers. *Does Miss Darcy press flowers and force her brother to admire her handiwork? He looks as if he is in pain. Or ill.*

Forcing her attention back to Kitty's description of a cake she once ate, Elizabeth wondered whether she would ever see the return of her beloved elder sister. She hoped God would forgive her impatience, but as *He* had yet to help with the muddle in Jane's head and heart, Elizabeth felt herself safe from punishment.

She heard the lyric of a nursery rhyme, and suppressed a sigh. Would Jane ever recover? Had yesterday's 'exposure' also exposed

Bingley to the full extent of Jane's illness? How long would he be patient whilst she appeared…mad? *How long can I distract him?*

I was not formed to play the role of deceiver. Mr Bingley cannot long pretend to be a disinterested suitor. His heart can only bear so much.

Mrs Bennet, who flitted between the two gentlemen in her parlour, announced to the room at large, "Lizzy, are you restless? You could show Mr Bingley the gourds in the garden You were quite pleased about those. Mr Darcy and Jane are discussing the roses of Pemberley."

"Oh," Elizabeth replied with a glance at the disconsolate man beside her. "Mr Bingley and I would also like to hear about the roses and gardens at Pemberley. Mr Bingley, you no doubt have plans for plantings at Netherfield."

He looked uncertain, but nodded with alacrity, peering hopefully at Jane.

Mrs Bennet had her own solution to maintaining the current company in her parlour. "Kitty, where is your sister's letter? Surely Mr Darcy would like to hear more about his friend's promotion!"

Appearing more put upon than eager, Kitty dutifully rose to fetch Lydia's latest missive. Mortified at whatever ordeal such a reading could put Mr Darcy through, Elizabeth nearly leapt from her seat. "Surely no gentleman wishes to hear Lydia's musings on ribbons and parties. I nearly forgot that my father asked whether Mr Bingley and Mr Darcy would join him in his book-room."

"He did?" Mrs Bennet looked confused. "Of course he did. He wants for the company of gentlemen able to match him in conversation."

"We must not keep Mr Bennet waiting," said Mr Darcy as he rose. "Please excuse us."

Mr Bingley followed him, throwing a wistful glance at the room as they disappeared—matched only by Jane's wistfulness at the sight of Mr Darcy's empty chair.

Jan Ashton

Jane's mood was improved when the men re-emerged with reports that Mr Bingley was the superior to Mr Bennet in a game of draughts. "Impulse and initiative," he declared to much laughter.

Darcy rolled his eyes. "As well as luck, for Mr Bennet and I are prone to strategic thinking even in children's games."

"It may not be chess or cribbage but draughts has its own challenges," Mr Bingley cried.

"Chess is the game of intellect, rarely requiring luck over skill," said Mary pedantically, whilst Jane threw dazzling smiles at Darcy before glancing down winsomely at the empty seat next to her on the settee.

Elizabeth watched as he ignored her in a graceful way that did not draw attention to itself and turned to his friend. "We must return to Netherfield. I fear a storm shall soon be upon us."

It was a cool farewell after such a light-hearted moment, and when Elizabeth looked at Darcy, she saw some intent in his brusqueness.

She moved with them towards the door, glanced up at the darkening clouds, and walked to the stables with the men.

"Congratulations to you, Mr Bingley. You were victorious over my father and in doing so, won the admiration of all my sisters."

He smiled. "Would that I won every game, every race, if that is what it takes to win back your sister."

"You have not lost her, sir," Elizabeth said quietly, mindful that the stables were tended by men whose interest in Bennet family doings was as avid as the ladies in the kitchens.

Darcy, who had remained silent, nodded his agreement to her avowals. Bingley took the reins from Samuel and stepped away. "I cannot help but notice that your sister's smiles all seem to be directed at my friend here."

Elizabeth winced. "You must not...she does not know what she is about!"

"I recall last autumn, how my highborn friend irritated the neighbourhood with his officiousness and arrogance...and stares." He glanced sullenly at Darcy. "Suddenly he is all politeness. Why do you seem to have charm and smiles to spare now?"

Darcy's expression held all the hauteur of which he had been accused. "Miss Bennet is quite obviously not recovered yet. Should I behave rudely to someone so injured?"

Elizabeth repressed a smile and held up a hand. "Even the best of men has bad moments and Mr Darcy cannot be faulted if his neighbours were too eagerly paying attention to his every expression. As to your notion of his behaviour towards my sister, he is only behaving as a gentleman ought. Jane thinks too well of everyone, and in her current, um, struggles, it is unlikely that she would notice if he did not." She must distract Mr Bingley from his wariness of Darcy's attractions; the only idea occurring to her was an obvious, if embarrassing one. "However, it might help with my mother's unrealistic expectations, Mr Darcy, if you were to more often display some of your former...um, taciturn nature?"

She looked up and saw him watching her with a smile in his eyes; his expression was so soft she felt her stomach swoop.

Mr Bingley was too caught up in his own ideas to notice the exchange. "Worry not, Miss Elizabeth, only allow nature to take its course. He cannot long remain pleasant in a roomful of company."

The target of his barbs rolled his eyes. "Or you, as Miss Bennet's suitor, could arrange some compliments, elegant little comments on her needlework and dried flowers."

Mr Bingley, his expression still mulish, nodded. "Right. I am happy to take on that task, but you must find another occupation that vexes you enough to sharpen your tongue. No lady can enjoy your company when you are in one of your humours. I can scarcely take it myself!"

Darcy smirked. "Thank you, my friend. Now I am in even greater anticipation of our confinement alone together this afternoon at Netherfield."

Elizabeth bit back a smile. Mr Bingley frowned as Darcy continued,

"What say you to a fencing match?"

CHAPTER
EIGHTEEN

The following morning, with the ground still damp from a night of rain and the predawn sky full of stars rather than clouds, Darcy moved rapidly down Netherfield's main stairs, anxious and hopeful that Elizabeth would be of the same mind as he was. They had not spoken privately since declaring their affections, and he was eager to see her, especially in the soft light of dawn before the rigours of the day's performance. In his haste to don his greatcoat as he moved, his steps were too loud.

"Darcy? Is that you?"

Bingley, clad in his nightshirt and banyan, stood in the doorway of the study, blinking sleepily. "Has something happened? Bad news?"

"No, no," Darcy assured him before asking with some worry, "Why are you here? Did you not sleep in your bed?"

"I was restless," Bingley said, shrugging. "I could not sleep and wandered down here. When the sky is clear, you can see Longbourn's chimneys from the study window, did you know?"

I have known that since last autumn, Darcy wanted to say. Instead, his conscience piqued by Bingley's plaintive tone, he simply nodded. "I believe Orion can be seen from that direction."

Bingley yawned. "Why are you dressed? Where are you going?"

"I rose early and thought to walk out."

"Walk? Not ride?" Bingley peered at him; was it suspicion in his tired expression?

"Yes, to look around the grounds closer to the park. After the rains we have had..." Darcy went on, describing the drainage issues that must be considered and the varied options that Bingley would have to study. Within three minutes, Bingley's eyelids began drooping. Darcy waved him off to return to his bed with the promise of a ride later, before breakfast.

———o o o———

Darcy moved swiftly through the tall grass, pleased to see Elizabeth already had arrived at the footbridge. He disliked that she was out and about when the sun had barely risen, but it was the kind of activity to which she was accustomed and his protective instincts would amuse, if not offend, her. The most important thing was that she was *here*.

While Darcy could imagine innumerable dangers lying wait for her in the dark—neighbourhood ne'er do-wells or lecherous highwaymen, angry boars or diseased foxes, tree roots to trip over or holes in which to plunge—while his fearless Elizabeth's only concern was being espied by a neighbour and word reaching Jane or Mrs Bennet.

She thinks less of her own safety and happiness than she does her sister's. If I had not discouraged Bingley's interest in Jane a year ago, her eldest sister could be wed to him and—and her youngest could be at home, untouched by scandal and safe from becoming Mrs Wickham.

Darcy slowed his pace, inhaling deeply to calm himself. Elizabeth held no such restraint. She flew to him, and within moments she was in his arms, his mouth upon hers, the anxiety and self-recrimination melting away. She fit in his embrace so perfectly, so sweetly; her kiss was a wonderful blend of excitement and affec-

145

tion. He wanted to shelter her, to protect her, to hold her, to love her. It was only a few minutes before he was in great danger of being carried away.

He owed her protection from his passion as well as from angry boars and tree roots, and forced himself to loosen his hold, resting his forehead against hers until sanity returned.

"We were almost found out," he said.

"What?"

"Bingley encountered me in the hall this morning. He asked my business, being dressed to go outside at such an hour."

"What did you say to him?"

He looked at her sheepishly. "I could not cause him any further jealousy by explaining that I was meeting with the most beautiful woman in the world to hold and kiss her before breakfast. Already he begins to be suspicious that your sister—"

"Bears an unusual attachment to your person. How suspicious is he? Does he begin to understand the state of Jane's heart and mind?"

"He has cautioned me more than once not to fall in love with Miss Bennet." Darcy shook his head, appalled at the very notion of such a thing. "I have assured him most vigorously that I will not, that I cannot."

Elizabeth looked up at him slyly. "That would be most inconvenient for all concerned," she replied in a deceptively neutral tone. "Mr Bingley would be at ends."

Of course, such teasing required that he kiss her again.

"When all is said and done, this charade is not easy for any one of us," he agreed. "I love you, and I cannot wait to make you my wife and to tell the world it is so. Especially, I wish to inform your mother." But seeing Elizabeth's dismay, he added, "It is difficult, not to listen to her—for she only tries to secure a husband for her eldest—but to be unable to contradict her. How can she be so blind to the sheep's eyes I make at you?"

Elizabeth struck a mirthful tone. "None of this has been easy, and I do not think it gives any of us pleasure—including Mama," she added. "Your reticence is a marked change from Mr Bingley's preference for constant conversation, and she finds the effort rather tiring. Perhaps you will be out of the running before you know it."

"Will I?" Darcy asked. "Perhaps I will have to show you other skills I have in order to hold your interest."

"Provoking man," she said, and he kissed her again until she was far too breathless to continue her teasing.

He made more of an effort to regulate his desires; he was far too easily...*provoked* in her presence. "You once expressed surprise at my friendship with Bingley, but he, like my cousin Richard and my school friends, are more garrulous than I, and they draw out my conversation. Your mother, Miss Mary, and Miss Catherine seem to have little more to say than your poor eldest sister, and the effort placed on me to initiate discussion is quite burdensome."

He grinned at her pretended outrage.

"All of that is well. If you are equally bored, Jane's interest in Mr Bingley's conversation may return. There remains the issue, however that even if she finds your conversation dull, she admires you far too greatly for your manners and intelligence and comely appearance."

He smiled.

"Come now, Mr Darcy. I have said nothing that you did not know about yourself. Be satisfied that it is you, rather than your wealth and place in society, that draws her attention."

"So I am to set aside those attributes she does admire and be less well-mannered and less intelligent? I am no actor."

Elizabeth smiled in what he thought of as her clever way. "No, and we cannot mask your handsome countenance, but I believe I know what to do. Rather than trying to lack manners and wit, perhaps imitate Mr Collins? We all of us considered him oafish and stupid, and we all disliked him, even Jane, who can find good in everyone."

"We want her to find no good in me."

"Well, you are taller than my cousin and more handsome and better dressed. Perhaps if you did not bathe..."

Darcy laughed. "I shall take a stand there, Elizabeth. I refuse to reek of horse and whatever was served at breakfast two days earlier."

"Oh my, truly the world is a-tilt. Jane is confused and you have become a wit." Elizabeth's light laughter was the sweetest sound Darcy could imagine.

"Did Bingley's gallantry in offering the carriage to your mother after church at all mitigate his faux pas in viewing what he ought not to have viewed when he arrived?"

Elizabeth's expression grew instantly troubled, and he was sorry he'd mentioned it. "I was so afraid he would never return! Even Mama was embarrassed, and my father, for once, apologised for his inattention. Jane, of course, seemed to have no idea of anything being the matter. I wonder…should we ask for Mr Tilden to visit again?"

Darcy took her hand in his, bringing it up to his mouth to lay a kiss upon it. "You ought to have known I would not allow Bingley to wallow in embarrassment. And if anything, he is more determined than ever to make your sister his wife." He waggled his brows. "Apparently he saw nothing to discourage him in the sight of her."

She tapped his chest in a chiding manner, but he saw the real relief in her smile, and had the triumph of knowing he had eased at least one of her worries.

"Unfortunately, as you might recall, Mr Tilden went to his daughter's home for the remainder of her confinement and delivery of her first child. He agreed to write to me once he was returned to town, but as yet I have heard nothing."

"I had forgotten." Elizabeth sighed sadly.

"However, his advice was rest for two weeks. It has scarcely been one, and it is far too soon for this dismay. She requires time, my love, and we shall give it to her."

Elizabeth visibly brightened and at that moment, with the atmosphere between them so warm and comfortable, Darcy could scarcely hold back from kissing her again.

"You are right," she said.

"Music to my ears," he replied, and she laughed before growing serious once more.

"I have had a thought."

"Only one?"

She took a step away from him and raised a brow. "About your interests and how they diverge from Jane's."

Although disappointed at the few inches now separating them, Darcy understood it was necessary. *Focus on solutions, as she is*, he reminded himself. *It eases her worry if she feels active, if she considers that we are doing everything that can be done.*

"I regret I paid little attention to Miss Bennet's interests when we were together at Netherfield. Is she fond of books?"

"Not particularly. She prefers embroidery, scrolling, and flowers—arranging them, drying them—to most things."

"Sedentary arts for ladies who are not great walkers?"

She nodded, and frowned again. "Although she has shown very little interest in anything at all, beyond sleeping and smiling at you."

"That is useful information for our scheme. I shall refrain from asking after anything that interests her. Instead, I shall read aloud the dullest of books."

Her frown disappeared. "Dull books? Such things exist for you?"

He shook his head. "Fear not. Pemberley has only the finest of books, with the finest bindings, and the finest words."

Elizabeth looked delighted. "There is truth in your looks—but not when you speak so of books. I suspect you quote Miss Bingley as your authority."

"A credit to you for both your rhyming and sleuthing skills, my love. Longbourn has a fine library. Your father must have some tomes on local agricultural practices that should be read aloud to Netherfield's new owner, or German philosophy that could enrich our minds, or perhaps—"

"My sister Mary would be happy to lend you her volume of Fordyce's *Sermons for Young Ladies*."

Darcy happily joined in her laughter. Even scheming was a fine thing, when one's partner in such an undertaking was Elizabeth Bennet.

———— ◦ ◦ ◦ ————

Bingley lay in his bed, warm and comfortable yet unable to fall asleep after Darcy's hasty and mysterious exit. His brief foray into sleep earlier in the night had led to awful dreams of Jane in her bridal gown, laughing with Darcy as they walked down the aisle and boarded their carriage to ride off as husband and wife. The images would not subside. His emotions were in tumult, anger and confusion and hopelessness at war; at the moment, anger was winning. For as much as Bingley liked and respected Darcy, and thought him to be truly the best of men—honourable and intelligent and loyal—he was beginning to hate him, just a little bit.

Seeing his friend receive Jane's smiles was more than unnerving—it was unfair. It was Darcy, along with Caroline and Louisa, who had encouraged him to leave Netherfield, to leave Jane. Yes, Darcy had confessed his error, encouraged him to return, open up Netherfield and seek out Jane's hand... But now, this was a perverse joke.

If I were a man prone to drowning my sorrows in drink, I would be in deep trouble.

Bingley had considered the situation from all angles. Miss Elizabeth was willing to spurn a man like Darcy, to hate him, for the hurt he perpetrated on Jane. Now she was willing to be a partner to Darcy so they could indulge her sister and guide her through her confusion and memory loss. How he hoped all the assurances Miss Elizabeth had given him would bear out. Jane had looked at him with such feeling the day before her accident; he could not bear to see how she now regarded Darcy. It was too hurtful. She gazed at him so fondly, as if anticipating his every word would bring her future happiness.

However, Bingley had also seen the small crease in Jane's brow, as if she was trying to work out not only Darcy's feelings, but her own. It was as if she was not certain how she was to feel, as if she too were acting—although in her case, without the conscious effort expended by the rest of them. Did anyone else see her struggle to make sense of events?

I have stood idly by, almost as a bystander to all the workings of my own life. For nigh on a year now, others have decided my path.

But I love her.

Darcy was a man of strong feeling, a loyal friend and a good man. Was he helping out to such an extent because he cared for Bingley's ultimate happiness with Jane or for his own hopes with Miss Elizabeth? It certainly seemed yesterday that there was some new connexion between them.

Darcy was not himself, or at least he was not the Darcy that Bingley knew best. *That* Darcy was droll and acerbic and impatient with those who wearied his vaunted intelligence and standards of behaviour.

This Darcy was, for lack of a better word, happy! And the only thing changed in his life was his proximity to Jane. The question now nagged at Bingley. *Is Darcy happy because of the time spent with my angel?*

He was in his robe, drinking his second cup of coffee in the drawing room, when Darcy strode back in from his 'walk', his hair damp and windblown, his cheeks ruddy and his eyes aglow.

"Your boots are wet," he said.

Darcy stopped and glanced down at his muddied Hessians. "Indeed they are." He shrugged and poured himself a cup as well.

"You are certainly in high spirits this morning."

Bingley's voice was unusually sharp but he had no wish to hide his irritation. He saw Darcy's brow crease as he considered the statement.

"Drainage ditches are cheerful things now, are they? Or do you anticipate seeing Jane today?"

"You cannot think I am enjoying this," came Darcy's incredulous reply. "I am here to assist you, *acting* on your behalf for the sake of Miss Bennet."

"And enjoying her company."

"I am your friend. Would you have me disparage her company, hurting her feelings and insulting yours?" Darcy did not flinch from Bingley's glare, but returned his piercing look. "What has happened? I understand this is difficult, but your spirits were more settled yesterday. Was the fencing not helpful?"

Bingley exhaled loudly, his anger and bitterness dissipated by Darcy's vexed expression. Unwilling to admit to having been shaken by his dream, he shrugged. "It is a muddle, and I am at times as confused as Miss Bennet. Not about my feelings for her, but how to simply hasten things."

He stared out the window at a pair of birds swooping down into the trees; he sighed, his resolution to blame Darcy for his unhappiness gone. Turning, he found Darcy staring at him, brows furrowed in concern.

"I know that Miss Elizabeth is the Bennet sister you care for most," said Bingley, "and that the two of you are doing what you can for Jane. You are a masterfully poor suitor, I must say. But at least I need not fear Jane falling in love with you."

Darcy only nodded, appearing a little unsettled.

Smiling weakly, Bingley yawned. "Caroline will be pleased to buoy you up in your suffering, I am certain."

"Pardon?"

"Caroline replied to my letter, and will be arriving soon with Louisa in tow. Hurst is at a hunting party and they were rather bored. My invitation came at the right moment." Bingley stared down at the sash on his banyan and began to adjust the knot.

"I know you mentioned bringing her here, but I thought you meant to wait until Miss Bennet is improved." Darcy's tone bespoke alarm. "You cannot think your sister will be anything except a hindrance to your suit."

"Miss Bennet and I spent many happy hours in conversation at Netherfield, which I hope she may recall when she visits, but I cannot invite her here until I have a hostess." He gave his friend a tired smile. "Besides, if anyone can distract Miss Bennet from admiring your very admirable person, it is Caroline."

CHAPTER
NINETEEN

D arcy, ensconced in his room, sans wet boots and jacket, mulled over Bingley's announcement as Stirling prepared to shave him.

Caroline, back at Netherfield, to be of service to her brother as hostess?

With her installed as hostess, Netherfield could welcome female guests and hold dinners, in rooms which might remind Jane Bennet of the time she had spent here in Bingley's company last autumn.

And I would have opportunities to spend time with Elizabeth without skulking about before dawn.

They could meet in sunlight—if not alone, at least in company. It was a much larger house than Longbourn, with grounds and gardens where he and Elizabeth could walk, make plans, and speak freely of their true feelings.

Pleasant as these ruminations were, they were overshadowed by the multitude of disadvantages to Miss Bingley's presence at Netherfield: her sharp and oft-expressed opinions, her cloying manner, her watchfulness over him and Bingley, and her open disdain for the Bennets. She had tolerated Jane Bennet best of all, but in the end had treated her abominably all the same. If Miss Bennet were to reveal the extent of her confusion and, well, irrationality, it would give Caroline more ammunition to lend force to her objections.

Worst of all, she would not be completely wrong. Miss Bennet was in no condition to entertain suitors. They were all relying upon Tilden's advice—but fine a physician as the man was, nothing could be completely certain.

Darcy suspected Caroline's efforts would be given over equally to mischief, trying to separate two lovers still trying to forge their alliance. He had avoided her company since leaving Pemberley in August. She had seen a different man then; that Darcy was certain his feelings for Elizabeth had been obvious to all in his party and he had not cared. He had thought he and Elizabeth would be engaged within a day.

No man is safe from romantic assumptions and ruin, he mused. *Ruin. Caroline would wish to ruin Bingley's hopes, again, even if she cannot ruin mine.*

How did Bingley think to explain their situation to his sister? How would she react, if she learnt Miss Bennet had forgotten Bingley and fixed her attentions upon himself?

What schemes would she perpetrate? Bingley's sister had plotted and flirted for years to earn society's notice and his favour. She was unlikely to gain the former and there was a cold chance in hell she could win the latter.

There were Elizabeth's feelings to consider. *'I do not imagine either of them would support their brother's suit.'*

"Sir, a little this way please."

Stirling's voice brought Darcy back to the moment. Seeing the man paused, blade in hand, awaiting his compliance, Darcy turned his head to the right and gazed out across the fields he had walked just an hour earlier.

If Miss Bingley learns Elizabeth and I are involved in our own schemes, not only to unite Bingley and Jane Bennet, but to unite with each other, her malice could possibly turn on Elizabeth. He could speak much to Caroline Bingley's lack of sensibility, but he would not dismiss her intelligence.

As if she will not immediately see, does not know, that my heart is with Elizabeth.

"All right, sir."

As Stirling wiped the soap off of his face, Darcy caught a glimpse of himself in the mirror and scowled. *If Caroline Bingley sees anything at all, she had best see this: I will do* anything *to protect Elizabeth. Anything and everything necessary.*

——— o o o ———

The announcement of Miss Bingley's impending arrival proved to be the spark igniting an otherwise dull visit to Longbourn.

A misty rain set in soon after the gentlemen arrived and kept them confined indoors. Kitty and Mrs Bennet both expended a good deal of complaint upon the weather until Mr Bingley revealed the news of his sisters' plans to join him at Netherfield, and host the Bennet ladies for tea.

"A dinner or two, as well," he added, looking at Mrs Bennet and then at Jane, "for without a hostess, Darcy and I have been unable to thank you adequately for the wonderful dinners we have enjoyed here at Longbourn."

Wearing a smug grin, Mrs Bennet's chin rose in victory at hearing such acclaim.

Elizabeth was not quite so sanguine. "Of course, Jane is not up to attending large affairs as of yet. Or even middling-sized ones. No one in the village has an understanding of her health, and I believe it should remain that way."

But at that moment, Jane smiled at Mr Bingley, in a curious sort of way—and it was the first time she had seemed to notice him at all. When she spoke, it was only to recite a nursery rhyme in a sing-song, dreamy manner:

"Boys and girls, come out to play,
The moon does shine as bright as day,
Leave your supper, and leave your sleep,
And meet your playfellows in the street;
Come with a whoop, and come with a call,
And come with a good will, or not at all."

Mr Bingley, beaming at the smile Jane had directed at him, nodded eagerly and continued as if she had spoken words of great sense. "Caroline will be pleased by your anticipation. She finds nothing more pleasurable than setting a fine table and ensuring her guests are comfortable and well-fed."

Then, perhaps sensing he had not lavished enough praise on Longbourn's hostess, he turned to Mrs Bennet. "As you, madam. Longbourn's table is the best set in the county."

"Our visitors say this often, and wish to remain in our company." After giving unexpected praise to Cook for her skills, Mrs Bennet said slyly, "We welcome all to return here, even Mr Collins, who nearly wept at the savoury excellence of Longbourn's sauces."

Elizabeth bit back a laugh as she glanced at Darcy; his grave expression was unmoved by the ridiculousness of the conversation, although she detected some merriment in his eyes.

"Charlotte and Mr Collins have their own cook to make sauces," Mary pointed out unnecessarily.

"It is said the sauce is the making of any dish," Elizabeth said solemnly, earning both girls a glare from their mother.

Darcy proceeded to read aloud, with a rather marvellous animation, from *A General Treatise of Agriculture, both Philosophical and Practical*, procured from Netherfield's meagre library, until Mr Bingley's relieved announcement that the rain had ceased. The visit soon concluded, somewhat to Elizabeth's dissatisfaction, as it came without a shared smile or quiet exchange with Darcy.

Her mother's energies were then put to use scolding Mary and Elizabeth for their defence of the Collinses' cook, before insisting Jane must lie down in her chambers and escorting her away.

Wishing for her own share of solitude, Elizabeth went to her room and curled up on her bed to try and sort through the afternoon's events. *Miss Bingley is returning here?* The implications of her presence, and the possibilities for her interference, were immense. Miss Bingley was a keen observer, but it would hardly take one to spot Jane's infirmities. Elizabeth knew the lady had seen her brother's sincere affection for Jane, and had heard, and disdained, Mrs Bennet's eagerness for the match. With a hostess at Netherfield, Kitty might get the ball she hoped for, but Miss Bingley could do more mischief than good if she learnt what was happening at Longbourn.

The lady despises our society. She would come to Netherfield only to keep her brother safe from Jane. What will she do when she learns of Jane's illness, never mind her apparent fondness for Darcy? How will she behave when she realises Darcy is in fact attempting to unite Bingley and Jane?

There could be no advantage to having Miss Bingley in their midst.

She saw Darcy's attention to me, and sensed his feelings for me, long before I had any idea. How long can it take for her to see that my feelings for him have undergone so material a change, and that his own have grown deeper?

In the privacy of her chambers, Elizabeth granted herself the luxury of thinking about Darcy and the feelings he engendered in her, and those she knew remained fervent in him. Less than a fortnight ago, she had found it nearly impossible to look at him. Now they had grown a comfortable camaraderie, a teasing, easy friendship, a joining of heart and mind. It was unlike any connexion she had experienced with those closest to her. No one but Darcy had ever created such a warmth of mutual regard and feeling. She loved him. He loved her. They had just barely begun, again, and Miss Bingley would not stand in their path either.

Nor will she mend his pen or dance a reel with him!

As Elizabeth recalled some of the odious woman's previous attitudes and misdeeds, a more recent event came to mind. She sat up, astonished that she had hardly noticed it at the time.

Did Jane smile at Mr Bingley and indicate—in her nonsensical way—

that she wished to go to Netherfield?

What did that imply? Or did it imply anything at all? Had there been *some* improvement to her memory, if only minor? If so, she might remember how terribly she was treated by Mr Bingley's sisters. Still, Elizabeth realised, Jane had made some effort with Mr Bingley rather than Mr Darcy! With a smile, she lay back down in glad anticipation of telling Darcy about her hopes. It must mean something, it must!

◦ ◦ ◦

"I must say, you selected quite the riveting choice of reading material." Bingley laughed jovially as they mounted their horses. "'Containing such observations and experiments as are new and useful for the improvement of land, with an account of natural productions as may help the ingenious in their studies, and promote universal learning?'" he parroted in the sonorous voice Darcy had used to bore them with. "I daresay your efforts to be tedious were wildly successful today, although you ruined Mrs Bennet's efforts to begin an oration upon the superiority of her cook over the Collinses."

"Oh, I quite enjoyed the author's thoughts on land improvements." *And Elizabeth's ability to stir up an argument so sweetly.*

"Longbourn's cook *is* highly talented. Even Caroline admitted Mrs Bennet sets a fine table."

"We shall remind her of her praise," Darcy replied. "In fact, perhaps we should write out every compliment and kind observation your sister made when she was last here, and keep it within arm's reach."

Bingley chuckled quietly before he asserted in a more solemn tone, "Caroline will not interfere this time, Darcy. She will not have you to support her."

Darcy coloured at the new reminder of that which he wished to forget. "Of course she will not."

"I have written to Hurst and summarised the situation," Bingley added. "I told him that if Caroline acts in any way to thwart my hopes of marrying Jane Bennet, or hurts Miss Bennet in any way, she will not be welcomed in my home and she will be his responsibility."

Darcy was incredulous—and impressed. "And his reply?"

Bingley shrugged and steered his ride around a rock. "I have not yet received one, but expect he will agree that my sister has both the funds and the character required to set up her own establishment. I will tell Caroline the same."

He kicked his horse and rode off quickly, without waiting for Darcy's reply.

Despite the lack of a moment alone with Elizabeth and some concern over her feelings on Miss Bingley's arrival, Darcy thought this afternoon had indeed been an improvement for Bingley's future happiness.

———— o o o ————

That evening, with nothing better to do than long for Elizabeth, he began to work on his correspondence. First he re-read the letter he had received from his cousin earlier that day.

Darcy,

It comes as a bit of a surprise to me that you have realised your own happiness whilst poor Bingley remains distant from his. I can only imagine your chagrin at selfishly experiencing joy as he is in the depths of despair. You must better focus on managing his affairs—his jackets, his hoped-for seat at White's, his leased estate, and, again, his romantic entanglements—and let others enjoy the company of Miss Elizabeth Bennet. Perhaps I shall be forced to abandon my own business in one lady's home and come to the country to assist. In the meantime, I have had happy letters from our dear girl, who believes that half-blind gelding my father wastes money on is the most perfect of God's creatures...

159

He reached for a fresh sheet of paper.

Richard,

Have you tired yet of sitting in my box and enjoying my good brandy? Have you determined your affections for the widow are such that you remain in town rather than joining Georgiana at Matlock or coming here to mock poor Bingley? Or is it duty that requires you remain? You mention nothing of the army nor your responsibilities, and in the past that has been somewhat foreboding. Tell me at least that we are not to make war with the Swiss or the Dutch.

My own duties remain the same, a seemingly endless waiting game. Forgive me, but you are the only one to whom I can complain. How I wish I was including a notice of my engagement for you to place in the Times!

Miss Bennet continues to be confused, and seems unable to recall Bingley at all. I continue to play the role you will think comes naturally: dull, indifferent, laconic admirer. As you know I am neither actor nor lothario, and lack a glib tongue and the ability to pretend an interest I cannot feel, much less behave as though impelled by unqualified, unalloyed inclination. Elizabeth recognises my weakness as well, and is my guide in her scheme to effect happiness for her sister and Bingley. Most unfortunately, Bingley's sister will be joining us soon, and I can only imagine what plots and pots she might stir to cause mischief.

Darcy paused before adding,

Elizabeth will be keen to overthrow any of Miss Bingley's schemes with her own. I am deeply fortunate to be her partner in any arrangements, and most especially her future.

I should never grumble again, for I am the happiest of men.

There, he thought. *A rhyme of which even muddled Miss Bennet might approve. Could I teach it to her, I wonder?* And he chuckled to himself.

CHAPTER
TWENTY

The following day, the early morning skies were dark with grey clouds after a night of wind storms and rain. Darcy, beneath his great black umbrella, hoped Elizabeth would not be at their meeting place. But he could not chance that she might wait out in the weather if he did not show, and so here he was, his boots sopping again, risking Stirling's wrath.

It was with both a tinge of frustration and a great deal of eagerness that he pulled her beneath the shelter of a towering oak, setting his umbrella between her and the wet sky.

"Darling, you shall catch your death," he lectured sternly, even as he opened his greatcoat and drew her within the added shelter of its warmth and plunged his mouth to hers. How he wished he could warm her in all the ways he knew. "Where is your umbrella? Think you impervious to damp and chill?"

She smiled up at him—somewhat dreamily now, he liked to think—and shrugged. "Someone is bound to notice a wet umbrella, and I did not feel like hearing the scolding. Silly me, to think I could avoid it."

"They will not notice a soaking hat, I suppose," he said, twitching the damp edge of her brim.

"This old thing will dry quickly before the fire in my chamber, while I brush out my plaits."

He was struck by the picture of it, her hair let down, flowing over her shoulders and cascading down her back—himself taking up her brush, playing lady's maid, the feel of her tresses between his fingers as he undressed her before the fire. He groaned.

"Oh, Elizabeth, what you do to me," he said, kissing her with a passion he had never felt before in his life.

When he released her lips, her expression was less dreamy than impassioned before she smiled again. "You must not blame me for any distraction. You look as if your man turned you out for a day on the town, whilst I appear as if I jumped in the stream after my sisters." She reached up to push her fingers through his hair—he had not bothered with a hat—and he nearly groaned again, her touch light, curious...and dangerous. It was vital that he remove his thoughts from their favoured direction. Her next sentence did the trick.

"I think we should tell Mr Bingley the truth—about us, at least," she said.

This was such a departure from her wishes of only a few days earlier, it caught him by surprise. "You know that I wait only for your sanction to shout my happiness to the world," Darcy said. "Are you certain he ought to know, even before your parents do?"

"I feel that Jane is improving. I know it does not seem so, and certainly her speech is still...disturbing. But something in the way she looked at Mr Bingley yesterday when he mentioned Netherfield, even the nursery rhyme she recited—about children playing, having fun—I think it stirred feelings of happiness in her, if not actual memory." Elizabeth cupped his cheek and gave him a tender look. "It is difficult, distracting him from her fascination with you, and he already suspects it. He should not have to also worry that you might ever return her feelings."

He was dubious about Miss Bennet's possible symptoms of recovery, but unwilling to lessen any of Elizabeth's hopes. "Will you allow me to speak to your father, at least? I believe I can impress upon him the necessity of remaining silent."

She bit her still swollen lip. "He will not like it, not at all. The very idea of a secret engagement will be an anathema to him."

"But these are unusual circumstances. I will not call it a betrothal, not yet—only make my intentions clear, and that you share them."

She laid her head sweetly upon his chest. "I am not yet ready to bear his teasing, even in private. And there is much freedom in having no scrutiny whatsoever upon us. I hate to give it up, whilst things at Longbourn are so unsettled."

Mr Bennet would not respect the tenderness of her feelings, Darcy knew, not if he could turn them into a witty rejoinder for his own amusement. And she had a point; if the Bennet ladies were allowed to come to Netherfield, it would be far easier to steal a few moments with Elizabeth alone if no one knew of their plans. While engaged couples were allowed some freedom to spend time together, he and Elizabeth were not engaged, nor could they be until Jane's future was more certain.

"I, too, am uncomfortable with secrecy," he admitted. "I hate to deal with you in this furtive manner, as if I were ashamed to court you openly."

"We both know that is not the case," she said fiercely, pulling back briefly before returning to his firm embrace. "I only want to give Jane the days she needs for her recovery. If, in another week, she shows no real signs of improvement, it might be time to...to accept that she might not recuperate within the usual time, and we may have to proceed with life as it *will* be, not as we hope it might progress."

He hated to see her discouragement, knew she was clutching to her optimism with both hands, especially so soon after losing her youngest sister to a man whom she knew to be a gross deceiver. It was a miracle that she had been able to give *him* so much of her affection, of her love, whilst so deeply anxious upon her sister's behalf. It told him something else, too—for her to have so great an openness of feeling for him at such a time as this meant her feelings had been engaged for quite some time. Otherwise, she never would have been able to spare attention and emotion for him in a new, deeper connexion. She had *told* him that her feelings had changed long ago, but this was evidence that came only from knowing her as he did.

"In a week then," he said. "I will admit that I have already informed my cousin, Fitzwilliam. In the meantime, I shall write to my solicitors so I am able to bring your father proof of a generous settlement."

Her eyes filled with tears. "So much," she whispered. "After all you expended in securing Lydia's marriage, that you should do so much, now."

His mouth gaped, and his arms dropped from around her. "I am sorry that you were ever informed of it," he said stiffly, embarrassed, looking away.

Elizabeth raised her hands to cup his face. "Blame Lydia for that," she said, and rose on her toes to press her mouth to his. She was not experienced, he understood that, but in her kiss she told him things he had *never* known, lessons of passion, of gratitude— yes, there was that as well, but not for worldly treasures, only for *himself*. He had never had such a kiss full of giving, of shared understanding. Her hat fell to the ground, and had its surface not been so muddy he might have followed it down, could not answer for what he might have done within that heat, that desire, that *gift*.

"I love you," he said, the words too brief for all he felt.

"As I do you," she replied. "I will marry you whenever you say. I trust you utterly. Tell Mr Bingley if you can, my father when you must."

His heart filled as a tear escaped and slipped down her cheek. He brushed it away. "Worry not, my love. The wife of Mr Darcy must have such extraordinary sources of care, of the best medical wisdom in the country necessarily attached to her situation, that any sister of hers could, upon the whole, have no cause to repine."

— o o o —

Darcy watched Bingley disinterestedly pick at his breakfast plate. The day before, he had seemed in a much better state of mind. Probably, like Elizabeth, he too had taken heart in Miss Bennet's first smile directed at him; possibly he had even drawn a similar conclusion at her rhyme. But in the grey gloom of a rainy day, he was apparently unable to retain his optimism.

Elizabeth wanted him to be informed of their intentions, and so of course he would do so. However, she only knew him as the genial suitor. She did not know the fits of envy Bingley occasionally suffered. He was not to be blamed, of course. He had been required to fight his way into acceptance at school and in society with his wealth and natural bonhomie, but it had never been easy. Darcy's birth gave him entrée to a world without any other qualification. He was required to be neither charming nor intelligent nor loyal nor even temperate.

Darcy once had believed Georgiana might do for his friend someday because her inherent kindness matched Bingley's; she would never look down upon him for his birth, and he would always respect hers. However, Miss Bennet could give him something Georgiana never could: she *needed* him. Bingley's constant disappointment that he had been unable to be the 'rescuer' of Jane Bennet revealed his desire to be respected, looked up to. In Miss Bennet, he had found someone who always would. While marrying Georgiana would have brought greater status to his children, Jane's birth plus his wealth and upbringing formed a net positive, and likely greater happiness for both.

Besides, as he had discovered, Georgiana was no chess-piece to be planned for and moved about without consideration, any more than he himself was. He could advise and assist, but she must learn to choose wisely for herself. And it would take much time before she was ready.

"Bingley, I have news."

Bingley glanced up from his plate and yawned. It was not an auspicious beginning.

"Miss Elizabeth has agreed to become my wife."

Bingley's expression changed swiftly from listlessness to astonishment.

"You are joking, Darcy. This cannot be!—engaged to Miss Elizabeth! No, no, you shall not deceive me. I know it to be impossible. She hates you. Well, perhaps hate is too strong a word. You have been speaking together, finally, regarding my angel's health. But marriage? She is sure?"

Darcy tried not to be insulted, but he had known, had he not, of Bingley's satisfaction that neither of them should be happy in love? His friend took no pleasure in Darcy's romantic difficulties, but at least his sense of fairness was gratified. Now it seemed that once again, Darcy had been handed life's greatest blessing whilst *he* was denied. And of course, he would tell the younger man nothing of what he had done for Lydia that had, evidently, proven to Elizabeth the depths of his devotion to her happiness.

"She is sure," was all he replied.

"I must congratulate you of course. But are you quite sure that she feels what she ought to do?"

"Quite sure," he repeated. Firmly.

Bingley's eyes narrowed. "The other morning…it was not about drainage, was it?"

Darcy was not about to put Elizabeth's reputation at risk, and made no answer. His silence, in itself, seemed enough for Bingley.

"I knew you were up to something! Drainage! Bah!" he smiled, a remnant of his former good humour finding the amusement in it. "I suppose you will be speaking to Mr Bennet today."

"As to that, Elizabeth desires to wait a week or so. She wishes her sister's health to be improved before her mother must cope with more excitement."

"What foolishness!" Bingley banged his hand on the table, rattling the spoons and unsettling Darcy. All of Bingley's liveliness seemed to be returning in service to the only decent news he had heard in days. "This is happy news! Mrs Bennet will be thrilled, and will talk of nothing else. Her worries for her daughters' futures will be lifted from her, and you know well that is a burden she has carried far longer than any illness. And you forget Caroline shall soon be here! It will be as well for her to be assured that her, um, hopes in your direction are futile ones. It will give Miss Bennet additional protection from any plotting, knowing that her sister is to be your wife, and if Caroline ever wishes to be invited to Pemberley again, she must maintain the connexion. You must talk to Bennet, and at once, Darcy! In fact, we should leave now!"

Darcy was dumbfounded. In coming up with an excuse for delay, both he and Elizabeth had failed to consider Bingley's whole perspective. They were protecting his feelings by clarifying that Darcy's heart was already committed to Elizabeth, but Bingley too hoped to become a member of the Bennet family. As a man in love, their concerns were his own. Yet so was his blindness. *They had been successful in their scheme, it appeared, to keep him from seeing Miss Bennet's childlike attachment to me.* Bingley had no idea of the true reason for deferral of the announcement.

"Elizabeth prefers to wait," Darcy said, in what he knew was a pedantic tone.

Bingley stood. "Then *I* shall tell Mr Bennet," he said defiantly. "You made a mistake, my friend, in not swearing me to secrecy first. This is excellent news, and I hope that Miss Elizabeth will soon be my sister. It is not in her own best interests that you be creeping around with her at all hours. If you care for her at all, you will go directly to her father, and save her the embarrassment of my intervention."

Darcy stood as well. "No!"

"You cannot stop me!"

"There are other reasons, Bingley, ones you do not know. I am not at liberty to tell you, but you must trust me that they are valid."

But Bingley was, evidently, caught up in his own image of himself as protector of the Bennet young womanhood. "Either you trust *me* enough to inform me of your so-called reasons, or I tell her father," he said mulishly. "Frankly, I cannot imagine anything that could be so important that it leaves their futures unguarded, Miss Elizabeth unprotected, and Miss Bennet without defence against Caroline's machinations.

"You are behaving most improperly, Darcy."

Hot fury flooded Darcy's usual calm. Perhaps Bingley did have some excuse for failing to trust Darcy wholeheartedly, after his deceit in the matter of Miss Bennet. But that he should skirt the edge even, of accusation against Elizabeth's *safety*, and hold up the excuse of sheltering Jane from *Caroline*—his *own* sister, whom *he* had invited here—was beyond the pale. He had done nothing to deserve that sort of censure and blame.

"If you care for Miss Bennet as you have repeatedly assured me, you will do nothing of the sort," he said coldly. "What has happened to the man who yesterday could protect Miss Bennet from Caroline himself?"

"What has caring for her to do with speaking to Mr Bennet regarding *your* actions?"

"I have told you, again and again, that Miss Bennet's mind is in disarray. You have seen it yourself. You know, of course, that she has gaps in her memory regarding you."

Bingley nodded sullenly but gave no other sign that he recognised Miss Bennet was filling in those gaps with more than simple nursery rhymes. Darcy could see that nothing except the full truth would do.

"Apparently—and in the most muddled of manners—she is in some way clinging to a notion of me with a sort of fascination. I suppose it is a matter of safety, somehow. I pulled her from the water, and she clings to the security of the notion. Miss Elizabeth fears that if her sister somehow believes that I am being taken from her before her senses return, it will adversely affect her recovery. Hence the wait of a week before she must cope with any more confusion."

Bingley turned utterly white; he even swayed a little on his feet, and Darcy feared he might faint.

"It is not romance on my part, Bingley, nothing to do with love or—"

"You have said quite enough. I perfectly comprehend your reasoning, and have now only to be ashamed of what my own has been. Forgive my presumption, and accept my best wishes for your future happiness with Miss Elizabeth."

And with these words Bingley hastily left the room, and Darcy heard him the next moment open the front door and quit the house.

CHAPTER
TWENTY-ONE

B ingley stormed down the hall and out the door, unaware of the concern and bewilderment he struck in the servants when they glimpsed the unfamiliar sight of anger on the face of Netherfield's affable tenant.

'If I am taken from her?'

How dare he! As if Darcy was the centre of the universe and everyone else existed to be his playthings. As if Jane's very being— her heart and her future recovery—was so engaged with, tied to Darcy! *He did not think her good enough for me a year ago and now he plays games with her heart, and with her sister's?*

Insufferable man! He already has won Miss Elizabeth, and will not claim it so that he may continue this tomfoolery with Jane?

Although hardly dressed for it, Bingley had his horse saddled and rode hard across the park; any hopes of the pounding hooves and discipline required to keep his mind on the terrain did little but exhaust his surprised horse, unused as she was to such a furious, uncontrolled canter. He had ridden some miles in what he would later realise was a large circle by the time sense arrived and he pulled up the reins, only to discover he was at that damned bridge connecting the estates.

If I buy Netherfield, I shall tear it down and build a new, sturdy bridge, further upstream, with a railing and gate to prevent wild animals and stray dogs from crossing on it.

He dismounted and began pacing.

Why will Darcy not announce his engagement? He thinks to protect Miss Bennet's feelings, but what of Miss Elizabeth's reputation? A secret engagement rather than speak to Mr Bennet and earn his blessing? Why do such a thing with the Bennets already at risk with poor, dear Jane's uncertain recovery?

Bingley leant against the railing of the cursed bridge, once again reminding himself of what he had been told—Darcy and Miss Elizabeth and the doctor all saying Miss Bennet will soon recover—and what he himself had seen. No, *not seen*, he thought, shaking his head to rid himself to the achingly beautiful vision of Miss Bennet in her lubberly grey apron. He had seen so much of her, enough to set fire to imaginings he tried to ignore. What he had *not* seen was real improvement in her mind, real recognition of *him*, beyond a smile the day prior.

A smile was something, wasn't it, in spite of the rhyme that accompanied it?

What if she does not fully improve? Can she be the wife I need? Can I be husband to a woman who is unwell, uncertain, unable to be in society outside of family? How do I protect her from Caroline and Louisa? Indifference would be the best I could hope for.

He looked up at the cloud-mottled sky and exhaled a deep sigh. Could he marry a lady whose affections were fixed on the man who will marry her sister?

'*It is not romance on my part, Bingley, nothing to do with love or—*'

"It has everything to do with love, you blasted fool!" he shouted. No one responded, of course, and in the silence, Bingley realised it was time, past time, he stopped relying on others and sought his own answers.

A visit to Longbourn, without Darcy, was in order. He was tired of being told how to behave, what to expect, how things ought to be. He needed to see Jane for himself, by himself.

——— ∘ ∘ ∘ ———

Elizabeth's face ached from all the smiling she had already done that morning, but she smiled again when she entered the morning parlour. She sank into the window seat and felt warmth flood her as she thought of all that was as it should be, and the expression of heartfelt delight she had seen on Darcy's handsome face. *And passion in his kiss...*

"Lizzy, are you well? You are flushed."

Mary's enquiry drew everyone's attention to Elizabeth. She straightened and acknowledged her family's curious gazes. "Of course, I was recalling something..."

As he turned the page in his newspaper, Mr Bennet chuckled. "You were awake with your thoughts late last evening and then out the door early, Lizzy. Do not catch a chill and bring Mr Jones here with his bag of leeches. We cannot lose another girl to her sickbed."

His wife reacted with alarm. "Oh Mr Bennet! Do not say such things! It is enough we have poor Jane, so affected by all the thinking and the sorting out of affections. She is not like Lizzy, able to stomp about in the mud and never beset by a sneeze. Jane is like her mama and has a delicate sensibility."

"Would that every lady had Jane's caution," Mr Bennet said drolly.

Elizabeth immediately took his meaning as a reference to Lydia, but for Mrs Bennet, it was a call to action.

"I am sick of caution and worry. If only those awful Gouldings took care with their dog, we would be in the thick of planning Jane's wedding breakfast and shopping rather than—"

"It has been less than a fortnight," cried Kitty. "What are ten days to a lifetime of happiness for Jane and Mr Bingley?"

Kitty's philosophical effort earned her a wink from her father, but Mrs Bennet would not be satisfied.

"Mr Bingley could make a larger effort," she said. "I begin to wonder if he has ceded the field to his friend and Mr Darcy has indeed taken an interest in our Jane."

Elizabeth frowned. "Just as Jane is all that is good, so is Mr Bingley in his patience and care as he awaits the recovery of her feelings for him. He has made clear he wishes to propose."

"Perhaps. Yet Mr Darcy remains steady. He too is in want of a wife and he and Jane make a handsome pair." Mrs Bennet shifted her skirts, a clear sign she was settling into her topic, and in an assured voice, said, "I believe Mr Darcy to be more handsome than Mr Bingley. He is the taller of the two, as well, and now that we have seen him smile on occasion, his comeliness is more apparent."

"As is his ten thousand a year, Mama?" Elizabeth said sharply.

From behind his newspaper, Mr Bennet made his opinion known. "Mr Darcy is all that you say, yet he is oddly inept at knowing how to speak to a woman's interests—although I grant that Jane's interests tend towards the domestic sphere and holds little interest for a man such as he. Yet few marriages bring together a match of true minds and affection, do they, Mrs Bennet?"

He folded the paper and took a sip of his tea. "Yes, we are agreed, then, that the tall, wealthy, handsome nephew of an earl would make Jane a fine husband if Mr Bingley fails to improve her opinion of him."

"Papa!"

"It is not only mothers who have opinions on a daughter's marital opportunities, Lizzy." He shrugged. "A son in law with whom I could play chess, and who dislikes card parties as much as I do? And his fabled library!"

Mr Bennet chuckled, tucked his paper under his arm, and strode out of the drawing room. Elizabeth gripped the arm of her chair, as desperate to go to her father and tell him *her* happy news as she was to remain and keep her mother from further specious speculation.

"What would Jane want with a fabled library? She would prefer he have a fabled still-room," offered Kitty.

It mattered little which Jane preferred, as the lady herself entered the room, smiling a little foggily and dressed in a pretty blue gown. Elizabeth rose to greet her sister and bring her to sit beside her, but not before Hill entered and announced Mr Bingley had come to call.

If he was a little dishevelled, it went unremarked on. Mr Bingley had purpose in his expression, and immediately asked whether Jane's ankle was healed enough that he could walk in the garden with her. Mrs Bennet agreed it was, hurrying Jane into her spencer and gloves, and ordering Mary to be their chaperon before Elizabeth could speak.

When the trio had exited, Mary looking irritated and Jane confused, Elizabeth turned to her mother. "You do too much talking, Lizzy. Mr Bingley is here without his friend, and whatever intention he has, it must not be interfered with by your clever conversation."

Mrs Bennet's rare forays into reason and sense could only vex Elizabeth, and she quickly took a seat nearest the window where Kitty had already positioned herself.

"Mr Bingley is doing little to advance himself with Jane," reported Kitty. "He is rather solemn."

Elizabeth peered out and saw the couple sitting side by side on the long bench nearest the rose arbour. Mr Bingley sat some distance from Jane, watching glumly as she plucked a dead rose and scattered its petals.

"Oh, why cannot all lovers come together as easily as Lydia and Wickham!" cried Mrs Bennet? "Their attraction was clear from the very beginning, and I knew he would marry her! They are so happy together!"

Elizabeth's mortification appeared to be shared equally by Kitty; Mrs Bennet, however, was encouraged by their silence.

"It is time Mr Bingley proposes. But if Jane prefers Mr Darcy, she should marry him."

"Mama!" Elizabeth lowered her voice. "I beg you not to share these opinions." She looked to ensure the windows were securely closed.

Mrs Bennet sniffed. "There are things that must be said aloud to be acknowledged. *You* may be too clever for Mr Bingley but I believe he would do well for Kitty."

At this, Elizabeth saw Kitty grow still with intense interest. She was rarely the centre of any conversation, especially one about herself and a gentleman.

"In fact," Mrs Bennet chuckled, "Mr Bingley's sister may prefer Kitty to Jane, as unlike Jane, Kitty is no rival to Miss Bingley's looks."

While Kitty whimpered, Elizabeth was speechless with anger. Mrs Bennet proclaimed her wisdom with all the self-assuredness of a woman with four unmarried daughters, two prospective grooms dangling within reach, and her own 'successful' match with a man who only tolerated her.

"Mr Darcy has ten thousand a year and he should have the handsomest wife," Mrs Bennet concluded.

Elizabeth jumped up. "Mr Darcy would take his ten thousand a year elsewhere if he knew he was the subject of such cruel gossip, and his friend was insulted by the young ladies' own mother," she cried. Turning to Kitty, she took her hand. "You, dear girl, are clever and sweet and among the handsomest girls in all of Meryton. When it is your turn, you shall not want for suitors."

Tutting, Mrs Bennet gave one daughter a consoling glance before admonishing the other. "Lizzy, it is none of your concern. You refused a most worthy proposal from Mr Collins, so your thoughts on a good match are of no consequence. What is meant to be shall be. If Mr Darcy desires Jane to be his wife, so she will be."

—— ◦ ◦ ◦ ——

Elizabeth fled to the garden, walking quickly around the back of the house until she could approach the couple unannounced and hear what was being said. Mary, seated on the opposite bench, looked up at her in surprise.

Mr Bingley rose awkwardly; Jane appeared oblivious of anything but the petals strewn at her feet.

"Miss Elizabeth, would you walk with me?" he said quietly.

Leery of Mr Bingley's desire to so quickly abandon her sister, Elizabeth nonetheless nodded.

"To my horse, please. I must go."

His sombre tone, too much like that of the old, implacable Darcy unsettled her. "What is it, sir? What has happened? Bad news at Netherfield? Your family?"

He looked at her as if she was mad and Elizabeth realised it was this genial man who in fact looked close to deranged. His face was pale with something akin to despair; his eyes radiated fury.

"In cases such as these, I believe I am to wish you joy, Miss Elizabeth. However, I understand your engagement to Darcy is to remain secret until my friend can rid himself of any obligation to...to your sister's fascination with him."

"My-oh! No, Mr Bingley, you misunderstand—"

"I understand nothing and everything. I came alone today to see Miss Bennet, and she has said nothing, nary a word, to me except to ask where my friend has gone and when shall he return. I am not a scholar like Darcy, I read few books and philosophy bores me. But I am intelligent enough to know when a lady has removed her favour and moved it to another. I have lost whatever love your sister once had for me."

"No!"

"Yes. Darcy, whether he wishes her love or yours or both, has destroyed my hopes. Your sister needs him. She wants him. This is a puzzle I cannot piece back together."

CHAPTER
TWENTY-TWO

E lizabeth paced the footbridge in the cold light of an early dawn, her thoughts racing faster than her ability to tame them. She could not feel the chill nor worry about the impending rain. Despite ruminating upon it all the night long, she could not understand how things had gone so suddenly, horribly wrong with Mr Bingley. Yes, it had been her idea for Darcy to tell him of *their* understanding, to allay his budding suspicions.

"I cannot help but notice that your sister's smiles all seem to be directed at my friend here."

But they had also spoken of protecting his feelings, of saying no more about Jane's symptoms; only that they had achieved amity together. Darcy was meant to move his friend's mind further *away* from the conclusion they—and Mr Tilden, for that matter—had drawn: that Jane, for unknown reasons, seemed...attached to Darcy. Surely, if he had simply told Bingley of their happiness, perhaps emphasising his difficulty in paying attention to anyone else *except* Elizabeth, it would have given Bingley ample sources of distraction? Why, why had he said anything more?

From a distance, the man himself strode towards her, tall and confident. He was a man who knew what he was about in anything he undertook. Darcy likely could not imagine what it was like for a lesser mortal such as Bingley, who was not possessed of those same gifts of steadiness and self-assurance—not born to them, as Darcy had been.

And yes, he was smiling at her...smiling, when Jane's hopes, her wishes, her dreams, her future had been shattered. It was no comfort that Jane did not yet know it. She would never blame another for her loss, only herself. But it was the fault, at least partially, of someone.

It is my fault, Jane, she thought. *I believed I could trust him.*

——— ◦ ◦ ◦ ———

After the wretched night Darcy had experienced, wherein Bingley did not come down to dinner nor answer his knock upon his chamber door, it was so cheering to see Elizabeth—dearest, loveliest Elizabeth—the only bright spot of light and hope within a decidedly gloomy period. It was beyond frustrating.

That Bingley should ever even imply that Elizabeth would not be *safe* with him...when the whole reason he was not already engaged to her was because of Bingley's sorry situation.

Which, yes, was partially his fault, in light of his actions the previous year. But not entirely. The insult of it, in the face of his patience!

The truth of it was, the man had been off chasing his hat instead of rescuing his girl, and he resented and blamed Darcy for it. Unfair! Threatening to embarrass and insult both him and Elizabeth before the mercurial Mr Bennet. Unjust!

He smiled at her, relief filling him that he was with her again; in her light and joyful presence, all his cares would slip away.

——— ◦ ◦ ◦ ———

"I do not understand how you could have revealed Jane's most private mortification," she blurted, as soon as he was within hearing distance. "Can you imagine how humiliated she will be once she recovers from her injury? To know she has lost everything due to a...a misconception beyond any influence or control! Mr Bingley knows! He knows and he was devastated!" She took a breath and frowning, demanded, "It was you who told him, was it not?"

His brows shot up. "Well, yes. But darling, if you would only calm yourself, I can—"

"Calm? You think I ought to be calm?" Elizabeth could hardly believe that he would be condescending at a moment such as this. "I realise it means little to you, but this is Jane's whole heart, stomped on, crushed! I asked for one thing, that you ease Bingley's potential for worry by telling him our news. We talked about this! We both agreed, from the very beginning of our scheme, that it was of the utmost import that he never learn of her...delusion! That she wishes openly for you to be at her side, instead of him!"

Darcy's appearance had turned to one of utmost hauteur. "I apologise, madam." He said nothing else, no explanations, and no real appearance of regret, either.

"Is that all you have to say?"

If anything, his expression grew even colder. "I make no excuses. I did, indeed, reveal that which we agreed would remain private between ourselves."

Elizabeth stared at him; he seemed to be looking at a point just beyond the sunrise. Even though he was within a mere arm's reach, he may as well have been a hundred miles away. It was obvious he would provide no further reasoning, nothing to account for his behaviour, no explanations.

He was Mr Darcy, master of Pemberley, who owed none to anyone.

What she wished to do was push him into the stream, but of course, she would never allow her temper free rein.

"I suppose I should be thankful that you do not mock my distress, as my own father would," she said stiffly. "As I cannot be 'calm', as you have requested, I shall take myself away until such time as I have gathered my sensibilities and not disturb you with them any further."

She turned on her heel and strode away, swiftly, that she might restrain her tears until she was out of sight. Nevertheless, she hoped...nay, she *expected* that he would call her back, that he would tell her it was all a misunderstanding. That somehow, she had misconstrued Mr Bingley's feelings or Darcy's part in them, or even that he was sorry to have disappointed her.

But no.

The only sound she heard was of her own footsteps, taking her farther and farther away, and the patter of rain splashing in her path.

———— o o o ————

After Elizabeth's abrupt departure, Darcy stood for a long while on the footbridge. When the rain began in earnest, pitting the surface of the water below him, he barely noticed, much less remembered to take shelter beneath his umbrella hanging forgotten from the bridge rail. He felt frozen, as if a layer of numbness prevented him from feeling the stinging drops.

How? he thought. *How did I manage to ruin everything after only a few days? I ought to have foreseen Bingley's response. I should have known he would proceed to Miss Bennet straightaway. What had he said to her?* That he had distressed Elizabeth beyond measure was obvious.

I may not be able to fix this, he realised, a sense of despair rising like the water at his feet, overwhelming the normally staid little stream, raising it to a torrent that nearly crested the little bridge. He ought to have known his brief current of happiness was much too good to last.

———— o o o ————

The morning passed in a dull, wet gloom. Neither gentleman graced the Longbourn parlour.

"Miserable rain!" Mrs Bennet cried, staring out at the downpour. "It keeps Jane's suitors from coming to the point!"

It matched Elizabeth's mood, however, and she was even grateful for the excuse of weather to explain the absence of callers.

It was startling to her how quickly time could pass when one was completely happy and completely in thrall, and how slowly it moved once when one was completely miserable. And if Jane sang 'O, where have you been, charming Darcy?' one more time, Elizabeth was going to lose her own sanity.

She looked with resentment at her father's closed book-room door, and bit back snappish comments at her mother's planning aloud of two different weddings, one for Mr Bingley and Jane, the other, twice as grand, for Jane and Mr Darcy. Nothing disturbed Mary's reading, or Kitty joining Jane in singing the nursery song's chorus and then giggling. Were they all lunatics?

Worst of all, could not they see that Jane was worsening? Her eyes were almost crossed in dazedness, her usual pristine neatness absent with tendrils of hair escaping her coiffure, while she sang the stupid song with all the gusto of a drunken seaman. It was a good thing that her callers were absent; she was more ill than ever. Even Darcy's company would likely bring her no calm.

Darcy!

She had not realised, not until this desolate, endless morning, how much quiet strength he gave her, how much of her optimism in Jane's recovery had been rooted in his caring, steadfast presence.

So, he had told Bingley the truth, and as could be predicted, Bingley had not taken it well. Why should it matter? Jane's health was deteriorating, there was no getting round it. It was only a matter of time before she betrayed herself with him, and what possible difference could a day or two make? She knew deceit was abhorrent to Darcy; perhaps Bingley had asked him outright? But she had been accusatory and emotional. Perhaps he believed her like her mother now.

Perhaps I am.

She had judged him in error, thrown angry words at him just as she had a year ago.

How terribly I have acted. No matter his mistake, mine is just as grievous. I have hurt him, but I cannot, will not, let it remain so. We will reach an understanding, an accord. I will not allow my feelings to proceed unhindered, without adding reasoning and rationality.

"'O where have you been Willie lad, Willie lad, oh where have you been, charming Willie,'" Jane crowed.

Kitty giggled. "Willie Darcy!"

Elizabeth buried her face in her hands.

———— o o o ————

Darcy was nearly soaked through by the time he re-entered Netherfield, apologising to the footman who took his sopping greatcoat and beaver. He was not sure what he ought to do; returning to London was a slight temptation, but his sorrow and grief would only travel with him. Besides, Fitzwilliam would call him seven kinds of fool, and hustle him right back to face her again. The point was moot; he did not want to leave.

I will not leave her.

He moved into the gold parlour where a healthy fire blazed, seating himself before it. After a time, feeling, rich and prickling, once again coursed through his breast, thawing his initial shock and filling him with determination. His interference in Bingley's life had contributed to his first separation with Elizabeth; he would not allow it to create another.

At that rather auspicious moment, Bingley stomped into the parlour. He said not a word, only slumped in another chair before the fire. Darcy did not pause to parse his words or carefully form his thoughts as he had when considering how to approach Bingley regarding his initial interference.

"Still sulking?"

Bingley turned towards him sharply. Just as quickly he looked away, but not before Darcy saw the resentment delineating his features.

"Blame me if it makes you feel any better to do so. I believe I am strong enough to bear up."

Bingley could not maintain his silence. "I do blame you, of course I do. Had it not been for you, I would be married to Miss Bennet long before now, and she would have been nowhere near that stupid bridge to be assaulted by a stupid dog!"

"Would she? And if so, and a dissimilar but equally unlucky accident caused her to lose her memories of you, would it still be my fault?"

The younger man would not answer.

"I understand your anger," Darcy sighed. "When Colonel Fitzwilliam and I were at Rosings last year, he told Elizabeth of my meddling in her sister's life—and yours. I was furious with him when I discovered that his loose tongue had materially lessened my chances with Elizabeth. But the fact remains, it was my own damned fault, for interfering in the first place. Just as the fact that your sisters and I presented any obstructions to your courtship is yours."

"I did not know she called!" Bingley cried, thrusting a finger at Darcy. "You hid it from me!"

"But you knew where she lived," Darcy said ruthlessly. "You knew how to renew the acquaintance when you still missed her after several weeks, did you not?"

"You had convinced me of its futility! That she did not care for me!"

"Oh, and a man can never court a woman whose interest is not easily won, can he?"

"And have her trapped by my intentions? Her mother would

have forced her to marry me had I betrayed any more of *my* interest!"

Darcy laughed humourlessly. "Do not pretend with *me* that you were *protecting* her. She lives in a small country village, without the influence of prestigious relations, on an estate entailed away from her family. She is too wellborn and too impoverished for nearly any man she is ever likely to meet. Her future is likely one of lonely, genteel poverty, and a man who truly loved her would have made protecting her from *that* his first consideration. You were protecting yourself, your family and your fortune, and you know it —or you ought to. I do, because I have been guilty of it myself. Marrying for love alone is a great risk."

Bingley opened his mouth as if to protest. Then shut it again. For some moments, they both stared silently into the flames.

"What should I do?" Bingley asked, on only a slightly plaintive note.

"You?" Darcy asked, shrugging. "The devil if I know. But as for myself…I shall do whatever it takes to get the girl."

CHAPTER
TWENTY-THREE

"I must set things to right," Bingley muttered. *I have failed Jane, again and again.*

"I am coming with you." Darcy's clear intent to fly across the fields to Longbourn churned up mixed feelings within Bingley.

"No, no, this is my error to correct. I must go and prove my steadfastness. I will do whatever is needed to stand by her—to stay with her in her tribulation."

"I have my own mistakes to address."

"Your rebuke was not only for me, eh? Miss Elizabeth has wrung your bell?" Closer examination revealed that Darcy's collar was damp. "Oh, I see. Either you have been crying, Miss Elizabeth has been crying on your chest, or—likeliest of all—you have been stomping about in the rain."

Bingley made some effort not to chuckle at Darcy's pained expression. His friend's quick journey from romantic bliss to despair should not cheer him but misery loved company, did it not? "She is angry with you?"

"Did I not just tell you I would do whatever it takes to get the girl? I need to 'get' her again."

They were both rational, lovesick men. "Of course. You tend

to your business with Miss Elizabeth and I will do all I must to prove my love for Jane, no matter her family or her state of mind. I am appalled at my own faithlessness. You cannot imagine—"

"Oh, I think I can—"

Bingley waved off whatever longwinded lecture Darcy was about to begin and strode towards the door. The man might think only his own ineptness in courtship was worthy of examination, but they both had work to do!

"I do appreciate your advice but do not test my good will for you and Miss Elizabeth. I simply have none to spare at the moment. I wish you happy—of course I do, once again—but at present I must do all I can for Jane, especially now that you have tossed the proverbial cold water upon me, awakening me to my own selfishness."

"Wish me luck," he added before taking Darcy's extended hand and shaking it. "I shall need it. My sisters are coming, and if they sense Jane's frailty or lack of feeling, their talons will emerge."

Unhappy was the quarter-hour Mrs Bennet spent in company with Kitty, Jane, and Mr Bingley. Just as she had assumed Jane would be Mrs Darcy, that man scowled and went off to the book-room with Mr Bennet; undoubtedly, they would have some dull discussion on books whilst she alone must manage Jane's affections towards Mr Bingley. Unless of course, Mr Darcy was speaking to Mr Bennet regarding settlements; she must not count out the notion. Longbourn was positively overrun with gentlemen, all there to pledge their hearts to her beautiful eldest daughter! Where was Lizzy? Did she not recall her responsibilities to Jane and her future felicity?

Kitty was doing her best to interest Mr Bingley in the art of remaking bonnets, but his attention kept drifting to Jane. Dear

Jane, who truly looked a little more peaked than she had earlier. *How pale and dull she is!*

Mrs Bennet glanced at Mr Bingley; he was frowning, his eyes intent on Jane.

This will not do. In the unlikely event that Mr Darcy has yet again abandoned our Jane, finding her company less desirable than Mr Bennet's, we cannot lose Mr Bingley. A few sips of beauty juice will do the trick.

She walked over to her daughter and held out her hands. "Jane, dear, you have had a busy morning. I believe you need a moment to refresh yourself. "

"No," she refused, with an unnaturally stubborn expression. "'Fair is the kingcup that in meadow blows, Fair is the daisy that beside her grows.' Fair, fair, fair."

"I do love to see a meadow full of daisies," Mr Bingley said, looking earnestly at Jane.

"Yes, yes, we all love a summer flower, Mr Bingley." Mrs Bennet grasped Jane's hand and tugged at the book. "I do need you for a moment. We must fetch Lizzy as well."

Jane pulled away, holding the book to her chest. "No! Fair, fair, fair."

"Mama, I shall fetch Lizzy," offered Kitty.

"No, Jane must come with me."

"Pray, Mrs Bennet, do let her remain." Mr Bingley turned to her with a far more pleasing expression than any he had worn since his arrival. "I do not wish Miss Bennet to leave. I am enjoying this more intimate company and would miss her voice, even for a few minutes."

Well. She nearly had forgotten how handsome and charming the man could be, and thus how well suited he was to Jane. Surely he would approve of any increase in Jane's beauty.

"Mr Bingley, it is just for a moment. Jane, you see, is showing signs of requiring a bit of her, er, tonic. Just a smidgeon, a few times per day keeps the doctor away. Now that is a pleasing rhyme, is it not, dearest Jane?" Mrs Bennet bent her head, pulling Jane's arm, whispering, "Come with me, just for a moment."

"Her *tonic?*" Mr Bingley repeated. Suddenly he was taking the seat beside Jane.

In a firm voice, quite unlike any Mrs Bennet had ever heard from him, he offered to keep Jane company while she fetched both the tonic and Miss Elizabeth. "I shall read the next of these little poems aloud to her whilst you are gone. I am certain Miss Catherine would like that as well."

"But—"

"My father suffered prodigious headaches," Mr Bingley said quietly, as though confiding a great secret to her. "When I was a boy, my own dear mother thought nothing of giving him his powders in our sitting room or parlour. It is a kindness to bring relief to anyone who is suffering, no matter where it be."

Perhaps he did understand, and was not so fussy regarding medicines or elixirs as the rest of her family; perhaps he did not even know that Mr Tilden had forbidden them. Mrs Bennet moved quickly and as quietly as possible to Jane's chambers and retrieved the hidden bottle. Hearing the floor creak in Elizabeth's room, she fled back down the stairs and into the parlour.

To her surprise, Mr Bingley greeted her just inside the door. "You are swift to aid your daughter. Let me assist you, Mrs Bennet." He plucked the bottle from her grasp, pulled out the stopper, and sniffed.

"Mr Bingley!"

"Good God!"

———— o o o ————

Elizabeth sat up, shocked to find she had been asleep for nearly an hour. She rose from her chair and stretched a bit. Her mind was alert, the awful memory of the morning rushing at her; she chose to focus instead on patting away the wrinkles in her gown and enjoying the thin rays of sun that were breaking through the clouds. She could hear voices below, a low rumble of a male voice.

Has Darcy come?

Then came a shriek from her mother. "Mr Bingley!"

Oh no, what has he done? Where is Jane? Fearing an outbreak of nursery rhymes or perhaps by now, rope skipping or worse—that Mr Bingley had permanently renounced her sister—Elizabeth ran from her room. She was nearly down the stairs when her father and Darcy emerged from the book-room, moving quickly, as she was, towards the front parlour. Darcy turned; when he saw her, his step slowed and his alarmed expression softened. She had hardly taken note of him when her father called out in a voice marked more by exasperation than concern.

"Mrs Bennet, whatever are you on about? Has Mr Bingley now decided upon Mary?"

Her father's poor joke only heightened the tension. There was Mr Bingley, arguing—*arguing!*—with Mrs Bennet.

"Give it to me," her mother cried.

"No, I shall not!" Mr Bingley stood in front of Jane as though shielding her. Jane, poor Jane, sat oblivious to the commotion; her eyes were unfocused, her nose red. Stricken with guilt for neglecting her sister, Elizabeth moved quickly to sit at Jane's side.

"What has happened, Mrs Bennet?"

She huffed and avoided her husband's eyes. "Mr Bingley is distressed that I take Jane to her room to rest!"

"No, I am questioning why you are giving her this!" Mr Bingley held up a bottle. "It smells strongly of laudanum! When was Miss Bennet prescribed a tonic? This is a large bottle, and it is nearly empty!"

Elizabeth gasped. Mr Bennet reached his hand for the vial; he had scarcely pulled the stopper before wincing, an expression that quickly turned to anger.

"Mrs Bennet, can you explain this?"

Despite her audience's incredulity, Mrs Bennet answered with the utmost confidence. "It is a beauty tonic, to ensure Jane will not lose her looks while recovering from her accident."

"A beauty tonic?" Elizabeth's arms slipped around Jane, pulling her closer. "How—?"

"*This?*" Mr Bennet thrust the vial at his wife. "Look at your daughter. Do you believe it is working? You have benumbed Jane's mind in a foolish effort to maintain her complexion!"

"Your daughter will always be beautiful," Mr Bingley protested. "You did not need to intoxicate her."

"I did not—"

Elizabeth felt Jane's head turn and look up at Mr Bingley. "I am pretty," she said happily.

"You see!" cried Mrs Bennet. "All is well."

A furious Mr Bennet was not placated. "Your idea of 'well' is better fit for Bedlam, Mrs Bennet. Did you concoct this potion? Must I fear you will begin dosing Lizzy or Kitty?"

"No! I-"

Mrs Bennet turned white, swaying on her feet; Darcy stepped to her side, leading her to a chair. She smiled nervously as he addressed her in a far gentler tone than the others. "Mrs Bennet, where did you obtain this tonic? Mr Tilden was very clear that time was all that was necessary for Miss Bennet's recovery."

"Mr Jones gave it to me."

Jane began to sing.

"My sister Lizzy and I fell out, And what do you think it was about? She loved coffee and I loved tea, And that was the reason we couldn't agree."

As arguments and accusations of neglect and stupidity began, Elizabeth whispered in Jane's ear. "Would you help me find a ribbon? You have the prettiest ribbons in your room."

Jane looked at her blearily. "Coffee or tea?"

Nearly shuddering in horror of all that she had misinterpreted in her sister's behaviour, Elizabeth turned and gazed at Darcy, beseeching him wordlessly to understand. He nodded.

By the time Elizabeth had managed to extricate herself from Longbourn and make her way to the footbridge, nearly an hour had passed. He stood next to the rail, holding it. No, clutching it, she realised. He was not so confident, nor so impassive as he appeared.

After all she had experienced and learnt of Jane today, what she *wanted* to do was throw herself into his arms—but he had yet to hold them out. After his last experience, and the way she had opened the floodgates of wild emotion before he could even say a word, she could not blame him for being wary of her. Besides, she could not speak of Jane as yet, not when the shadow of their own disagreement stood like a wall between them.

"I am sorry for my outburst this morning," she said tentatively.

"I am the one who must apologise," Darcy said quickly. "You are correct in that I ought to have never informed Bingley, not for any reason. I should have anticipated the direction of our discussion—it was hardly surprising that he would...well, it does not matter."

Elizabeth could see that he was eager to set the whole matter aside; she wished to do so as well, but there was no point in having a squabble and not coming away from it with a better under-standing of each other. Naturally, her instinct was to be agreeable, but neither did she wish to repeat any past mistakes—nor suffer for them again in the future.

"Actually, you have already apologised. But it does matter, to me," she said softly. "I should like to understand."

"Oh, I did not mean that your opinion is unimportant, of course it is. Absolutely." He still would not meet her eyes. "I wish for you to trust that I am a man of my word. We agreed, as you said, that I would not reveal your sister's, er, inclination to Bingley. I did. No other consideration signifies."

Plainly, he was unenthusiastic about further discussion of the matter.

"You do not trust me, I see, to keep 'calm.'"

She had meant it as a tease, but evidently he could not tell.

"No, not at all. Truly." He looked genuinely alarmed.

He had *always* been able to tell; he had understood her odd sense of humour—even before he understood her in other ways.

She sighed heavily. *I have damaged our easy connexion, our friendship, even.*

"I have disappointed you. Again, I apologise. I..." he began.

"You what?"

"It is not important."

"It is *very* important."

He looked frustrated. "I have not the words to explain, as some so easily do. I am ill qualified to—"

He stopped mid-sentence, looking at her directly for the first time, scrubbing his hands through his hair in something like exasperation. He had forgotten or mislaid his hat, she realised.

"To recommend yourself to strangers," she recalled aloud. "But I hope I am no stranger."

"You remembered," he said quietly. "But neither can one learn to argue in ballrooms, except for the polite coquetry we shared. I would much rather hear your vexation, all of it. I did hear a bit of it this morning, but in essence I told you to stifle yourself. I was not prepared to hear your distress. I reacted poorly. I am heartily disgusted with myself."

"As am I. Disgusted with myself, that is." She held up a hand, seeing that he was about to argue the point. "No, truly. I did not even give you a chance to explain before I began screeching at you like a shrew. I allowed myself to become upset, frantic even. All over circumstances that neither you nor I can control."

He moved a step closer, giving up his death grip on the railing. "You did not screech, I can assure you. And of course you were upset. I behaved abom—"

"Stop!" she cried. As soon as the word was out of her mouth, she regretted it. His dear face, which had only just begun to ease in its severity, lost all expression.

She closed her eyes. "I am sorry, I am sorry. A lifetime of living with my sisters has taught me that it is often the loudest voice who is heard the most clearly. It is not wise, and I pray you will be patient with me as I unlearn the habit."

He nodded stiffly, plainly uncertain what had caused her outcry.

"You blame yourself for our squabble, it is obvious," she began.

Again, he nodded.

"And yet I, upon further reflection, had already concluded that you must have had a reason for acting as you did. I would like to hear it. Hear what happened when you spoke to Mr Bingley."

He looked as though he wished to protest, but did not quite dare, and she felt a thread of sorrow for her earlier quarrelsome manner. She was no fading violet, but there were means of expression far more effective than outshouting one's partner. Elizabeth believed in her own ability to communicate without 'stifling' herself; she must practise, however, with peaceful, patient persistence. Thus far, only the persistence came naturally.

At last, he broke the silence.

"He...Bingley...believed he should immediately inform your father of our happy news, rather than wait another week."

"What is this? He actually threatened to go to *my father*? Why would he? What right had he?"

He appeared uncomfortable, possibly unwilling to make his friend look any worse than he already did in her eyes. "He was upset, has been, from the beginning, that he was not your sister's rescuer. I think it likely he...in the moment, at least, wanted to see himself as yours."

Elizabeth was speechless.

"At the time, I could not think of any other reason to delay him...he was very determined."

"Of all the..." She was flabbergasted. Such an action from the normally placid Bingley had never crossed her mind—although in his dealings with her mother today, he had shown himself to be less *manageable* than she had supposed.

After a moment of shock, she looked up at Darcy; he regarded her with concern, leaning towards her as if holding himself back from touching her. She wanted no such restraint. The next moment she was in his arms, within his sheltering embrace, the strength of it seeming more like home than Longbourn ever had.

He simply held her, his strong heartbeat a pounding reassurance in her ears. Her sorrow for Jane's troubles was still great, but all was out of their hands. They had tried their best, had they not?

"I am so sorry," she said, her voice muffled by his coat. "Of course there was nothing else to be done, except tell Mr Bingley the whole of it. It is his own fault if, in attempting to play God, he earned additional burdens."

He looked down upon her, his eyes soft. "As all we who habitually attempt it eventually learn."

She grinned, wrapping her arms about his neck, but quickly sobered. "Why did not you tell me? I know I was too emotional, too upset, and too judgmental when I confronted you. I ought to have given you the benefit of the doubt. I am very sorry, very angry at myself that I did not. I only wish you had tried to talk to me, to tell me what happened. Were you protecting your friend?" She held him tightly, wanting him to feel her affection, her care, her willingness to be his and her acceptance—regardless of the mistakes they both would make.

"I…a gentleman never contradicts a lady. I could not."

"Even if she is completely, astonishingly wrong?" She met his eyes. "There have been times in our shared past where we have both contradicted each other. One particular moment, at Hunsford cottage, comes to mind."

"And look how well that went," he replied drily.

She touched his cheek, feeling the stubble of his beard even though he had probably shaved not all that long ago. "I will learn to regulate my excessive emotion, as a sign of my commitment to our united, *peaceful* future. I would only ask one thing of you."

"Anything," he said roughly.

"Please talk to me. Tell me what you think, what you feel. Even if your feelings are not perfect ones. I would rather know them, than be shut out."

"I…I *was* angry," he admitted, after a long pause, as if it were a shameful confession. "Angry at you. For being angry at me." He shook his head in apparent self-disgust.

"Oh, of course you were. I accused rather than listened."

He looked at her, seeming amazed.

"We will not quarrel for the greater share of blame annexed to this morning," said Elizabeth. "The conduct of neither, if strictly examined, was irreproachable. My hope is that we learn from our mistakes, so as to make fewer of them in the future. So that we might spend more time doing this."

She tilted up her head, her hands in his curls, drawing his lips to meet hers in a deep, wonderful kiss, a kiss of welcome, a kiss of reprieve, a kiss of reconciliation, a kiss of new awareness and new feeling. It was some moments before they broke apart for air.

"Tell me that again," he said, and brought his mouth down to hers.

CHAPTER
TWENTY-FOUR

The bright early morning sun peeked through the curtains and beckoned Jane awake. She sat up on her elbows, shielding her eyes from the beam, and slid to the edge of the bed. The room, unfortunately, refused to stay still. Rather than try to stand and begin her ablutions, she sat, wondering why she felt so strangely. Splaying her fingers upon the distinctive lines of sunshine marking stripes across her bedcovers, she blinked.

Her world had been an odd dream, of headache and strange sensation...for how long now? Days? Weeks? A year? Her belly roiled, and for a moment she looked about for the chamber pot.

My head hurts. The sun is too bright...

She leant to the nearby window, pulling on the curtain to limit the bright light hurting her eyes. She moved her head, and despite the megrim, there was no flash of pain. She had expected there would be, but she had no idea why.

If only my stomach would settle.

She tried to think, to quell the nausea and confusion. In her most recent memory...or was it a dream?...she was crossing the footbridge with her sisters. Something happened...a dog? Kitty screaming? Falling? The cold chill of water, being unable to move.

A sharp pain in her ankle. For some odd reason, Mr Darcy was in the dream, too.

But the harder she tried to remember specific details, the more confused her memories became.

Carefully, slowly, she stretched out her leg, expecting her ankle to pain her. It seemed perfectly well. If only the room would stop spinning! Finally, she cautiously made her way to her dressing table and peered into the mirror. Her hand rose to stroke a purplish bruise blooming on her forehead; a small bump rose at its centre. There was another above her ear, but nothing was tender to the touch.

I have been ill, she realised. *Those injuries had been painful ones. I do not remember much, but I know this. And despite the nausea and awful headache, I am better now.*

Smiling, and with a feeling of peace that she had not felt in ever so long, Jane slowly washed her face and brushed her hair.

Her stomach settled a little, although she was unsure about breakfast. The effort to do even what little she had was rather exhausting. Should she ring for Molly to help her dress and join her family? She was just about to pull the rope, when Mrs Bennet's voice rang out from just beyond her chamber door. Jane paused when she overheard her name.

"Lizzy, where do you think you are going? It is enough we have poor Jane still abed this morning, exhausted from the exertions of all her callers yesterday. She has so many decisions to make. We have a wedding to plan! To someone."

"It is still quite early, Mama. And Jane is most likely overcoming your overdoses of opiates."

Opiates? I do not even do well with a glass of wine! What has happened?

"No one wants to hear your fussing, Lizzy. You must sit with your sister, and prepare her for the gentlemen who will take tea with us today. If Mr Darcy desires her to be his wife, so she will be."

Mr Darcy?!

"She needs time before such notions are broached," her sister replied, rather sharply.

"I am sick of pauses and postponements! We ought to be deciding upon the dishes to be served at her wedding breakfast, rather than tip-toeing by her bedchamber. If Jane prefers Mr Darcy, she should marry him. He may have rescued her but at what risk to her reputation?"

"Mama!" Elizabeth lowered her voice so that Jane could barely hear her pleading. "Jane is sleeping. I beg you to keep these opinions to yourself."

Jane collapsed upon her bed. *What was all this?*

"There are things that must be said aloud to be acknowledged. You think yourself too clever for Mr Bingley but I believe he would do well for Kitty."

Mr Bingley...for Kitty? Jane covered her mouth with her hand. She could not hear Lizzy's response, only a low, fierce murmur.

"How many times must I repeat this? Mr Darcy has ten thousand a year and he should have the handsomest wife," Mama replied.

Lizzy's response to this was easily heard. "Mr Darcy is not for sale or auction, Mama! How many times must *I* remind *you* that he is not yours to manipulate? He will do as *he* wishes, not as you wish, nor as Jane wishes!"

"The dull turnip should *be* so fortunate as to win my dear Jane. What is meant to be shall be. If Jane desires Mr Darcy to be her husband, so he will be. She has made her preference for him as clear as the sun at noonday."

Whatever Lizzy responded was indistinct, but Jane was conscious of her mother's voice growing fainter and further away; it sounded as though she was still bleating about Mr Darcy.

Mr Darcy!

Before Jane could think further or suss out the meaning of what she had heard, Elizabeth opened her bedroom door, smiling brightly. "Good morning, dearest. It is still so early, and yet you are awake! Are you well today? Would you like a tray in here?"

Jane leant over the edge of the bed, and cast up her accounts.

———— ○ ○ ○ ————

It was not for another hour that Elizabeth was able to leave care of Jane in Mary's capable hands and go walking out. Thankfully, Jane had fallen immediately asleep once her illness was past, and remained sleeping peacefully. No one was anxious to call in Mr Jones, for however Mrs Bennet had misconstrued his instructions, they could not be easy about his potions at present. And although anxious to know whether Jane's full memory was yet returned, it seemed very likely that time and rest, as Mr Tilden had first claimed, were the best possible restoratives.

She set her hand on the knob to the side door which let out on the kitchen garden; from there was the shortest route to the footbridge. It was much later than her usual time of meeting Darcy; he was likely long gone by now, but she must at least verify his absence.

"Lizzy, where do you go now?"

Startled, Elizabeth turned. Mr Bennet stood in the doorway behind her, an amused expression on his face.

"Are you off to fetch yourself a husband?"

"Papa!"

"My dear daughter," said Mr Bennet, "with as many suitors as are hanging about Longbourn, I expect that you are now growing them in our kitchen garden. Where is your basket to collect your harvest?"

Elizabeth summoned a smile, but her father was not finished polishing his wit upon her.

"I have always thought to fetch a high price for the beauty of my daughters. I may now double my price for Jane. Her head is broken a bit but as you know, her heart appears to be strong, she would never bother her husband regarding fashions and refurbishing, and she can recite all the nursery rhymes her children could ever wish to hear."

"Papa..."

"All will be well, my Lizzy. You worry too much. Mr Jones was unwise not to include you or myself in all discussions of my partially drowned offspring, but Jane is now off the tonic. And while I do not think much of London physicians, even Tilden advised us to give it more time."

More time. It was what they needed, but would they have it?

"Your poor mother is watching the hourglass, however, and fears the sands of time." Mr Bennet chuckled at what Elizabeth thought a mean-spirited jibe.

"I only want what is best for Jane," she said. "Mr Bingley was heroic yesterday, but I hope he will give her the time she needs."

Mr Bennet was regarding her in amusement; she knew her expression still wore anxiety, but she covered it with a smile.

"Come back to the parlour where the fire is blazing," he said. "Allow Mr Darcy to collect his stares in the warmth of the indoors. He turns up often enough so that Jane might admire him, but I notice him address his remarks to you quite frequently."

"Papa." Elizabeth spoke in her sternest voice, knowing her father only thought of his jokes and took little seriously. "Mr Darcy and I have been discussing the current state of affairs and how best to address Jane's confusion and conclusions."

"Have you? Well, protecting Bingley from Jane's misapprehensions can only lead to a happy outcome," Mr Bennet agreed complacently. "Darcy is the cleverest fellow in Meryton, to be sure, but he has met his match in you."

——— ∘ ∘ ∘ ———

Darcy glanced up at the sun; he and Bingley were to go shooting this morning, so would not be able to grace the Longbourn parlour any time soon. There was no sense in expecting Elizabeth to appear at the footbridge at this late hour, but he hated to miss her. Looking up from the hypnotic current flowing at his feet, he was both astonished and thrilled to see her tripping down the forest path towards him. He showed his approval in affectionate greeting.

"I was beginning to worry that Miss Bennet had worsened," he said, once they broke apart.

"Not worsened, precisely," she replied, and explained the morning's illness.

"Sleep is likely the very best thing she can do," he agreed. "And to be frank, attending her conversation—such as it has been—being in her company, while you sit nearby enjoying the company of Bingley and your sisters *has* been rather unbearable."

"If you wish to know whether my envy is equal to yours, I can assure you that it is."

Darcy rewarded Elizabeth's avowal with a gentle kiss. "Thank you. I cannot help but hope that in even less than a week, I might speak to your father. Not to hasten our betrothal, you understand —but I am eager to enjoy your mother's praise and endearments."

"I did not realise a man of 'ten thousand a year' was equally blessed by wit," she laughed before turning serious. "I cannot help but feel that without the doses of elixir, my sister will soon recognise Mr Bingley, her heart returning to the man who rightfully claimed it last year."

He gave her a silly grin. "I *would* be glad, but all my happiness is currently occupied now that I have claimed *your* heart."

Elizabeth arched an eyebrow as if to scold him, but at his last words her expression melted into a dreamy smile that deserved another kiss. Or three.

"How does Mr Bingley?" she asked some time later, her voice languorous.

"Hopeful, lovesick, and hopeful still more. He has rescued Miss Bennet from excessive elixirs, you see, and no longer gives his hats —or me—accusatory stares."

She laughed exuberantly, a sound he rejoiced in.

"When I asked after Mr Bingley," she finally managed, "I wondered as to his expectations for the arrival of Miss Bingley and Mrs Hurst. They arrive today?"

"Yes, probably any time now. His temperament should improve

after we go shooting this morning, and he shall be ready to meet them with optimism," he admitted. "With Miss Bingley in residence, he can host a dinner as he has been longing to, allowing your sister to perhaps recall happy hours spent in his company at Netherfield."

"That will be ideal if *his* sister does not discourage such engagements, and *if* Jane is in her right mind. She shall be even more spiteful if she sees that two Bennet sisters wish for your attention, and ready to pounce upon a Bennet weakness."

Darcy pulled Elizabeth back under the shade of a copse of trees and kissed her.

"Only you shall ever have my heart."

"I am glad." She stroked his cheek lovingly. "Bring them to tea today. My father will not be home to practise his wit upon them, and Jane will still be abed and unable to betray any remaining peculiarities. Miss Bingley cannot come between us, but we can yet protect Jane and Mr Bingley—"

"It is for him to take charge of his sister," Darcy said happily. "May we cease speaking of unhappy lovers and sour sisters, my dear Elizabeth? We have, after far too many months, declared our mutual affection, and you have agreed to be my wife, and we have yet to fully discuss our own happy future."

Her tiny hand squeezed his arm. "I greatly anticipate announcing our joy to my family and the neighbours, but we must be careful and keep our secret for a few more days."

He nodded, resigned to playing the part in which she had cast him for a *bit* longer. "I understand we must stay quiet. And yet I do not know how to pretend. *You* are all I can or wish to see."

"But you must not look at me," she laughed. "Here is what you must do so that Jane does not see the happy light in your eyes and mistakenly think it is for her. Oh!" she cried. "And you must apply all that I say to your other faithful admirer, Miss Bingley! Heaven forfend that she learn of our understanding."

Darcy rolled his eyes. "I am your servant."

Elizabeth glanced at the sun and began to speak quickly, as if realising how soon they must part. "You must remember that a little distance keeps you safe. You must not hover over Jane *or* Miss Bingley."

"'Tis a simple request. I have never 'hovered' near any lady but one." He gave her a meaningful look.

Elizabeth's attempt to look stern dissolved in a giggle. "Anyone in your company knows you prefer to stand near walls and windows."

"Indeed. I shall take a chair some distance away and leave you or one of your sisters as my go-between."

"Women dislike hovering, even when it is a suitor."

"All women?"

She looked at him, grinning. "Mayhap I speak from the experience of the last lady of my acquaintance who was wed. Mrs Charlotte Collins."

He smirked. "I see. Keep my distance. Do not hover. What else must I know of how *not* to court a Bennet girl?"

"Never, ever gaze at her lovingly," she said, her expression glowing with merriment. "Your eyes must not meet her eyes for long moments nor rest on her lips."

Darcy stepped closer. "You ask much of me, madam. As you know, I am disposed to staring, and thinking unknowable thoughts prone to others' misinterpretation."

"You also prefer to manage the affairs of others, and I am asking you to continue to allow *yourself* to be managed in order to manage my sister and Mr Bingley." She bit her lip, as if knowing the response it would elicit from him. "Are you able to set aside your own inclinations and desires and do what I have asked?"

He nodded, all thought and feeling having run southward from his brain.

"Good, then." Elizabeth took a breath and stepped away. "Your gloves must stay on at all times, unless dining or turning the page of a book certain to bore my mother and sisters."

"But not you."

"I am never bored by a book read aloud in a pleasant voice."

"Ah, so had only Mr Collins been in possession of a more pleasant, sonorous voice, he would have won your heart."

"Oh, he would have surely won my heart," she replied in a sly voice. "He is everything a young man ought to be, unless one also wishes for a man to be well-mannered, clean, clever, educated, handsome, and kind."

Darcy arched an eyebrow in amusement. "And more discerning of his company and perhaps, less obsequious, as well as less fond of his own voice and the opinions of his patroness."

Elizabeth, clearly delighted by his teasing, returned it eagerly. "Yes, an agreeable young man would have all of these qualities, as well as something in his air..."

"I have much to learn indeed about courting a lady. Had I only some means to write notes to myself."

"I shall remind you," she replied happily. "Now then, when you speak or are standing near, your breath must not quicken, nor your words stutter."

"I shall read no poetry nor speak words of love." He stepped closer, running his finger along her cheek. "Not to your sister."

"Indeed, none of us should like that."

He leant down and touched his lips to hers.

"I shall think only of you, of our happiness."

And for several happy moments, that is all they both did.

———— o o o ————

It was fortunate all hunting weapons had been put away before Miss Bingley's carriage rolled up in front of Netherfield later that day.

An expression of repressed fury marked her countenance as she was helped from the vehicle. Mrs Hurst cringed behind her sister as Miss Bingley stared up at Netherfield, nearly sneering, before noticing her brother and Darcy emerging through the doors. She greeted them with a tight smile and stepped swiftly towards Darcy with a questioning look.

"I am sorry my brother's stupidity has compelled our return here, Mr Darcy. He is ridiculous."

If Darcy had not been happier than he ever remembered feeling, and hellbent on suppressing any hint of it so as not to upset Bingley or betray his promise to Elizabeth, he would have been far more offended by Miss Bingley. Good humour, he decided, was all that could carry them through the next few hours.

"What has Hurst done now?" he asked.

"As you know, Hurst does nothing, but *he* at least knew how to choose a wife." She pierced Bingley with a glare. "You know I refer to Charles. Why have we returned to this backwater?"

Bingley would have none of it. "Come, Caroline. You may wish to change into your best gown and slippers. In their eagerness to renew their acquaintance with you, the Bennets have invited us for tea."

He turned and sauntered up Netherfield's front steps. Darcy bit his lip to keep from smiling, quickly realising his lips were somewhat tender from Elizabeth's loving ministrations earlier that morning. That memory brought a smile to his face, piquing the already enflamed curiosity of Miss Bingley.

"Mr Darcy, if you recall, once you were anxious to leave this place," she said heatedly, gesturing broadly at Netherfield. "I beg that you tell me what amusement you take from our predicament."

"Well," he began, albeit too slowly for Miss Bingley; she tucked her arm into his and leant too close for his comfort. The feel of *her* hand clutching his arm was so unpleasant, it proved helpful in recalling him to his more customary gravity. He took a step towards the house, practically dragging the lady with him.

"Your brother is his own man and has determined Miss Bennet is the lady who gives him his greatest happiness. He is determined to make her Mrs Bingley, and I am here to support him in his efforts."

Her fingers tightened their grip as she tried pulling him to face her. "You cannot agree that Jane Bennet is suitable for Charles! Her family is appalling, she has no education, no wealth nor connexions."

Bingley's driver may have been from Scarborough but Netherfield's housekeeper, footmen and other servants were local. They knew, or knew of, the Bennets. Darcy made a careful reply in a voice loud enough to reach the ears of those Merytonians pretending to hear nothing of his conversation with Miss Bingley.

"Miss Bennet has not been to school nor had a governess and she lacks the generous dowry of many ladies whom your brother has admired briefly but who would not wish to be connected to a man scarcely a generation removed from trade." Darcy ignored the change in Miss Bingley's colouring and continued. "However, Miss Bennet is the daughter of a gentleman, whose estate goes back many generations, and she is kind-hearted and all that is good. Beyond that, she shall not lack connexions, for she and her sisters are my friends."

With that, Darcy led a stunned Miss Bingley up the steps and into Netherfield, moving away and loosening her hold on him as the housekeeper stepped forward to escort the estate's newly arrived hostess to her rooms.

Smiling again, for his elation outweighed any small discomfort, he walked down the corridor, slipped into the ill-used library, and sprawled in a chair, content to await the time to depart for the Bennets' ruminating over the impossible happiness that had finally become real.

Real and true, between us.

It was, he realised, the first *happy* secret he had ever held.

CHAPTER
TWENTY-FIVE

E lizabeth hummed as she watched Mr Bingley hand down his
sister to Longbourn's groom. Miss Bingley and Mrs Hurst
did not disappoint; they had dressed to remind the country folk of
their access to London's best shops and milliners. Miss Bingley's
blue silk gown was trimmed in some dark fabric that appeared to
match her black velvet spencer; it was a pretty look that would
look prettier on Jane or Kitty, or any one of a dozen ladies of Elizabeth's acquaintance. A smile or a disinterested expression may
have lent Miss Bingley some appeal; the sneer she wore instead
was rather ugly. Standing in the window as she was, Elizabeth felt
safe in her judgments; no one knew she was watching and the
Bingleys were not the centre of her interest. The man on the horse
now approaching filled that role. Mr Darcy rode up and delivered
his steed to Longbourn's groom, brushing his trousers and
straightening his back as he glanced up at the house, gazing
intently at the front windows as if searching for her. Elizabeth
managed to refrain from lifting her hand to the pane, and instead
left her rooms to join her family downstairs, where Mrs Bennet
was loudly preparing herself for an encounter with the lady who,

nearly a year ago, had broken her hopes and Jane's heart for a match between the families.

"Everyone knows I have a compassionate nature and always encourage comity between friends and neighbours," Mrs Bennet declared. "We may require more armour to withstand Miss Bingley's petty compliments."

"Now that he has a hostess, perhaps Mr Bingley will hold a ball at Netherfield," added Kitty.

"They are here," Elizabeth announced as she joined her mother and sisters. Oh, how she wished the ladies would not prove a hindrance in their efforts to reunite Jane and Mr Bingley.

Her own efforts to encourage civility would be taxed by an equal struggle not to let her gaze or attention drift to the tall, handsome Mr Darcy. Miss Bingley was a consummate hostess but a less skilled visitor; her disinterest—perhaps it was disgust—was apparent to any sharp-eyed observer. Of those in company with Miss Bingley and Mrs Hurst in Longbourn's drawing room, Elizabeth could count only herself and Mr Darcy as sharp-eyed, but sharp tongues were plentiful.

After all, if Miss Bingley was to endure Longbourn's hospitality, we must not further her enmity towards the Bennets. Elizabeth feared her diplomatic skills, such as they were when challenged by the clash between her mother's audacity and Miss Bingley's conceit, would be sorely tested.

———— ○ ○ ○ ————

Elizabeth returned the Bingley sisters' greetings; Darcy perceived them to be given reluctantly.

"And how does your sister do?" Bingley asked her, with the greatest concern.

"She is resting," Elizabeth explained. "She has done naught but sleep since...since you were last here, but her rest seems very peaceful. My sister Mary is with her."

"Miss Bennet is ill?" Miss Bingley asked, a note of scorn in her voice, as if she had always guessed the lady to be a weakling.

Bingley explained the accident, fortunately saying nothing of the symptoms Jane Bennet had demonstrated, nor the 'tonic' her mother had administered. He had raged enough about that startling discovery to Darcy.

Miss Bingley spoke few words and displayed little interest in Miss Bennet's health or the events in Meryton since her departure the previous autumn. The lady's attention in fact rarely strayed from himself; Darcy had found a seat by the window, too close to her, but across from Bingley and Elizabeth, where he could look at his intended to his heart's content.

Mrs Bennet filled in any quiet moment by regaling Miss Bingley with the past year's events in Meryton society, including four weddings, two deaths, and one shocking impropriety involving the nephew and heir to Purvis Lodge. As she began to weave in complaints against the Gouldings along with hints for a ball at Netherfield, Elizabeth's interventions showed her skill; she agreed with her mother about the pleasures of dancing to *Mr Beveridge's Maggot* and quickly steered the conversation away from neighbourhood gossip by asking Mrs Hurst about the health of their Scarborough relations.

Elizabeth may disparage her proficiency with a needle or paintbrush but no one can challenge her talent at gentle persuasion.

Bingley, who had been nursing his worries for Jane Bennet during most of the meeting, beamed at Elizabeth, seemingly as impressed with her conversation as he was. Or perhaps admiring her. But who would not? Darcy would never understand an attraction to the elder sister when the younger one was Elizabeth. Nevertheless, he knew Bingley had set his heart upon the other, and would not be truly happy until his angel was restored to full health.

Unfortunately, Caroline was not as prepared to be impressed as the gentlemen.

"You are rather quiet, Miss Elizabeth. Did the marriage of your youngest sister diminish your spirits? I can imagine that as the second eldest of five daughters, it would be difficult to watch the youngest—by some five years is it?—wed before you do."

Darcy felt fury filling him, but his beloved seemed less wounded than amused by Miss Bingley's query. Clearly, the lady had lost none of her spite, but she was imprudent to display it at Longbourn, and in his presence.

"Miss Elizabeth shall have no lingering delays upon the marriage mart. In fact, I predict her stay shall be an extremely brief one." He lifted his teacup in a slight toast to her. She smiled, and Darcy returned it, feeling his anger fade away. Caroline was simply unimportant.

By the startled look upon Miss Bingley's face, he saw that she understood him, although no one else seemed to have. He only wondered how long it would be before she decided she had not heard what she thought she heard, and reframed the entire conversation to her own liking.

But her sister took up the gauntlet.

"Such a pity that Miss Bennet is unable to join us today, when we had so looked forward to renewing our acquaintance," Mrs Hurst said, her voice heavy with polite scorn. "But then, she is subject to every complaint, is she not? I suppose it is a miracle she has lived to see her...twenty-fifth birthday, is it not?" She had purposely added years to Jane's age.

Bingley appeared angered by her words, and he spoke immediately, and as sharply as he could upon such a public occasion.

"Caroline, Louisa, Miss Bennet has the grace and manners of a lady, and her family has welcomed us here today despite the way you neglected her company in London, and as you will recall, your failure to inform me of her presence in town." Bingley turned his attention from his now white-faced sisters and gave the Bennet ladies a gentle smile. "I miss the jolly presence of Miss Lydia, and hope that she has found joy in her marriage. She and Mr Wickham acted as their hearts demanded. May we all do so and find happiness."

"Hear, hear," said Darcy.

——— o o o ———

"Well said," agreed Elizabeth. From the corner of her eye, she spotted white fabric from the angle where the staircase met the landing, the point from which she and her sisters had often spied upon their mother's company when the parlour door was left open, as it was today. Blonde tresses showed, peeking above the rail. *Jane!* For a few moments she tensed, worried that her sister might betray her earlier symptoms. Where was Mary? She was supposed to be at her side!

But after a few minutes of the desultory conversation that followed, the fabric and the hair above it disappeared. Jane, evidently, had gone back to bed without ever betraying her presence.

Mrs Bennet began lamenting her own sadness at Lydia's absence from Longbourn. "But what happiness she has in Newcastle with her dashing Mr Wickham! Parties and dancing—"

Darcy stood, followed quickly by Mr Bingley. After thanking the Bennets for their hospitality, the two men promised to call the following morning and ushered Miss Bingley and Mrs Hurst to the carriage. Once the door had closed and enough time had passed to assure the ladies their words could not be overheard, Mrs Bennet exhaled loudly.

"And not a thank you or a compliment from Miss Bingley! She has never had a finer plum tart, I tell you." She picked up her fan and waved it rapidly back and forth. "Truly, I pity her. She is jealous of Lydia's happiness and growing older and more bitter."

Elizabeth tsked. "Truly, she has grown no sweeter whilst ripening on the branch another year."

Kitty snorted and the three ladies were united, for once, in shared laughter; it was all the postscript the Bingley sisters' visit deserved.

———— ∘ ∘ ∘ ————

Darcy was surprised that Miss Bingley's temper held for the length of the three-mile journey back to Netherfield; as soon as her brother handed her down, she stalked angrily into the house, Mrs Hurst trailing her. Bingley sauntered in behind her, threw his gloves down on the table, and paced across the rug before returning to stand before his sister. Darcy stepped through the door, his attention torn between mediating the impending hostilities away from overhearing servants and reading the newly arrived letters sitting on the silver salver. Taking a deep breath, he pocketed the missives and steered them all into the library. He closed the doors just as Bingley's raptures began.

"Things went well today at Longbourn," he crowed. "It will not be long, I predict, before Miss Bennet recovers fully and we may host their family for dinner."

"Dinner?"

"Yes, very soon. You were there when I said I would be issuing the invitation, Caroline!"

The lady lifted a hand to her head and sniffed. "I told you this country air was affecting me. Clearly it has affected you as well, for I have no recollection of that event. You are delusional."

Darcy looked between the brother and sister before resting his gaze on Bingley. "Mrs Bennet does set a fine table. Your sister clearly does not wish to seem in competition with her."

Miss Bingley received his challenge as he had known she would, with a brittle smile, and offered, with great reluctance, assurances that a dinner with their neighbours from Longbourn would be planned once Miss Bennet was able to attend.

"Soon," Bingley said, one finger in the air, "with lemon tart and apple loaf. Miss Bennet is fond of them and I recall she especially enjoyed Netherfield's fruit desserts when last here."

"Yes, *apple loaf* is just what I would have chosen to serve at a formal dinner."

The contained fury he heard in Miss Bingley's reply raised the certainty in Darcy's mind that something would be broken in her rooms later today. *A vase, most likely...something she can hurl against the wall.*

———— ◦ ◦ ◦ ————

She had broken enough twigs to float an armada but Elizabeth took no notice, snapping another stick and tossing it in the stream. She had walked almost a mile, across the fields and halfway back again to exercise her emotions and work out her thoughts. Now she paced the infamous footbridge, willing Darcy to join her; after the time spent in company with the Bingleys, including the unpleasant conversation she was certain followed their visit to Longbourn, she assumed he too would have need of some exercise. But she had yet to see him.

The events of the past two days ran like a strong current through her mind: the endearments, promises and kisses between herself and Darcy; the clear disdain Miss Bingley still held for the Bennets; Mr Bingley's defence of Jane, and the pleasure she hoped Jane had taken in it.

When she had returned upstairs, Mary was asleep in the chair beside Jane's bed, and Jane was apparently sound asleep too. But she was rolled to her side, her arm cast over her face. Elizabeth would bet good money that she was wide awake, and yet avoiding conversation.

Why?

At least I have hope that my sister is returning to herself. She is awakening, as if from a long sleep. Naturally, she will have some confusion.

Her longing for Jane's incipient happiness was heightened by what it meant for her own; Elizabeth would not dispute it. Her love for Darcy had been reciprocated only days ago; keeping secret their attachment was no great ordeal. She could only hope Mr Bingley would soon know similar contentment with Jane.

The thumping of hoofbeats caught Elizabeth's ear and suddenly, there he was. Darcy dismounted, led her off the bridge and over to a more secluded spot under an oak tree, where he expressed equal pleasure in seeing her. After a few daringly long moments, their embrace loosened and Elizabeth looked up at Darcy, smiling.

"How I have wished to encounter you!"

"How I have wished to kiss you." He kissed her nose and returned her smile.

Elizabeth's gaze rose past him. "It shall soon be dark, so we must address the main topic at hand." At Darcy's amused nod, she began to enthuse. "How is Mr Bingley? Has his sister fled back to London or is she barricaded in her rooms? It was certainly a lively visit."

"Lively? I would say vexing and discourteous."

"Ah, but the reaction Miss Bingley prompted was quite opposite what she intended," she said, nearly laughing. "You did not see it, but Jane heard Mr Bingley speaking to defend her! It was wonderful!" She explained about the hiding place upon the landing, and seeing Jane there. "I do not know why she hides from us, as she seems to. Although she was definitely ill this morning, and surely needs more time to recover."

"Bingley is well-pleased," Darcy said. "While he has no definite assurance of improvement in your sister's sentience, he has hope that when the tonic is no longer affecting her, he will be able to begin again. He feels as though he is able to say all that which he feared to say the first time he was here, and it has mended his entire disposition. He has instructed Miss Bingley to be less a hindrance than a help in speeding along the denouement we all anticipate."

Although she suspected an entertaining explanation lay behind his words, Elizabeth was all too aware of the time and moved on. "I am quite looking forward to dining at Netherfield. Perhaps we can ensure Jane and Mr Bingley have some time separate from the others. Perhaps we can seat my father near Miss Bingley. That would provide diversion for—"

Darcy put his finger to her lips, then replaced it with his own lips as he murmured, "Such a mischievous maker of schemes."

As the shadows grew around them, he stepped back and gently tucked a lock of hair back into her bonnet. The tenderness of the gesture flooded her with such warmth, Elizabeth could only nod her agreement as he offered his arm, seized his horse's reins, and led her back to Longbourn.

CHAPTER
TWENTY-SIX

The following morning, Elizabeth was shocked when, just as Mrs Hill announced the arrival of the gentlemen of Netherfield, Jane came downstairs dressed for callers, followed by Kitty, who was looking very pleased. Jane had been sleeping and unwilling to waken when Elizabeth sat with her earlier; only her mother's insistence that Kitty remain with her sister during the hours for visitors had driven her from Jane's side.

Jane looked lovely, if a bit pale, avoiding the eyes of everyone as she murmured her greetings. At least her lips were free of nursery rhymes; Mr Bingley appeared deeply enchanted.

They had scarcely taken their seats when Mr Bennet entered the drawing room.

"Lizzy, I would see you in my book-room."

Elizabeth had not heard her father so grave since Lydia had run away. The lack of humour in his voice silenced the conversation in the drawing room. Mr Bingley paused in his explanation of his sisters' absence as they planned their future dinner party, and looked curiously at the older man. Elizabeth felt all eyes on her as she rose from her seat. She could not look at him, but assumed Darcy wore a worried expression; only her own concerns kept her from sending him the reassuring smile she gave to Jane.

She followed Mr Bennet into the familiar room, swallowing when she saw him sit behind his desk. *This will be a truly formal interview.*

He tapped a finger on the desk and began. "I have just met with Mr Woodcock to collect the rent he owed from the summer. The reasons for the delay are of less concern to you than the other purpose of his call. He spoke of seeing my daughter in company with a certain gentleman. You and Mr Darcy were alone, and seen by him *arm in arm* on two separate occasions."

Elizabeth took a deep breath, relieved that Mr Woodcock had witnessed so little with Darcy, and certainly nothing of the true nature of their meetings.

"I see I have left you speechless, Lizzy. I suspect you would prefer to ask questions rather than offer me an explanation."

"Papa, you know that Mr Darcy and I were working together to stir Jane's memories and reunite her with Mr Bingley."

Mr Bennet leant back in his chair. "You apprised me of a scheme but sketched in few details. Clearly it involves frequent meetings to consult one another? Arm in arm?" Drollery gave way to more serious paternal sentiments when he asked her to explain the alliance. "Have mud puddles and slippery stones assisted you and Mr Darcy in forming a friendship of sorts during this exercise? I fully trust in your sense, my girl, and Mr Darcy has acted with honour since his return here from London, but I do not know this man well and to have you wandering about the estate with him? It is not wise."

Her chin rose in defiance. "He is a good man, and a wise one. How many men of his station would send for his physician from town, and return to support his friend and play a role in such a curious charade? If anyone's reputation is at risk, it is Mr Darcy's!"

"You defend him with vigour," Mr Bennet replied with surprise. "If I need not worry about your reputation, must I worry about your heart?"

At this, she blushed.

"I see."

Although her gaze was anywhere but on her father, Elizabeth could sense his disquiet; he shifted in his seat, rubbed at his face, and then noisily cleared his throat.

"What of Jane?"

She looked up to find him looking at her, bemused.

"What of your sister's feelings? Your mother believes Jane may now truly prefer Mr Darcy to Mr Bingley."

"My mother is both wrong and impatient. Her desire for a quick resolution—*any* resolution—impairs her understanding of those whose felicity is at stake. It is to be hoped that Jane's memories of what she felt for Mr Bingley will return, now that Mama is no longer *drugging* her, and his feelings for her are unchanged. Perhaps they will very soon recognise it. But Mr Darcy is not Jane's to love, nor will he ever be."

Mr Bennet's wry humour reappeared. "Will Kitty's tender heart be bruised if she is not Mrs Bingley?"

"At least your family never fails to amuse you, sir."

"And you, Lizzy? Shall you be amused?"

"I shall be happy." A rush of feeling flooded through her as she spoke the words aloud. She gripped the skirt of her gown, heedless of the creases she would make in it, her favourite blue; although she tried to hold in her bubbling joy, she could not mask it from her father.

"Is it Mr Darcy who will ensure that happiness?"

"Yes."

Mr Bennet's surprised expression turned cautious. "Does he feel as you do?"

"Papa, he loves me, and he is helping Jane and Mr Bingley for my sake."

"And his friend's, I would hope." He shook his head. "Mr Darcy is wealthy and shows great loyalty to Mr Bingley, but you do not owe him your hand."

"He agrees with you, and insists I do not. But he already owns my heart, so I wish him to have my hand as well."

"He '*owns*' your heart, Lizzy? That is a worrying choice of words."

Never had her father looked at her with suspicion but Elizabeth could see it now, peeking out just underneath his concern. How had love, from its very beginnings, turned her into such a goose? First, and for far too long, she had been unable to find the right words to speak to Mr Darcy, and now she was using the wrong ones to explain him to her father!

"Papa," she began, "you mistake my meaning."

Elizabeth could see by the anger in his expression that Mr Bennet did not doubt his understanding nor care a whit for hers. "You have spent mere hours in Mr Darcy's presence since last autumn when he spirited himself away with the Bingleys. Has some spell been cast, Lizzy, making all the Bennet sisters fall in love with the man? Ho, this is a fine scheme he has...charming penniless but amiable sisters to what—? Fight one another for his favours? Shall I worry next for Mary?"

"No!"

Elizabeth, her eyes bright with indignation, stared across the desk at her father. He stared back at her, as startled as he was angry.

"Papa," she said softly. "You are fond of a good story, and I believe it is time to tell you one about Mr Darcy."

A quarter of an hour later, when she returned to the drawing room, Elizabeth found her mother and sisters listening to Darcy reading Milton aloud. Only Mary was proving an attentive audience; Mrs Bennet's head was as drooped as her fan and Mr Bingley appeared to be dozing in his chair. Kitty's head rested on Jane's shoulder; both girls looked up at Elizabeth's entrance as though hopeful of a respite.

Darcy paused and reached for his tea. "Miss Elizabeth, will you join us? We are nearly to Book Five."

Stifling a grin, she replied in a voice as solemn as his. "I regret missing all of the third and fourth, sir. May I take you to my father? He wishes to speak to you."

As Darcy stood, Elizabeth watched Mr Bingley sputter awake

and give him a small smile; Jane's sleepy gaze moved between the two men before she levelled a curious look at her.

"Is all well, Lizzy?" Jane struggled to shift a yawning Kitty off onto the cushions. Mary and Mr Bingley both rose to assist her, but Elizabeth strode quickly towards the door, Darcy right behind her. He bowed and they were gone.

○ ○ ○

Laughing, Elizabeth pulled him into a small alcove, so small their bodies were mere inches apart, and it was all Darcy could do to keep his hands to himself.

"That was a masterstroke, sir," she whispered. "*Paradise Lost*, read aloud to the Bennet ladies?"

"In under ten minutes, all were asleep or trying desperately to keep their eyes open. In your family's defence, I will have you know that Bingley was the first to succumb."

"Ah, your deep, dulcet tones lulling my family into the arms of Morpheus."

"Except for the stalwart Miss Mary."

"Well, my father thinks you have charmed all of the Bennet ladies."

"Except your mother." He leant closer and breathed in her scent. "I shall never live up to Wickham as her favourite son-in-law."

"Nor I to Lydia, but you have a much larger house and carriage, so her vexation will subside."

"Your father appeared unhappy when he called for you. Is all well?"

Elizabeth lowered her voice to the merest whisper. "It is...now. I have laid bare our joy."

Oh. *Oh.* The unease underneath the elation in her reply matched his own. "Your father...is he greatly surprised?"

"He is...as much by our mutual felicity and wishes as by the revelation of your assistance with Lydia. I felt he must know," she said hurriedly.

"Ah." *Damn.* He took a deep breath. "It was necessary, to achieve his blessing?"

"No. It was necessary for *me* to boast of your goodness." She lowered her voice even more. "If you wish to charm him, speak of your libraries."

"I had better go talk to him," he said, smiling, before turning more serious. "I love you," he whispered in her ear.

Then, after kissing her brow, he disappeared around the corner and took the final steps to the book-room. He knocked once before he was beckoned inside, where Mr Bennet sat behind his desk, clasped hands across his midsection. Before Darcy could even close the door behind him, Mr Bennet's tired voice cut through any promised tension.

"Is Mary to be the only Bennet sister unsaved by the valiant Mr Darcy? In case you wish to prepare for what appears to be the inevitable, she is frightened of owls, low necklines, sin, and eager dance partners."

Darcy pushed the door firmly shut and approached the older man. "I hope the only inevitability is that Mrs Bennet soon shall have two weddings to plan."

Mr Bennet appeared amused. He replaced his spectacles and looked expectant. "Three daughters married? Lydia will be unhappy to lose her exalted status. Which of her sisters have you chosen?"

"Elizabeth, sir, is the Bennet sister I love and wish to marry." Darcy grinned, realising the thrill of saying his thoughts and wishes aloud.

"I see. Well, if Mary is to be spared your heroics, I insist you employ them for my own sake and take on the duty of telling Mrs Bennet the happy news."

Taking this as Mr Bennet's implied blessing, Darcy nodded. "I shall, sir, but I am under strict orders from Elizabeth to withhold any announcement until her sister and Bingley have their own."

After a chuckle that sounded more like a scoff, Mr Bennet leant back in his chair again. "Ah, the endlessly tangled web of deception and pretence. Let us hope Cupid's arrow soon pierces it. Poor Mr Bingley has had much to contend with as a suitor. If only he had been as quick and direct with his proposal as you, and spared us all of this spectacle."

——— ◦ ◦ ◦ ———

Jane had felt nothing but relief when Mr Darcy was called from the room. Had there ever been a less compelling book to listen to, even if read in Mr Darcy's rich, deep voice? She did not want to admire his voice, nor his reading nor his form, nor his handsome mien. *Intelligent, kind and well-looking he may be, but I do not love him, and he shows no signs of romantic affection towards me.*

Surely I did not behave unseemly towards him! Please, no!

Jane looked at Mr Bingley. He had been as drowsy-eyed as she had felt during the reading, but like her, had rallied when Mr Darcy left the room. *Our tempers are by no means unlike. We neither of us care much for books and dry histories and philosophy.*

He is capable of a show of temper, even to a most deserving sister! she reminded herself. *He stood for me yesterday, and reprimanded Miss Bingley and Mrs Hurst for their treatment of me last year.* Jane wished she could ask Mr Bingley his thoughts; in the next moment, as his eyes found hers and his expression brightened, she realised she knew them. Rational thought abandoned her as they continued to gaze at one another.

Before Jane could speak to or return a smile to Mr Bingley, Elizabeth entered, smiling—radiant, really, in a way that Jane scarcely recognised. Her sister exchanged a nod with Mr Bingley as she took a seat beside him. He smiled at Elizabeth, glancing at the door and nodding his head. Dimly, Jane could hear Mary speaking to Elizabeth but her own attention was on the unspoken exchange between Elizabeth and Mr Bingley.

How very odd.

Moments later, Mr Darcy returned from the book-room. Jane watched as he moved back to his seat, picked up his book, and held it on his lap, listening with the others to Kitty's long-winded story about the mischievous Lucas boys' 'borrowing' of a meat pie from Mrs Robinson's windowsill. Mr Darcy looked at no one and his cool expression betrayed nothing of consequence to what had been discussed behind closed doors.

It could not mean what it appeared it meant...could it? But Lizzy hated Mr Darcy! Oh, what had happened whilst she was lost in that dream world! The not knowing was terrible!

"What did my father wish to speak to you about, Mr Darcy?"

They all looked at her with some amazement, and she realised it was the first thing she had spoken, really, in all this tongue-tied morning. But surely it was a most innocuous enquiry?

Mr Darcy tore his gaze away from Elizabeth, who broke in before he could reply. "Papa wished to speak to Mr Darcy about an estate matter, Jane. All the advice he has given to Mr Bingley for Netherfield has made some impact on my father's plans for Long-bourn. Apparently."

"Yes, he wished to discuss the worth of some especially vital part of the estate," said Mr Darcy, with a small smile that bewildered Jane. Mr Darcy was not an especially smiling sort of man.

"Well done, Darcy," cried Mr Bingley. "You are the man who knows all about managing an estate's lands and parks."

He does. Mr Darcy is the man everyone turns to in their hour of need, or with questions, or to seek advice. He is a man who provides his knowledge and strength to others. I wonder who he turns to and relies upon? But it was an idle thought; Jane had no real interest in learning anything of the great Mr Darcy's inner workings; she only hoped she had not embarrassed herself before him! If only she could remember!

As Mary began reminding them of the important role shepherds play in managing land, Jane turned and watched Mr Darcy, tapping his book—such a very dull book! As impatient as he appeared, his gaze was relaxed, even amused—and it was on Elizabeth.

Lizzy!

Does Lizzy love him? The thought was so startling that she lost her place in their conversations.

"Miss Bennet?"

She turned dazedly; Mr Bingley stood in front of her, holding a skein of thread. Elizabeth, Kitty and Mr Darcy had disappeared; only Mary remained in her seat.

"Darcy and your sisters have gone outside for fresh air," he said softly. "You dropped this. Are you well?"

Thinking how very kind he was to assist her, and how handsome he looked standing there, Jane gave Mr Bingley a small smile and reached for the thread.

"Thank you, sir." Her eyes moved from his to the empty chair beside her.

Mr Bingley understood quickly and sat down. "I admire how well you concentrate on your work. I wish that I had something to employ my hands as Darcy reads. He chose to entertain us with a very dull story, and I believe he nearly put himself to sleep as well," he confided quietly.

Something shifted within Jane as Mr Bingley spoke; some forgotten tendril of connexion returned. She turned to him and whispered, "I rarely understand half of what he and my sister say, let alone read."

He stared at her for a moment, and Jane feared he thought her stupid. Then he nodded, and directed a huge smile at her. "Although I admire them for it, they are too clever for me. I am more comfortable to sit with you and talk of dancing and flowers, or that pretty needlework you do."

"I would be pleased by it," she replied, her heart pounding. "It has been too long since we enjoyed such a conversation together."

CHAPTER
TWENTY-SEVEN

O nly a day passed between the call on Longbourn and the Bennets' arrival for dinner at Netherfield.

"Sit down, Bingley."

It was the second time Darcy, who himself was acting restless as a colt, had requested he find a chair and sit in it; Bingley had ignored Caroline's earlier demand.

"No, I cannot!" Bingley stalked across the room again, lost in remembrance of his most recent exchanges with Jane and the anticipation that their travails were at an end. *Why must I be still when everything inside me cries out in joy? She loves me. I see it.*

"Charles, do be still. The carpet is already rather worn, and it would be a shame if you put a hole in it before the Bennets arrive."

Bingley heard the sneer in the way Caroline said 'Bennets' but chose to ignore it. His sister's misery could not dampen his hopefulness.

"I am all anticipation for dinner. I believe some games afterwards would be pleasant."

Caroline looked appalled. "Games."

"Oh yes," he replied, waiting for Darcy to support the idea, but his friend remained too distracted to notice.

His sister stood, and came close to him. "I arrived here three days ago and was immediately forced to return to the carriage to visit the Bennets. Thereafter, I was compelled to extend a dinner invitation and I have spent much of the past two days planning the menu and arranging the details so that you may play out this fascination with Miss Bennet. Am I to have not a moment to unpack my things, to rest in the country, as one does?"

Louisa murmured her agreement in support of her sister's tirade.

Struck by a sudden wave of guilt over the many tasks he had given Caroline, Bingley acceded to her previous request and sat down. "We shall not have games, but if you would play for us, I am certain Miss Mary and Miss Elizabeth would exhibit as well."

"A splendid idea," agreed Darcy, finally joining the conversation from where he stood staring out the window. "We are a small party. There is no need for us to separate after we dine."

Bingley was quick to agree. "I do not wish to separate, not when Miss Bennet is welcoming my company."

"Bingley?" Darcy walked towards him. "What has happened?"

He looked at his friend with some astonishment. *At last Darcy sees my barely suppressed joy! He has been too caught in his own expectations to notice.*

"She began a conversation with me..."

Caroline rolled her eyes and looked as if she might throw something at her brother. Instead, she glided out the door, followed by her sister.

Bingley smiled. "Darcy, I have a favour to ask of you and the clever lady you admire."

○ ○ ○

A quarter-hour later, Jane stepped last from the Bennet carriage and found Mr Bingley handing her down. Her mother was already leading their group up the steps, trailed by her father and sisters.

Miss Bingley, walking quickly behind them, glanced back at Jane—and at Lizzy, following on Mr Darcy's arm. Jane could see the displeasure in her hostess; she smiled. As one who had lost everything once and nearly again, she had no room in her heart to indulge Caroline Bingley's temper.

"Mr Bingley."

"Miss Bennet." Mr Bingley pressed her hand. "I am pleased to have you here at Netherfield. It has been too long. It was last year, the twenty-sixth of November, when we were together last."

"At the ball."

"Yes." He smiled and began to lead her up the steps.

Jane looked at him and she saw the earnest hesitancy she had seen weeks ago, when he had first returned. She remembered it from last year, even, and when she looked more closely, she saw hope as well. "I remember dancing with you there," she said softly.

"Do you?" He looked close to exploding with the revelation. "It was glorious! Two sets."

"Indeed." Jane fortified herself as she said her next words. "It was a wonderful evening, the last you would spend at Netherfield for nearly a year. You left the following day, and did not return until a few weeks ago."

She watched as Mr Bingley's hopeful expression clouded; he stopped and closed his eyes briefly before opening them to stare at her intently and reply.

"Less than a year, yet it felt like eternity. I was away for ten months, eleven days, and—" his brow wrinkled and he glanced up at Netherfield's front door—"well, far too long." His head did a little shake and he stepped closer. "I went to London on business and planned to return within three days, but when my family joined me, I was a fool to be persuaded you did not return my feelings."

"I did return them."

"And your feelings remain just that, in the past?" Bingley swallowed. "When I learnt only a few weeks ago that I had been wrong about your feelings, I returned here with Darcy to see you, to see whether it could be true that you might still care for me." He shook his head. "You appeared to, but since the incident at the bridge, I have scarcely been your friend. You did not remember me and..."

Jane's mind raced. *Mr Bingley had returned as more than a friend, he had returned to...*

"What did you determine about me when you returned to Longbourn?"

"That you were as handsome and kind and lovely as I recalled—"

"—Are you certain? Even now? Time effects many changes."

"I am not much changed."

"But I was!" She looked up at him, knowing her despair was apparent in her eyes. "I do not recall much of anything of the last two weeks. But I have heard my mother say...imply...that I was... that I may have..." she trailed off, hardly able to put into words the terrible idea that she may have expressed fondness...or worse, for Mr Darcy.

"No," he said, touching her cheek. "You were and ever have been my angel."

—— o o o ——

Mrs Bennet was well-pleased with her evening. Her hostess did not disappoint in either her deportment or her menu; Miss Bingley was all that was polite, if not gracious, and she had clearly taken Mrs Bennet's advice on her dishes. Perhaps not the partridge —but even there, Mrs Bennet held her tongue. There was no need to complain of heavy sauces when there was a tension in the air characterised by side glances and swallowed sighs from her eldest daughters, nervous titters from Kitty, and knowing nods from Mr Bennet.

She looked from Jane to Mr Bingley; there was a pronounced alteration in their behaviour. They had arrived in the drawing room later than the others, and although separated at dinner, now were sitting together, talking quietly. Jane looked more beautiful than ever. It was a grand moment for Mr Darcy to give up on his attentions to her! He now sat by Elizabeth, undoubtedly entertaining her with his talk of museums and oats. Pleased with the picture before her, if too anxious to rejoice in her accomplishment, Mrs Bennet bent her head to Kitty's.

"This is how it should be," she said in a low voice.

"Yes, it is," Kitty replied. "Jane has chosen well in Mr Bingley, but now poor Lizzy must fight off Mr Darcy's attentions."

○ ○ ○

Pleased as Darcy was to shed the mantle of Longbourn's dullest suitor and most tedious conversationalist, it had been impossible to display either wit or warmth when seated at dinner between Caroline Bingley and Mary Bennet. Miss Bingley had employed her skills well and had escaped censure from Mrs Bennet—not an easy feat for such a fine, vain hostess. But ample as the meal had been, conversation had suffered as it happens when numbers—and understanding—were uneven. Now, returned to the drawing room for coffee, salvation arrived when Miss Mary rose with some alacrity to take her place at the pianoforte and abandoned the chair she had taken beside him.

He stood and made his way over to Elizabeth and was quickly warmed by her welcoming smile.

"Finally," she said. "We have been apart all evening."

"I wish to forget the past hour. My ears are quite worn out."

"Yes, Miss Bingley was rather devious with her place cards."

Darcy nodded, glad for Elizabeth's full understanding of the lady. "She neglects to list scheming among her arts and allurements."

He watched her laugh prettily before she replied. "As to scheming, you were very sly, sir, urging my mother into the house and herding everyone away from the doors. Jane and Mr Bingley appear well on their way to a renewed understanding."

Darcy shrugged, allowing him to shift close to Elizabeth and touch his finger to hers. "Bingley deserves every effort I can make on his behalf, but in this instance, all effort has been his."

"As has all success," she replied, tracing a finger over his wrist.

He failed to reply, too overwhelmed by the sensation she was creating, with the soft tip of her finger on his skin. "You undo me," he finally managed to whisper.

A cough from Mr Bennet recalled Darcy to himself and he asked Elizabeth whether she would like coffee. They busied themselves while Mrs Bennet incited an argument across the room.

"Mary, choose a piece to play or allow Miss Bingley her turn to exhibit!"

"It is all too baroque," complained Mary, "and requires a mastery that I have yet to achieve."

"One must practise in order to improve themselves and ensure pleasure to others," said Miss Bingley. "There are no simple airs or hymns among the sheet music at great houses like Netherfield or Pemberley," she said, turning her gaze on Darcy. "Perhaps I could send a servant to the nursery to see its inventory?"

While Darcy absorbed the insult more angrily than its intended target, it was Elizabeth who was prepared to parry it.

"I believe the mistress of a great house should always have ready whatever pleases her guests. Perhaps one must practise a proficiency at hosting as much as guests must practise the art of conversation, or shooting, or playing."

It was as clever and cutting an insult as Darcy could imagine and one he wished had been addressed to Lady Catherine. Mr Bennet, however, chose to effect further injury.

"Mary, come away if you will not play. You have made Lizzy missish."

Elizabeth paled. The angry trembling Darcy felt in her stilled. "Please, excuse me," she said, hurrying towards the doors.

"Elizabeth!" Darcy glared at Mr Bennet and dashed after her.

"Hold, Lizzy," cried the older man. "I have grown tired of charades and schemes." He rose from his chair and held out his hands. "Come, Lizzy, come, Jane."

The sisters exchanged glances and stepped towards him. Mr Bennet smiled at his two eldest daughters and took each of their hands. "A father dislikes it when a daughter leaves his house. We do not like to be neglected, you know."

His words were met by nervous laughter. "This has been a fascinating fortnight, and I am pleased to see our Jane recovered," he continued, looking at his eldest daughter. "I believe you now fully remember where your heart lies?"

She blushed and nodded; she smiled at Bingley.

"And you, Mr Bingley?"

He did likewise.

"Ah, well done. I have not a doubt of your doing very well together. Your tempers are by no means unlike. You are each of you so complying, that a proposal is scarcely required as you are both in agreement."

"Well, I would *like* to propose," Bingley cried.

"Off with you then." Mr Bennet gestured for Bingley to take possession of Jane's hands. As the couple moved away, beaming at one another, Mrs Bennet's cry of joy nearly masked Miss Bingley's groan.

"Now then, Lizzy."

In the fog of anxious expectation over Mr Bennet's next words, Darcy's eyes found Elizabeth's. Whatever anger or mortification she had felt earlier was gone; he saw only love.

"It is time for another declaration, is it not?"

Unwilling to allow Mr Bennet to profess their mutual sentiments, Darcy stepped towards Elizabeth; she moved towards him as well and took his outstretched hands.

"If you will have me."

— o o o —

"You love Mr Bingley? You are certain of it, Jane?" Elizabeth took the few moments of privacy offered by the arrangement of furniture to quiz her sister.

Her bold surmise, she soon learnt, comprehended but half the truth. The anxious affection between them, which she was conscious of having continually watched in Mr Bingley's every look and action, had finally received the delightful confession of an equal love from her sister. Jane's mind had recalled all that had previously passed—with the possible exception of a few recitations and rhymes—and her heart and faith were similarly engaged with his. All was well, all was as perfectly wonderful as it should have been not two weeks prior—nay nearly a full year ago!

Not since Darcy had revealed to her his own love and hopes had Elizabeth ever listened to anything so full of interest, wonder, and joy. The happiness of having such a sister, and one who was returned to her former self and able to share in similar joy, led them to a tearful embrace.

"Darcy will be so pleased," she thought, not realising she had said it aloud until Jane fixed her with such a look.

"Lizzy? You and Mr Darcy? You truly love him? Why...I thought you hated each other!"

Elizabeth burst out laughing.

"Do not laugh! Tell me the truth."

"The truth is that I am very pleased with a man as good as Mr Darcy loving me."

At that moment, Miss Bingley stood. "This is madness," she cried, jumping out of her own seat so that all the company looked at her. Mrs Hurst put her hand out, as if to stop her, but Miss Bingley shook it off.

"Love often is, hence poetry and novels," Darcy said coldly.

"I had a very interesting conversation with Mrs Philips in the town square today," their hostess announced. "She was delighted to inform me that it was not Shakespeare raising the rafters of Longbourn these past weeks...but Mother Goose." She stared accusingly at Jane, who looked confused.

If Elizabeth had been upset before by Miss Bingley's ill nature, it was nothing to how she felt now. She stood at once, and her opponent was in very great danger of losing her hairpiece. Darcy stood as well, his eyes narrowing upon her. They both opened their mouths to speak—but were halted by the peremptory hand held up by Mr Bingley.

"Caroline," he hissed, moving directly in front of her. "Not another word. Not unless you wish your allowance to be cut into the tiniest slices imaginable. You say one more ill-natured syllable regarding Miss Bennet, her illness, or anything else to do with any other Bennet, you will discover just how awful the taste of eating your words."

"Only those on the best of terms with both my future wife and her sister will ever again receive an invitation to Pemberley," Darcy added sternly.

Miss Bingley looked from one to another of the assemblage. Not even Mrs Hurst would meet her eyes, and Mrs Bennet was opening her mouth to deliver a rather large piece of her mind. There was nothing else for it.

———— ◦ ◦ ◦ ————

"Miss Bingley was quite vexed," said Jane. "It was fortunate the sofa caught her swoon."

"She would have preferred a handsome man catch her, but there are none left untaken in this house!"

"A footman, perhaps."

Elizabeth laughed at Jane's sly joke. "You are well-prepared to be sister to dear Miss Bingley. She is at least as vexed by the Bennet sisters' engagements to the men she most cares for as she is by the missed opportunity to use a runaway dog to thrust herself into Mr Darcy's arms and affections."

Their laughter went on long enough to attract the attention of the two gentlemen pacing in the corridor. The door opened and Mr Bingley poked his head inside.

"May we enter?"

"Of course," the sisters said together. Elizabeth laughed and rose to meet her beloved before he advanced much farther into the room. Jane, blushing, stood as Mr Bingley came to her side.

"How is Miss Bingley?"

"Your mother and Miss Catherine are attending her."

Elizabeth stared at Darcy in disbelief. "Truly?"

Mr Bingley nodded, his own gladness clearly overwhelming any worry he felt for his sister. "Mrs Bennet had the foresight to carry salts in her reticule, and has provided them to Caroline. Miraculously, she is far calmer."

"Two glasses of sherry surely helped." Darcy's comment provoked a giggle from Elizabeth that he answered with a fond smile. "Miss Catherine reported Miss Bingley is now far more amenable to not only the attachment she had long thought herself victorious in thwarting, but feeling herself to be the matchmaker whose schemes brought together Elizabeth and myself."

"That is a pretence I am happy to see her entertain for the next many decades." Elizabeth laughed softly and laid her head on Darcy's shoulder.

"Many indeed," he replied.

Neither took notice of the couple standing somewhat awkwardly next to them. After a moment, Elizabeth heard Jane's voice.

"I wish to speak to you both."

Elizabeth and Darcy drew apart, their eyes meeting in mutual recognition of Jane's need for resolution, and took seats on the settee. She watched as Jane and Mr Bingley followed suit, and gave her sister an encouraging smile.

Her hands in her lap, all of Jane's serenity appeared to flee as she looked from Elizabeth to Darcy to Mr Bingley. "I have been the centre of much distress these past two weeks, I think, and I feel I must apologise. I do not know what Caroline was implying, but if she knows, and my aunt Philips knows, I would rather be informed."

They all looked at one another. Finally, Elizabeth nodded. In fits and starts, with the gentlemen filling in forgotten details, the tale unfolded. When it was finished, there was a moment of silence.

"Oh, such a soft-headed mullion I have been." Jane covered her face, her head shaking. Mr Bingley immediately began to speak reassurances, but Elizabeth shook her head, shushing him; smiling, she grabbed her sister's hands.

It was immediately obvious to all. Jane Bennet was laughing uproariously. "Charming Willie?" she burst out, tears of mirth streaming down her face.

Elizabeth joined her, and then, suddenly, they were in hysterics, riotous, side-splitting laughter overwhelming them all.

"It is one of my sister's very best qualities—she has always been able to laugh at herself," Elizabeth said, when she could finally speak. "Although, Mr Darcy is very gifted as well. Much as he has disavowed any talent for the stage, he was quite effective in performing his role as a 'dull turnip', as my mother has designated him. I am pleased that all will again know him as the most interesting and charming man of my acquaintance."

Mr Bingley decried being bested as most charming, and they all broke out in laughter once more.

"Whatever schemes were hatched, whatever vegetables had their reputations besmirched," Darcy said, winking at Elizabeth in a way that gave her a rush of warmth, "is in the past. The mutual affection between Elizabeth and me—"

"—and Jane and I," Bingley interrupted eagerly, "are established and shall not be torn asunder by rocks, roguish dogs, or our relations."

"All scheming, all pretence is at an end." Darcy smiled at Jane and Mr Bingley before turning to gaze warmly at Elizabeth. "No acting is needed to fill the roles of true-hearted lovers. All is as it should be."

The End

Get a free ebook!

Receive a free ebook when you sign up for the publisher's newsletter! *For the Enjoyment of Reading* contains short stories by Jan Ashton, Julie Cooper, Amy D'Orazio, Linda Gonschior, Lucy Marin, and Mary Smythe. Its yours, free, for signing up for the Quills & Quartos Newsletter HERE.

Acknowledgments

I must thank everyone who knows me well for the patience, grace and support over this past year–chiefly and as always, my family, and my friend and Q&Q partner, Amy. Thanks as well to Gail Warner for her kindness in reading and commenting on what turned out to be a draft of this finished work.

The largest share of much deserved thanks, gratitude and warm hugs is for my friend and editor Julie Cooper, who found comedic and romantic gems where I could not see them and pointed out, ever so gently, the bits of rubbish plot or writing that did not fit.

About the Author

Jan Ashton didn't meet Jane Austen until she was in her late teens, but in a happy coincidence, she shares a similarity of name with the author and celebrates her birthday on the same day—if not the same century—*Pride & Prejudice* was first published. She's yet to find any Darcy and Elizabeth candles on her birthday cake, but she does own the action figures.

Like so many Austen fans, Jan was an early and avid reader with a vivid imagination and a well-used library card. Her family's frequent moves in the U.S and abroad encouraged her to think of books and their authors as reliable friends. A former journalist, she is a life member of the Jane Austen Society of North America, and co-founder of Quills & Quartos Publishing.

facebook.com/author.janashton

twitter.com/jancat10

bookbub.com/authors/jan-ashton

Also by Jan Ashton

A Match Made at Matlock

A Searing Acquaintance

In the Spirit Intended

Mendacity & Mourning

One Minute More

Some Natural Importance

The Most Interesting Man in the World (*with Justine Rivard*)

ANTHOLOGIES AND COLLECTIONS

'Tis the Season

Happily Ever After with Mr Darcy

Made in the USA
Las Vegas, NV
04 January 2023

64797920R00144